KID CHAOS

SEAL TEAM ALPHA

ZOE DAWSON

BLUE
MOON
CREATIVE
LLC

Kid Chaos

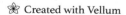 Created with Vellum

ACKNOWLEDGMENTS

I'd like to thank my beta readers and editor for helping with this book. As always, you guys are the best.

To all the unsung souls out there. This one is for you.

The thing about chaos is that while it disturbs us, it too forces us to roar in a way we secretly find magnificent.

Christopher Poindexter

1

Somewhere in the Darién Gap

Water, water everywhere—normally for a Navy SEAL that was heaven on earth, but in this situation, in this part of the Darién Gap, it was hampering their movements.

The only other good thing about the incessant rain was that it also screwed with the slew of *Clan Los Piratas* who were on their tails.

Son of a bitch! Kid Chaos, aka Ashe Wilder, shifted his gaze from the deluge outside the cantina's door to the other patrons in the smoke-filled bar: no one here was going to stop them. Not some old whore that had seen better days or the two small kids—in a bar, no less. The only thing they would do was challenge him to a coloring contest, and he could win that hands down. His nieces could attest to his coloring prowess, not to mention how proficient he was at pairing up Barbie's rad miniskirts with tiny heels. Yeah, he loved the ladies, even eleven and half inch ones with plastic bodies.

Of course, he would never admit to playing with dolls,

and he much preferred the real ones to any child's toy or blow-up for that matter.

He moved over a seat and reached out. Cowboy was slumped in his chair, and Kid was getting real worried. He'd been going in and out for the last hour. Still dazed. They had ditched all their gear for these civilian clothes to better hide out from the CLP bastards that weren't too happy they had just nabbed their second-in-command.

Just a few months back, Hector Salazar, who'd been bagged by Kid's team, had given up Angel Nunez, his second-in-command. Angel had planned the murders of DEA agents who had gotten too close to their operation and even pulled the trigger on one of them. Hector was trying to save his own ass, and now they had both of the bastards by the short hairs.

That op had been fun, and it had brought together his LT, Lieutenant Bowie "Ruckus" Cooper, with his fiancée, Dana Sorenson, a reporter and videographer who wrote and filmed on the human condition. She was doing a migrant piece in the Darién Gap, got herself kidnapped and held hostage in Hector's stronghold until the team had rescued her and her crew.

Cowboy jerked when Kid touched his forehead. He'd slapped a makeshift bandage over the bullet graze, but Cowboy's brain might have sloshed around in his noggin' a bit from the RPG explosion that knocked him out.

He needed medical attention. But first, they had to get the hell out of here. Kid wouldn't rest until he was out of danger and safe aboard the USS *Annenberg*.

"Where are we?" Cowboy asked, his voice low and strained. He blinked a couple of times.

"Hey, man. Welcome back." Kid gave him a smile. "We're in a bar in the middle of nowhere, Panama."

"Where?" Cowboy asked, looking around.

Kid realized that Cowboy had some memory loss. "We're in the Darién Gap. We were giving Angel Nunez a one-way trip to prison."

"Right. The mission. Did we get it done?"

"Yeah, man. Tagged and bagged. He's outside tied up. But we got separated from the team, and you got hit by a graze to the head."

Cowboy blinked some more, as if he wasn't sure he'd heard Kid right. "Outside?"

"Yeah, he carried you for miles with my weapon in his back. Then we found a Jeep, and it was smooth sailing all the way here. Except the Jeep was full of coke, and the drug runners were pretty pissed off."

"Kid, you are fucking crazy."

"Have we met?" Cowboy just glared at him. "All I know is this ain't no damn garden party. Not a finger sandwich in sight."

In spite of Cowboy's condition, he laughed. "Dammit! When I have my head on straight, remind me to kick your dang ass."

"Get in line, partner," Kid said with a smirk.

"How about you?" Cowboy asked, his dazed whiskey brown eyes going over Kid's midriff just above the tech vest's waist strap where a red stain had spread.

"Yeah, we got friends on our tail, and they nailed me." The blood on his "borrowed" T-shirt was nothing but a little nick. "Had to ditch the body armor for speed." It had bled some, would need stitches to close, but it wasn't going to slow him down one iota.

Cowboy swallowed, his movements slow. "Man, I ain't going to be no help. I got my bell rung dang good. Maybe you should cut Nunez loose."

"Don't worry about him. We're all getting out of here."

With a strong gaze, Cowboy murmured, "I have no doubt about that."

"Damn straight," Kid agreed. They had their orders. Two SEALs caught in Panama adding insult to injury by snatching another one of Panama's uglies was something the brass wanted under wraps. Not that Panama would cry a river over losing both Salazar and Nunez, but they would have to make some response, and the SEALs didn't like broadcasting their missions.

"I'm going to get us some chow and something to drink. Something really cold if I can manage it."

Cowboy was taking a few minutes to process what Kid had said, then he nodded.

Of course, feeding Cowboy might not be the best course of action. He'd already puked up his guts on the way here. But he had to get something into the big man. He needed the fuel.

Kid walked up to the bar and said in Spanish, "Four fish plates. Energy drink?"

"*Sí, bebida energética.*" The toothless bartender nodded. Kid held up his fingers to indicate six and grabbed the cans he set on the bar, flinching when his wound protested the twisting motion of his torso. With thanks to the bartender, he headed back to the table, the cans burning icy, the condensation wetting his palms. He brought one of the cans up to his forehead, the cold soothing. Such a small thing.

He left the bar, handing one to Nunez and the man he'd paid to watch him.

Cowboy was drifting when he got back, but still upright in his chair. "How you holding up?"

"I'm doing great," Cowboy said with a flash of a grin. The man was tough as nails. Kid knew he'd grown up on a ranch, honed from riding fences and muscling ten-ton beef. A branding, riding, roping legend. He set the drinks down in front of Cowboy and popped the tops. "Drink up, bro."

Cowboy reached out and set his big hand around the can making it look small and slim. He took a sip, then gulped some. "Don't drink too fast. You need to keep it down. Are you still dizzy?"

"Some." Cowboy wiped the back of his hand over his mouth.

Kid figured it was more than some. But nothing would slow Cowboy down as long as he had breath to move. Kid was the closest to Cowboy on the teams. They often did things together while on R&R. The Texan was as into extreme sports as Kid. With his steady whiskey eyes and his dark, thick hair, he was twenty-nine. He had a wide mouth, high cheekbones, and a deep-voiced drawl that made the ladies swoon. Kid was lucky he was cute, or Cowboy would get all the attention.

Cowboy had obtained his chief rating in three years. The rank was an honor. It was about service and required a peer review of master chief petty officers to achieve. That he had done it so young was nothing short of miraculous.

Where Kid was quick off the mark, Cowboy tended to be more thoughtful.

The good news—and there was some—was neither one of them had bullets in them.

"Do we have transpo?"

"Working on it. The bartender said there's a crazy banana boat guy that comes along here. Come rain or shine, he's working the river. We'll have to squeeze in among the fruit, but he can take us upriver as close to the LZ as we can get. We'll have to hoof it the rest of the way."

"Roger that." Cowboy chuckled. "I think we can safely say the guy is bananas."

Kid threw his head back and laughed for a couple of seconds. "You slay me, Cowboy."

"Yeah, I'm good at the jokes," he said with his deep, radio announcer voice.

The bartender called that his food was ready, and Kid went back to the bar. The fish still had their heads attached, and he pinched them off, dumping them in the trash. It was enough that Cowboy's gut was churning with nausea, he didn't need to see a dead fish eye looking up at him.

He placed the plate in front of Cowboy, and he looked down at the meal. He swallowed hard.

"Want me to debone it for you?"

Cowboy gave him an amused look and said, "Sure, Mom. Thanks."

Kid laughed and reached out for the plate and pulled the fish off the bone with his fingers.

"Ewww, cooties," Cowboy said with a grin.

He looked like hell, and Kid's jaw tightened. He wasn't losing him. They'd been traipsing through the jungle for three days, then four hours of running full out. At first, Kid had been carrying Cowboy across his shoulders, and he had five inches on him and thirty pounds. Then, Nunez had taken over.

This quick rest was warranted, and Cowboy needed better first aid. Then they would put themselves in the hands of a crazy banana boat distributor. Kid liked crazy. He associated with crazy.

They would take their chances on the river, because it was certain when the CLP caught up to them, they were dead. Sitting in this lighted cantina was a calculated risk. The patrons kept shooting them wary looks. They might have ditched their gear, but no way were they leaving behind the lethal sub automatics they carried. Kid's was in easy reach. They had both kept their side arms as well, a simplistic but lethal weapon in their hands.

Kid was certain that these people were used to seeing armed men in this hole-in-the-wall town. Nothing but a few rundown shacks in a muddy joke of what passed here as a road. They were also no friends to the CLP, which really suited them fine.

When Cowboy started eating, Kid walked out of the bar and handed two plates to the man. Nunez glared daggers at Kid. "Here's some food for you, Angel buddy. Eat up. We've got many more miles to go."

The now leader of CLP spat at him. Kid crouched down to get at eye level with him. "Have some respect, you son of a bitch, or I'll carve you up into little pieces, keeping you alive as long as I can. Rules of engagement be damned."

Nunez blanched. He tried not to show it, but he was a little spooked by Kid, and that suited him just fine.

"I should feed him?" Nunez's guard asked.

"Put the plate on the ground and let him eat like the dog he is for all I care."

He went back into the cantina, pulling the first aid kit out of his pared down pack. He shoveled in fish and rice. Then he leaned forward, and Cowboy looked like the fish and rice weren't sitting quite right. "Keep it together, *compadre*."

Cowboy sat back, and Kid pulled off the bandage to his forehead. The graze was long and deep. Definitely would need stitches. He closed it with four butterflies, then pressed a waterproof bandage over it. Pulling out his knife, he cut the self-adhesive bandage in half and wrapped it around his head, pressing it to seal it closed. Cowboy moaned, and his head dropped to his chest. "Come on, buddy. You can't sleep on the job." He smacked Cowboy's face until he roused.

"I'm okay," he said.

"I need you to stay with me. I know it's hard and your brain is hamburger right now. But when that boat gets here, we've got to be on it. We're running out of time."

"Boy howdy. I can barely see straight."

"Well, you're going to have to cover me, so do the best you can." As he argued with Cowboy, he was tending to his own wound, swallowing down his own hurried meal as he cleaned the graze the best he could, then slapped a bandage on it. He grunted and clenched his teeth as he curled the other half of the self-adhesive bandage around his torso. He wiped the blood from his hands with the napkins. He downed the last energy drink.

"What? I'm sure there are some guys on the teams who want to shoot you, but I don't happen to be one of them. What if I kill you?"

"Then I'll come back as a pissed off ghost and haunt your ass."

"Kid!"

The bartender called out the boat was here. "Go time, big man." He muscled his shoulder under Cowboy's armpit and helped him to stand. Shoving his weapon into his hands, they left the bar.

And it was go time. Men were coming out of the trees. He dropped with Cowboy, murmuring, "They're at twelve o'clock. Spray your cover from ten to two."

"Talk about shooting blind," Cowboy mumbled, then said louder, "Where are you going?"

Kid pulled out his knife and said, "To even the odds."

Kid was in full out commando mode. He was the only thing standing between Cowboy and his maker. He was determined the maker would have to wait just a bit longer for Cowboy's soul. Currently, it belonged to the SEALs. When he was done with paring down the threat, he returned to Cowboy.

"You're still alive."

"You sound surprised. Never bet on the house," Kid said. "Get up, Nunez." His tone brooked no back talk. The CLP bastard rose, the makeshift rope around his ankles only allowing him to take normal strides. There would be no running for him.

Kid saw the boat pull up to the dock. Shoving his gun into Nunez's back, he said, "Keep moving."

When the banana boat guy saw them coming, he continued to unload his bananas in spite of the rain and the armed conflict happening right in front of him. Nerves of steel, this guy.

More CLP burst out of the trees. Or they might have been the pissed off drug runners coming for the men who had taken their Jeep. It was a tossup. Didn't matter. Their bullets would kill them just as easily.

When Nunez hesitated, Kid put his boot into the middle of his back and kicked his sorry ass into the boat. He landed on the bananas. Gunfire ripped up the dock, and without hesitation, Cowboy returned fire. He helped him into the boat and propped him against the dock. "You're taking us upriver."

The man calmly nodded. Geez, he was really starting to like this guy. "Let's go, *amigo*!" As Nunez tried to fight his way out of the yellow fruit and Cowboy reclined in the bow, the banana boat guy motored them into the center of the river in a downpour, sheets of heavy rain obscuring them from view as the darkness swallowed them up.

An hour later, he dropped them three miles from the LZ.

Unfortunately, Nunez had been hit in the leg. Kid had bandaged it during their trip, but he'd lost a lot of blood and was very weak. On shore, Kid dropped his pack as he shouldered both men. He heard the chopper before he stumbled into the clearing, weapons immediately trained on him by the steely-eyed men of his team: Ruckus, Scarecrow, Blue, Tank, Wicked, and Hollywood.

"Son of a bitch!" Ruckus said. "I don't believe it."

"Believe it, LT. Chaos reigns!" Wicked said.

"Geez, Kid, what took you so long?" Hollywood needled.

"Screw you, bro," Kid replied, his breathing labored.

"Fuck, Kid. You are my hero." Scarecrow laughed and radioed the USS *Annenberg*.

Blue climbed into the helicopter. Tank, Wicked, and Hollywood rushed to him, and a set of hands took Nunez and another set tried to take Cowboy. But Kid shouldered them aside and walked the last few paces, his legs burning and his body about to give out, to the waiting chopper and laid his team member and friend down. Blue slipped his hands under Cowboy's shoulders and took his head onto his lap.

"Bullet graze. Concussion. Dizziness, vomiting, blurred and double vision, short episodes of unconsciousness, badass to the bone."

His team members all chuckled. As Blue shined a light into Cowboy's eyes, Kid sank slowly to the ground, but he didn't make it all the way—his team caught him.

ONE MONTH LATER

Kid opened his apartment door and froze. Cowboy, who was just behind him, slammed into him. The place was empty except for a folding chair in the middle of the room.

"What the fuck?" Kid said, the shock of seeing all of Mia's furniture gone slamming into him like a high velocity round. Straight up head shot.

"She's gone?" Cowboy asked.

Kid was trying to breathe around the pain and sense of loss crowding his lungs. He turned on his heel and slammed the door.

"Uh-oh," Cowboy said at the look on his face.

It didn't take him long to get to the mall where Mia worked as a buyer for one of the high-end clothing stores. When he got to the head of the store, she was coming out. A man greeted her, and they kissed. Kid felt as if someone had given him a shot to his solar plexus. Cowboy put his hand on Kid's shoulder. "Kid, don't. You could easily kill the guy, and then you're going to jail. It's not worth it."

"It's not his fault," Kid gritted out, his eyes on Mia. The beautiful, soft Mia who had kept him going through all that shit that had gone down in the Darién, then the highly covert op that had followed shortly after that. Granted, he'd been out of contact for months, but this...this was wrong.

He strode across the space that separated him from lovely Mia. When she turned, she saw him coming and her eyes widened, her mouth forming a perfect O.

"Ashe!" she said, breathless as if she couldn't help herself.

When he reached her, the guy turned to him. "Who is this?"

"None of your goddamned business. Mia, a word." The guy was dressed like a corporate lackey with his expensive suit and tie. Even though it looked like the bastard was in the dark, Kid wanted to deck him to release some of this explosive anger, the pain that was tying his insides up into knots. Even though he'd told himself never again, he'd gone and fallen in love with her. Now it was too late for any kind of retreat. He was completely caught flat-footed and dead in the water.

"Mia?" the suit asked, his perfectly coiffed features and his ruthlessly shaven face a deep contrast to Kid's own shaggy black hair and dark stubble. He looked more like a street thug than a SEAL. He'd just come off deployment, and the first thing he had to deal with was a bare apartment and a Dear fuck you John message in that empty, echoing space.

"It's all right, Chad. I'll be right back." There was confidence in her voice. Of course she knew Kid would never hurt her, even though she'd just torn out his guts.

When Chad went to move forward after Mia, Cowboy grabbed his arm and said, "Out of millions of sperm, you were the fastest? He had a relationship with her, amigo. So, back off for a bit."

Even in civvies, Cowboy commanded attention, and Chad...Chad? *Fucking* Chad? What the fuck...backed off.

Her eyes went over Kid as if she couldn't seem to get enough of looking at him. She raised her hand, but at the tightening of his jaw, she let it fall back to her side. "I've forgotten how beautiful you are."

"I didn't forget about you for a freaking heartbeat." He shot her new boyfriend a derisive look. "Chad? Really, Mia. You could have had the decency to break up with me before you took up with him."

"And how exactly would I do that, Ashe?" She set her hands on her hips, her eyes snapping with both pique and pain. "You're always gone, and when you're here, there's always the threat you'll be called in. I can't wait around for the rest of my life worrying about whether you're dead or alive. You take such chances. You're not unbreakable!"

"Yes, I am."

She let out an exasperated breath. "I'm sure you think that's some kind of SEAL mental exercise. But you can die just like anyone else. I can't live with that. Losing you like that. I don't have that kind of strength. I just want to remember what we had." She looked over her shoulder at Chad, and Kid wanted to howl at the top of his lungs. "He's easy, a banker. He has normal hours, and he's good to me. I can make a life with him. You and I never really meshed except in bed. We were good there." She rubbed at her forehead, closing her eyes at the memory. "So good." At the flash, he grabbed her hand.

"You're engaged?" The rock sparkled under the lights, and his heart shattered.

She bit her lip when she met his eyes, tears welling. "I'm sorry you had to find out this way. I tried to tell you the last time you were here." She brushed at her tears. "You looked so tired and banged up. I knew I couldn't handle it anymore. When he asked me out, I said yes, and things progressed."

"While I was fighting and risking my life for this country and you!" He couldn't believe what was happening. This was the second woman in his life that was walking out on him. He closed his eyes.

The minute he'd seen her after BUD/S was over, Caitlin had become distant. He kept trying to tell himself that it was his imagination, but when he woke up two days later alone, her closet and drawers cleaned out, he knew.

He'd gone after her using their GPS app; he'd tracked her down, and there on a lonely highway halfway to Virginia, he'd caught up to her. She had told him she couldn't and pressed the ring back into his palm. She said she wasn't strong enough to handle his absence, that the worry would kill her and kill their relationship. She would resent him, and she didn't want that. Then she'd gotten in her car and driven away.

"I know," Mia shot back, breaking him out of that flashback. "But the thought of breaking it off and then having you go into danger with that to deal with was just too cruel. You were gone so long. I just couldn't wait anymore. I'm sorry, Ashe."

He watched her stoically walk away as he fought with the betrayal, the pain, and the loss.

Cowboy came up to him and said, his voice subdued, "I'm sorry, Kid."

Love was a freaking crock. Trying to keep a relationship going was tantamount to climbing Mt. Everest. She wasn't wrong. He was deployed approximately two hundred and forty days out of the year. He was always on call, always in danger, but she'd been wrong. He was unbreakable. They just had different meanings for it. But he was serving his country, giving his all for her and people he didn't even know. It was what he signed up for, was dedicated to doing.

He guessed he was more in love with the team than he was with her.

"It's okay, Cowboy," he said. "I'm okay. I'm just pissed I lost out to a banker." He buried his disappointment, his betrayal, and his pain, but he knew he wasn't fooling anyone, not even himself.

Cowboy deposited Kid on his bed after he force-fed him ibuprofen and water. Made him brush his teeth. That's when Kid had broken down, and Cowboy had held him in a tight embrace like the brother in arms he was.

The guy who had saved his life many times, most

recently in the Darién Gap. It was Mia's loss, and, he would admit to himself, she knew it. Even as she'd walked away with her banker, she couldn't keep her eyes off the boy wonder. Yeah, the kid was male eye candy and packed a lethal punch to the fairer sex, but he was also noble, smart, considerate, and a freaking amazing catch.

At least she'd left him a place to sleep, the callous, back-stabbing bitch. The boy was wasted, had passed out after the sixth bar they'd visited. Long before he'd done the sweet babe in the john and had been making out with another one shortly after that. There were plenty of strap hangers, or frog hogs as they were referred to, in line. He was on a crash course, and Cowboy would be there to pick up the pieces stone cold sober. Kid had wounds and scars; this was a fresh one and completely invisible. He ached for his teammate, but all he could do was administer the alcohol, pick up all his pieces, and try to help put them back together again. They only had so much leave, and Ashe needed to be one-hundred percent when they went back to work.

Distractions in their job could kill them. Cowboy had to fight his all the time.

He knew all about the heartache associated with coming home, and he hadn't been back to Galveston in a long time, but the shame was always there, lurking. His agitation only intensified when he thought about going back home for his cousin Michele's wedding. He'd gotten the notice only days before their last deployment, and now it was only months away, but he was already dreading it.

He stripped Kid down to his skivvies and pulled the covers over him. Setting his Stetson on the bed post, he pulled off his shirt and toed off his boots. He went to Kid's closet and pulled out the camping cot he kept there along with a sleeping bag.

He finally shucked his jeans and thought about the one woman he'd never been able to get off his mind, going all the way back to high school. Kia Silverbrook, a beautiful freak. She dressed like no one he'd ever seen—goth inspired, sexy-ass, downright stirring leather and lace garments that Cowboy, in his teenaged hormone-laden years, often wanted to strip off her body and see what she was hiding underneath. She looked like a storm with her pitch-black hair, cloud-gray eyes, and alabaster skin.

He'd heard in his senior year that she had a tattoo on her butt, and he was dying to know what it was. She was a hacker extraordinaire with the kind of skills MIT grads salivated over and had been suspended once for hacking into the school's grading system just to prove she could. She was brilliant, sexy, and she scared the hell right out of him. She was in the freak squad, and he was on the football squad. But that's not what stopped him from making a move. No, there was something about her that spelled danger in big red letters. His plan had been to go to college and then take over the ranch, but two years into his degree, everything changed. The ranch had been in heavy debt, and as a result, the ranch had to go up for sale after his father's death. Feeling ashamed of his father's action and unable to focus on his studies, when a recruiter for the SEALs had come around, Cowboy had enlisted.

But it had been ten years since he'd seen that girl. She was probably married with a passel of children.

Kid stirred, the sound of his fresh heartache muffled into his pillow, touching Cowboy as he drifted off with Kia's dark eyes on his mind, wondering what might have been had he taken a chance.

2

Six months later, La Paz, Bolivia

Paige Sinclair pulled up the booking for the guest who would be arriving today. Ashe Wilder. He was going to be here with them for a week on various bike trips around the area. His flight had already landed, and he would be taking his trek down the most dangerous road in a couple of days. He hadn't planned out the rest of his trips. He said he wanted to be spontaneous. Not something Paige was used to in her life, but to each their own, she supposed.

The tour company brought in the adrenaline junkies by the boatloads. Some talked about climbing Everest or visiting an Incan temple on a mountaintop in Machu Picchu. Paige got plenty of adrenaline with her real job as a Special Agent with the Naval Criminal Investigative Service, or NCIS. She was in La Paz undercover with the tour company, investigating the theft of a large cache of military weapons out of Naval Amphibious Base Coronado. NAB Coronado was a huge naval installation across the bay from San Diego, California. Paige worked out of the West Coast

Headquarters for NCIS located in Oceanside, California, at Camp Pendleton, the Marine Corps Base.

One of the armories on NAB Coronado had been robbed, two military policemen murdered. It was an expertly executed job, but one of the robbers had been shot and had left his blood behind when he'd escaped. The weapons hadn't been recovered, nor had they showed up on the international market.

The DNA of the blood found at the scene matched Corporal David Duffield, a former marine, but he had disappeared along with the weapons. The only other evidence found at the scene was the flight manifest to La Paz, a key piece of evidence the wounded man must have dropped during the robbery. After exhaustive research, Paige discovered that Duffield had connections to a former CIA officer, Bryant Anderson, who was part owner in a tour company based out of La Paz. He was co-owners with a Bolivian native, Cris Oyola. Anderson was rumored to also be a mercenary for hire as well as a provider of arms and ammunitions. It was enough to convince the Director of NCIS to allow her to go undercover at the tour company to surveil Anderson and investigate the connection.

She'd been here for two weeks, and no sign of any illegal activity, the guns, or Duffield had materialized. This made her wonder if the wounded marine had been unable to complete the flight and crashed in the Andes. The rugged terrain around here could easily have concealed the downed wreckage. That was a daunting task, and it would involve more than just her undercover. She'd need proof before the Director would contact the Secretary of the Navy and start the wheels rolling for a search of approximately thirty-four thousand square feet of mountains. Not to mention it was possible the plane could have dropped into the ocean, and then those weapons would never be recovered. The pilot wouldn't have sent out any kind of mayday or turned on a beacon to follow. No, he'd wanted to fly under the radar, but his wound could have been fatal... Still all speculation on her part. She wasn't going to involve any kind of official channels until she had something concrete to go on.

Especially with her promotion hanging in the balance. She was on the cusp of getting her own team. She'd put in the years and the time, given up everything to her job, including her personal life. So, she had few friends, and she spent all her time working. Her father had done the same, and he had been her role model. Her dedication had made her stand out at NCIS, and she fit into the team seamlessly.

The bell over the door rang as a group of people came into the office. She looked up to see it was one of the tour groups from the US. She smiled and started to check them in, confirming their reservations. After the last person, she made the necessary adjustments to the record. Just as someone came up to the counter, she dropped her pen, bending down to retrieve it. When she came back up, her breath backed up in her lungs. Wow was all her brain could come up with at the moment. Just wow.

He was tall, six two at least, and lean that hinted at the kind of muscular described as "ripped." He was insanely good looking, boyish, but those eyes of his told her that he was much older than he looked, closer to thirty maybe. He had a well-formed nose and beneath that a rebellious mouth, the bottom lip fuller than the top. But it was those piercing eyes that gave her the warning that he was dangerous, with the kind of stare that was usually reserved for interrogations—intent, potent. It was just a natural extension of his personality. He had on a baseball cap, the brim shadowing his features, but it couldn't conceal his strong, angular jawline.

He looked like he'd just come off a climb. He was dressed in olive green cargo pants, a gray T-shirt, top-of-the-line hiking boots, and a black jacket tied around his slim hips.

Who was this guy?

"Ashe Wilder," he said, as if he'd read her mind, his voice low and melodious, a pretty sound out of an arresting man. "I have a reservation."

He gave her a half-smile from that sexy mouth and leaned forward, extending his hand toward her.

"Yes," she managed, placing her hand in his. "Paige Sinclair." She was bombarded by disturbing new impressions. There was a compelling attractiveness about him, an appeal that was unfeigned and indestructible. His eyes were a deep cobalt blue, and the long, thick lashes accentuated their hypnotic intensity.

There was something very intriguing about his face, something that touched her in the most profound way. It revealed a depth of character, an inner strength, but it also revealed an imperviousness that had been carved by experience. Paige felt an immediate affinity for him that she had never felt for another human being. Her keen awareness of him as a man had an immobilizing effect on her, and she was conscious of nothing except the warmth of his touch and his unwavering gaze.

"Don't tell me you can't find it, ma'am? I didn't just fly almost five thousand miles to be a tourist," he said, the look of irrepressible mischief in his eyes. "It's not my thing."

His words broke the spell, but Paige was unwilling to break physical contact with this man, and she reluctantly withdrew her hand from his grasp.

He stared at her for a second longer. She realized he was waiting for her answer.

She looked down, typing in his name. The record popped up, and she just stared at it, trying to regain her shaken composure. Right, the American from San Diego.

She looked up and got flustered all over again. She never got flustered, even when she worked with some of the biggest jerks on the planet who thought a female agent was a pushover. Especially now when she had a job to do and didn't need any gorgeous distractions.

His brows rose as he stared at her, waiting for her answer. He pulled off his baseball cap, revealing a shock of dark hair, heavy with just a tad too long bangs, but short in the back. He ran his hand through the silky strands.

"No, we've got your reservation. No bazaar shopping sprees for you unless that's something you want to do."

He flashed her a smile that was pure charm. "I have some things to buy for friends and family, so I guess I can work the shops a bit." Oh, God, this man could charm the pants off a nun...that's if nuns wore pants...did they?

She handed him his welcome package.

"I didn't make a hotel reservation. Can you recommend one?"

"Oh, that was risky."

The change in him was immediate. It was as if some vital link had been broken, and his expression was suddenly shuttered as he scrutinized her. "I live on the edge."

It was obvious that he had, for some reason, withdrawn behind a wall of cool politeness, and that bothered Paige more than she liked to admit. Her voice was uneven when she responded. "That's why you're here."

Their eyes connected, and for a split second his guard was down, and Paige experienced a sudden galvanizing rush that set her heart hammering wildly against her ribs. But beneath the electric undercurrent of sexual chemistry, there was a distinct push-pull dynamic. Whatever initial attraction there was between them, he wasn't sure about pursuing it.

"The hotel?" he asked. Bending down, he picked up a worn leather duffel and set it on his impossibly broad shoulders, his biceps pulling into a thick, hard bulge.

"Yes. I could recommend Hotel Petite Hacienda. It's close by and has all the amenities."

"Could you point me in the right direction?"

"Of course." She came from behind the counter and went to the front door, conscious of every move he made. What the hell was wrong with her?

The bell tinkled as she went outside into the cool June air. It was winter in the Southern Hemisphere. She hadn't quite gotten used to the traditional "summer" months to be the opposite here. He didn't seem to mind the chilly air even in his short sleeves. A light drizzle coated the streets. A long line of mountain bikes that would be loaded for the trip tomorrow stood by the front door. He came up beside her, leaning down slightly as she pointed down the street.

"Right down to the end of the block. You can't miss it. It has an arched entrance and is a tan colored stucco building. It's next door to a quaint church." She turned and brushed her hand across his chest when she gestured down the street. He was too close.

He went stock still, taking a breath. She did her best to ignore his reaction. "That way is where the bazaar and all the shops are, and you can shop until you drop. Just don't wear high heels."

Oh, Lord. Why did she provoke him? He was too damn close. A warped grin appeared, and there was a touch of humor in his voice. "Well, ma'am, I'll have to pass on that. I left them in my other duffel."

"That's a shame."

"Now what will I wear with my pretty dresses?"

She laughed, and the spark of humor in his eyes faded. "You have a nice laugh, Paige Sinclair."

She experienced a weird sensation in the pit of her stomach. His voice had a peculiar huskiness to it that jangled her nerves.

He backed toward the street, his eyes on hers. "Thanks. I'll see you tomorrow."

"Seven-thirty sharp at Café El Mundo. Hope you enjoy your stay."

He kept backing up, his eyes glued to hers.

"Oh, wait—" she called out, but it was too late. His butt hit the first bike, and the rest of them fell like dominoes with a crashing clash of metal and leather.

He landed on his back on top of them in a heap. She rushed over. "Oh, my God. Are you all right?"

He looked up from the chaos he'd made of the bikes and grinned like a fool. "Nothing hurt but my pride."

"Let me help you up," she said as she reached out and clasped his hand.

There was that jolt again, as if she'd been zapped with lightning. He came up a little faster than she expected, tangled up as he was in the wreckage of the bikes. His dexterity surprised her, caught her off guard and threw her completely off balance. She was the one now in jeopardy of falling. She wasn't exactly sure how he did it, how he kept them upright. But he did, and before she knew it, she was jammed up against all that hard muscle.

She clutched his broad shoulders as he gave her a solid base to cling to. Once her mind was free from keeping her on her feet, her responsiveness to his body jumped up a million notches. She went still rather than move away, every cell in her body throbbing.

They stared at each other, and everything but the sound of her heartbeat faded away, her world narrowing down to his face, those eyes, something expanding between them, the air thickening until she could barely breathe around the awareness locking her...them...in place. He was just as affected as she was, and that sent a frisson of warning down her spine. Her normal guardedness when it came to men who had an interest in her seemed to desert her here. She was all about working hard, and that meant long hours and no personal life. Getting ahead in her job was worth every long, hard hour, every minute it took away from pursuing...pleasure.

She found it hard to maintain direct eye contact in the face of his rather intense focus. There was a wealth of vibrancy there, like he was a man who rushed at living as if it would be his very last chance to wring every ounce of exuberance, a man who couldn't be contained.

Oh, man, don't go down that road, Paige. That road led to a loss of control, and rules and discipline would get her where she wanted to go. She had a plan and getting hot and bothered with adrenaline junkie Ashe Wilder wasn't a good move or a smart one. She was working. But did he have to look so good, so alive, as if he could infuse her with the kind of energy that would fuel her, take her places she had never gone, energize her beyond her imagination?

Maybe if she just got physical with him, it would take the edge off everything. A fling in beautiful Bolivia with a very intriguing man. What could be the harm? She could see what it would be like to juggle sex and her job. Maybe it wasn't as difficult as she thought. Her body craved the weight of him instantly.

Once her mind went there, she couldn't stem the images of touching him, every inch of the body that was so intimately pressed against hers. This close, the blue of his eyes seemed as wide and deep as the ocean, and, boy, did she want to swim. His skin was incredibly smooth, despite the hint of five o'clock shadow, with such a downright sun-darkened richness to his skin, it made her fingers and palms itch. He had such a cute, boyish look to his face, but those eyes told her that he was no boy and he knew exactly what to do with a woman.

Without warning, longing washed over her, and she recognized the feel of it from the years she'd spent helping to raise her brothers with her overworked and tired father. He had praised everything she'd done to keep their family together. But loneliness, that was something that pulled at her now. He blinked a couple of times as if he'd seen the vulnerability in her. She swallowed, and her heart lurched, the dynamic changing between them as if he'd identified with the emotion in her eyes. That gave her the impetus to push away. A fling with him? What the hell was she thinking? He would suck her in like a vortex, and the distraction could cost her everything—her promotion, her job, her very life.

"Is everything all right out here?"

She looked over her shoulder to see Mr. Oyola, the co-owner come rushing out.

"Damn, I'm sorry," Ashe said. "I wasn't looking where I was going."

Mr. Oyola gave her a knowing sidelong glance. "That happens around Paige."

She nudged him, and the mischief maker only grinned.

"Yeah, I bet it does," Ashe said, a smile flirting with the corners of his mouth—a beautifully sculpted mouth.

A mouth she had no business looking at.

There was a tremendous pull between them, the kind of pull that was almost impossible to ignore.

"At least I didn't end up on my ass." The words came out of her mouth before she could stop them, and they were filled with a teasing breathlessness that she was unaccustomed to hearing in her own voice.

He laughed, and the sound of it tightened around her like gentle but tough vines. Flirting with him came much too naturally.

"Thanks to me." The husky inflection to his voice only made her tingle more, and that wasn't what she wanted. She could still feel the imprint of his arm around her waist and his hand tight around her arm to keep her from falling to the street.

Mr. Oyola reached out his hand and said, "Cristopher Oyola." She was thankful for him breaking up this flirt-fest.

"Ashe Wilder. Nice to meet you." Reaching for Mr. Oyola's hand meant he gave her even more breathing room. She stepped back, and they shook briefly.

"Mr. Oyola is part owner of Going Down Wilderness Excursions," Paige said, taking another step back, then going around Ashe bending down to haul his duffel from among the fallen bikes.

It was heavier than it looked, and even as she went to move it, Ashe took it effortlessly out of her hands.

"I'm looking forward to the trip down *Camino El Muerte*," he said as he propped the duffel against the office wall.

Road of Death. It was no joke. She drove the van, and she could attest that the narrow road was harrowing at the very least and in bad weather, downright treacherous. But there was genuine challenge and pleasure in Ashe's voice. She shook her head. Adrenaline junkies and their crazy ways. She reached for the first bike and righted it, moving on to the next. Ashe and Mr. Oyola went farther down the line and began to pick up the other downed bikes.

"I'm really sorry about this. If there's any damage, I can take care of it."

"That's generous of you, but it looks like there's no harm really done here," Mr. Oyola said.

"We can take care of this," she said, wanting him to move along. She had work to do. "We're sure you must be tired and hungry from your long trip. The hotel is just down the street, like I said." She pointed in the direction of the quaint, well-regarded hotel.

He looked at the bikes as if he felt responsible for helping them. "Really, Mr. Wilder. No harm done."

"Mr. Wilder?" he asked, walking to his duffel and hefting it once again to his shoulder. "It's Ashe, ma'am." He took a few steps and then turned back. "I'll see you both tomorrow." But he was looking at her the whole time. There was that intense gaze again. She was in for some kind of day tomorrow. It didn't have anything to do with the Road of Death and everything to do with Ashe Wilder.

She watched him walk away, that broad back supporting the duffel. She couldn't help thinking that the man looked just as good from behind as he did from the front.

Mr. Oyola nudged her. "Something distracting you?"

She dragged her eyes from Ashe's retreating form and gave him a sidelong, don't-go-there look.

"Not anything I can't handle," Paige said. She reached for another bike.

"I have no doubt about this," her boss said. "You might stop being so controlled and give yourself permission to let loose every once in a while. What's the worst that could happen? You get your heart broken. It builds character."

"What would you know about broken hearts?" She smiled. "You and your wife still act like newlyweds."

"This is also true, but faint heart never won hunky man."

She laughed out loud. "You let me worry about my love life—and hunky men." She picked up another bike and gave him an affectionate look. "I've got this, Mr. Oyola."

"How many times do I have to tell you, Paige, to call me Cris?"

"It doesn't seem professional to call someone I work for by his first name, but if you insist—"

"I do." He gave her a warm smile. Mr. Oyola—Cris had the warmest brown eyes, and he was always teasing his employees in that soft, earnest voice of his. Working for him was so completely different from working for NCIS where the atmosphere was always tense and driven. Of course, Mr. —Cris had the kind of business that was conducive to relaxation. This was what people did when they were on vacation.

He inspected the bikes very thoroughly. She had no doubt he wanted to make sure they were sound for tomorrow.

"Okay, Cris it is."

"Then you need to start calling me Bryant."

She stiffened at the deep, commanding voice behind her. She turned to find the other co-owner, Bryant Anderson, the man she'd come to investigate. He looked every inch of what he was—a mercenary. Big, honed, thick muscles bulging everywhere. But unlike Ashe Wilder, he was arrogant and smug, giving off a vibe that told her he was more dangerous than she could imagine. She had disliked him from the get go, and nothing had changed. She couldn't understand what had possessed Cris to go into business with such a man, convincing herself that Cris just didn't know what was going on. He was a family man, strong supporter of his community, ran his business with the kind of joy that showed he loved what he did. He was the people guy, and Anderson, well, he was the hard-ass who took the bikers down the side of a mountain. So maybe he was the necessary evil.

He gave her a once over like he always did. So the opposite of Mr. Oyola, who had eyes only for his wife, Ariane. Together they embodied true love and had two kids, Riky and Jhosselin, whom Paige adored.

"What happened here?" he asked, coming to stand next to them.

"Nothing serious, just a little mishap with one of the customers."

"Doesn't bode well for him riding down a mountainside. What a joker."

"It was an accident," Paige said more harshly than she meant to, retreating toward the front door as three men entered.

His eyes narrowed as he tracked her toward the office.

She'd always been respectful of Anderson only because her job was to get him to trust her, but she couldn't help defending Ashe. Damn, he was already getting her into trouble. She smiled to lessen the impact and then ducked inside to handle the new clients.

Ashe Wilder. Yeah, some trouble, indeed.

3

That was so freaking smooth, man, he said to himself as he walked away from the carnage he'd left behind. That woman had taken over his senses. Hell, he could still smell the floral, enticing scent of her.

All the way up the street, Kid resisted the urge to turn around. He wasn't too far gone that he couldn't recognize some potent attraction when he felt it. That girl was five feet eight inches of sexy brunette knockout—a one-two punch to the chin.

After his breakup with Mia, he'd gone on a binge for the rest of his leave, trying to understand how he could keep getting it so wrong. Cowboy was just simply there for him, not judging and wholly supportive. Kid had exhausted his mind with constant movement and sated his body with countless women, the kind that had no problem with a short-term affair with a SEAL. Sex was the answer and still was for him right now.

But that wasn't the vibe he got off the beautiful brunette with the stunning golden green eyes. She was more than an affair, and that was reason enough to steer clear. He was here for a vacation. That was it. Not that he wouldn't want some kind of a hook-up. He just suspected that Paige Sinclair came with plenty of complications. More than Mia. A lot more than Caitlin.

Right now, he wanted hot and reckless and easy in his bed. She might slide over him hot as hell, and it would be just as easy to let the scenario in his head play out in real mode, but some alarm, deep in his brain, sent out warning vibes. Kid might pull out all the stops when it came to ops, but matters of the heart were much trickier.

And a whole helluva lot more painful.

Sex wasn't love, though, and it wasn't trust, and though he didn't know a damn thing about love anymore, and in retrospect doubted if he ever had, he did know about trust —and he wanted that in a relationship.

Mia had been easy and uncomplicated, or so he'd thought until she'd blindsided him six months ago. Now, he figured he didn't know squat.

He'd convinced himself he needed that type of woman, the kind who was always waiting for him, keeping home and hearth warm while he went to bad places and did bad things to bad people, and so far, every time, he'd come back alive—he and his elite team. It's what his mother had done for his father, and that was all he'd had to go on.

Even though he'd been only ten when his father had died, he remembered him, a big, bold presence in his life and the way his mom had loved him. With anything that was tied to his dad, he wanted to be worthy of that memory, of his dad's sacrifice, but as for his doubts about being as good as his dad...that was something he kept private. Not even Cowboy knew that information.

What would it take to be that man he had built up in his head over the years? The ultimate sacrifice? It certainly required him to go in with both barrels blazing and damn the consequences. All-out war with that image was something Kid battled in the darker moments when he allowed himself to think about it.

As he passed the first block through a mad carnival of jostling pedestrians and honking, diesel-spewing minivans, feeling as gritty, congested, and cosmopolitan as New York City, it was clear this was the urban jungle. A jumble of cobblestones and concrete, Gothic spires, sharp-suited businessmen, and shoe-shine boys. Amidst streets lined with vendors, he glimpsed the steeple of the church and waited until the street traffic had slowed enough to cross.

La Paz was the highest capital city in the world with immense, scrubby plains flanked by barren, even more intense mountains, all of it under a flat and penetratingly bright sky. He'd seen some harsh places in his travels all over the globe, but this area was stark and harsh—yet also stunning, the sort of landscape that put people in their place, in the very best way possible.

The altitude had nothing to do with his giddiness at being here with the prospect of biking in challenging terrain. He'd spent a lot of his normal training as part of a SEAL team in San Diego, riding the steep and winding trails, climbing and running through the rolling hills and mesas that rose from the Pacific shore. With his constant PT and his preferred training, he'd be able to handle the steep mountains here with virtually no problem. The trick was staying hydrated and getting plenty of rest.

He spied the boutique hotel, the arching doors and the sign with the name in flowing gold letters on a black background.

He checked in easily and left once he'd set his stuff in the bathroom and unpacked his clothes. He went downstairs to get a meal, then walked through the city to the bazaar because he was a bit bored.

Near the intersection of *Calle Max Paredes* and *Calle Graneros*, the streets were filled with peddlers hawking clothing, handcrafts, and household goods. Making his way through the twisting maze of knock-offs and cheap imitations he made a mental note to come back when he was settled and pick up some good gifts for his family back home. Tucked into the alleys and courtyards were *tambos,* thatch or tin roof structures, meaning 'place of rest' where shoppers could purchase oranges, bananas, and coca leaves. The leaf was chewed by farmers and miners and sometimes tourists to ward off hunger and the effects of the altitude. Being in the military, he avoided the leaves but bought three oranges.

At a booth, he found some cute stuffed llamas and bought two, one for each of his nieces, a necklace for his sister with pretty blue beads and silver stars, a jaguar pendent for his mom, who was very fond of them, and for his brother-in-law it was organic coffee. The guy loved his caffeine, and it was his hobby to try different beans from around the world.

Once Ashe was back in his room, he prepared to sleep. Relaxing on his bed, leaving the curtain open so he could see the magnificent icebound peak of Mount Illimani rising imperiously to the southeast, the beautiful Paige glided through his mind. As he drifted into sleep, he thought about how many mountains he'd scaled in his life, the pressure to climb even more pressing at him, conquering every challenge. It's what his dad had done up until he'd died.

Failure lay heavily on him, his relationships ending with him not understanding why they had ended. The were answers tantalizingly close, lost behind some kind of barrier he couldn't seem to breach.

He wanted to be the kind of man his father was—loyal, strong, dedicated, and fearless—yet he was plagued by the thought that he always fell short.

Until the day he proved himself.

He woke early, as natural as breathing. He showered and dressed for the day, noting the drizzle. So much for a dry run down the mountain. He was psyched, his body restless and his mind completely focusing on Paige Sinclair from the moment he opened his eyes. He tried to ignore that buzzing along his skin, but when he was attracted to a woman, his inclination was to go after her hardcore.

Dressing in layers, he left the hotel and headed back toward the office and Café del Mundo, his hands deep in the pockets of his cargo pants. He was going to be early, but that would give him time for some breakfast. He would need the fuel.

He breathed deep of the cold mountain air, the sun barely up in the gray light of the new day. Kid had always been comfortable in the shadows, and it was where he did his best work.

The streets were quiet, so much quieter than the day before with the hustle and bustle of the late time of day. But that was okay. Chaos lived in the quiet times so that when the frenzy began, it was already comfortable.

He approached the café, and there she was, striding toward the door. Their trajectory would bring them to the same space in a matter of moments. Of course, he expected her to be here, but not this early. Mia hadn't gotten out of bed until probably nine on a good day. But here Paige was, living in his early morning world, looking good enough to eat for breakfast. She had on purple hiking tights that hugged the curve of her thighs, a short, black jacquard miniskirt tight around her hips and curvy butt, a green pullover hoodie, and a pair of black, stylish hiking boots. He clenched his jaw to make sure his tongue was still safely inside. He should really be focusing on the ride. That wasn't a damn leisurely Sunday trek. It was an adrenaline pumping, treacherous hurl down a narrow mountain path on a slick surface. Certainly nothing with the word *slick* in it was going to be safe or easy. SEALs knew that the only easy day was yesterday.

She made the door just a fraction of a second before he did. "Ma'am," he said. His training and mission readiness took over because he was off the charts, pure, unadulterated havoc here. He reached in front of her and went for the door handle to hold it for her, but instead of doing that, the edge cracked her right in the forehead.

She took a step back. "Ouch," she said, her hand coming up to her face, rubbing at the spot he'd hit, that long, dark hair rippling around her like liquid silk.

"Oh, geezus," he said, immediately contrite. "I'm so sorry!" *You are so freaking smooth, Kid! Yeah, banging her was the idea, but not in the head for Christ's sake.*

She turned to look up at the idiot who had just cracked her skull. Her eyes squinted at him. "You?" She chuckled, and he liked that she had a sense of humor about this little mishap. "Are you sure you want to go on this trip? It's going to require balance *and* coordination."

He laughed softly. "I'm beginning to think the same thing. But the only two times I've lost my balance and my coordination have been around you. Normally, I'm a badass."

She stepped out of the way as he pulled the door completely open and waited until she moved. But she didn't, and for a moment, he thought she might be exercising caution. He couldn't blame her. Instead, she just looked up at him, color flowing into her cheeks. Damn, she was beautiful. Not pretty. Not cute, but freaking gorgeous.

Her eyes were so amazing, unique and contrasted with her dark hair. Even with the gold color shot through with rays of vivid green, she gave him a direct, penetrating stare. She was no shrinking violet, not a woman who blushed but then wouldn't make eye contact with him. If she was nervous, she showed none of it. Bold, beautiful, and in charge of herself. He didn't like the last part so much. He was nothing but restless energy right now, as if he could explode out of his own skin.

She gave him the once over, and damn if he didn't like the way those eyes took him in in a smooth, hungry slide. He was used to women looking at him like that. It wasn't ego; it was just fact. He'd lived with female attention his whole life, and he *always* loved it. What red-blooded man wouldn't?

He wanted to fuck her right now just from sight and smell. He couldn't imagine what it would be like if he touched her. She was stirring up the chaos in him that was never far from his center...it *was* his center.

"How about some breakfast?" he asked when he really wanted to say: *How about some hot, incredible, the-best-you-ever-had, mind-bending sex?*

"Sure," she said in passing, throwing him a simple look over her shoulder. He grinned. He couldn't help himself. Then in the next instant, his grin faded completely.

She'd walked on by, leading the way through the door and into the café, leaving him to follow the black skirt, behind the languid movement of her boots, shapely calves, and the smooth rolling motion of her hips, behind the finest ass he'd ever seen—shapely, tight. And he was dying, the awful, wonderful feeling from yesterday rearing up again and swamping him in one big crashing wave.

Pure lust had never come so close to dropping him to his knees. Never. He could handle lust, so this had to be something else, but he'd be damned if he'd put any kind of label on it. Not after those previous relationship wrecks. Whatever it was, it didn't relent, not all the way past the tables and chairs or across the polished wood floor and into a booth. It was like a fist around his heart, a tight, aching feeling in his balls.

She kept up a casual, mostly one-sided conversation about what he could expect on the trip, lamenting the weather and driving the van. He heard himself agree—yes, ma'am, it was going to be an adventure—all the time trying to tear his gaze away from the movement of her butt and the barely-there fragment of black cloth trying to cover it—and failing. The only success he could call his own was the impulse he overcame to be able keep his hands to himself and his tongue in his mouth; he didn't jump her. Yeah, that was a win, a pitiful, embarrassing win.

She made him feel like a sorry, out-of-control teenaged boy. He'd like to think he was more in control of the measured chaos in him, but she was taking him down with every step she took.

He tried for sniper focus, to absorb her words and reply in some format that was close to an answer. But it was like falling over those bikes yesterday as she filled his senses.

BUD/S, combat, training, or badassery didn't prepare him for Paige.

He'd never, not once while a SEAL, scrambled for sanity, not like this. He wanted this girl like he'd never wanted anyone—not Caitlin, not Mia, not all those women he'd done since he'd broken up with Mia.

But he wanted temporary, even a controlled temporary. This woman was definitely not into risk, not with her comment yesterday about his lack of hotel skills or her caution about driving the van down the mountainside. That was all he could handle right now, and a fling with a beautiful woman like Paige would take the edge off. He was always running hot, and his edge was as hard as granite and sharp as a knife.

"How long have you been driving the van?"

"Two weeks," she said, focusing more on the approaching waiter than him. "Hello, Marco." The waiter flashed her a bright, white smile, the kind of hope in his eyes contrasting with Kid's confidence.

Yeah, back off, buddy. You can't compete with Kid Chaos, even with those pretty boy looks. Hoo-yah. Paige was obviously used to getting hit on. Kid was sure it was a minute-by-minute problem for her.

She didn't open her menu but instead said, "Go ahead. I know what I want."

He glanced down at the offerings.

"Coffee?" Marco asked.

"The usual," she said to him.

"Carrot juice," Kid said.

"No coffee?"

"Nah, I'm wound tight enough." He closed the menu. "I'll have pancakes, scrambled eggs, and bacon."

"Now, you're talking." She handed her menu back to Marco. "I'll have the same."

Kid did the same with a smug look on his face. He and the babe had stuff in common. Wasn't looking good for ol' Marco.

"I've only seen pictures and a couple videos on the ride. Looks pretty intense."

"It's pretty hairy going around some of those hairpin turns. Had some close calls, and I'm an excellent driver, but with the drop-offs and the sheer cliff walls, the narrowness of the road...well, it's hellish."

Her version of hell didn't even scratch the surface of his.

"I bet you do it very well," he said. The calm, matter-of-fact tone to her voice told him she liked to be in control, and when she wasn't, that pissed her off. Control was an illusion. People might think that was strange coming from a guy in the military. It was all about control and discipline. But Kid did what was necessary in his own way. For that alone, the SEALs fit him like nothing else ever would. The bonus was working with his elite team members who embraced the exact same philosophy.

She met his eyes, and something intangible flowed between them. She blushed at his frank, steady gaze.

"I'm not much into four-wheeling with a minivan, but I do all right."

Damn, he'd never felt this way before, and it sent a shiver over his skin that had nothing to do with the cold of this place. She smiled, a smile that was meant completely for him, and his heartbeat tripled. He drew in oxygen, and for the first time in the Andes, he was feeling the thin air. When Marco came back with their drinks, he had a sour look on his face.

Paige gave him a conspiratorial smile when Marco turned away, and regardless of the complications he could literally feel coming his way, he wanted this woman. A week in bed with her would certainly take the edge off.

Kid's plate landed with a rattle. Mario gently placed

Paige's in front of her, and Kid couldn't help but grin. *Eat your heart out, pretty boy. I'm way too cute for her to resist.*

She dug into her food. After a few mouthfuls and a sigh, she asked, "What exactly are you good at, Ashe Wilder?"

"Things that matter the most," he said after inhaling his own food.

"That so? Like what?"

"Work, family, friends. Coordination and balance."

She nodded and laughed. The sound of it resonated and made him quiver. "Right." Her eyes danced a bit, a wry smile playing across her face. And a mouth he couldn't stop noticing. Looking at. And wondering.

"What exactly do you do for work?"

"Government."

"Vague." She sipped her coffee.

He shrugged, downing the last of his carrot juice. "It's a job." He didn't go around broadcasting he was a SEAL. He wasn't going to be here long enough for her to find out that much about him. It didn't really matter at this point. He snagged the bill Marco had set on the table.

"You don't have to—"

"I got it," he said. He figured out the money and a generous tip. The guy could use something to brighten his day. They rose and headed for the door. When he reached it, she stepped back, giving him a dubious look. He laughed. "I promise I won't give you another concussion." When she went in front of him, he couldn't resist setting his hand against the small of her back.

Outside, the day had brightened some but still had a gray cast to it. "And this adventure? You do this a lot?"

"Yes, I do. I love the challenge."

"People like you always do."

"People like me?"

"Adrenaline junkies."

"The adrenaline is a by-product of the experience, not the goal," he said.

"Oh, how do you mean? What is the goal?"

"I'm more interested in the challenge."

"Why?"

"It makes me feel alive."

"So these trips are a way for you to seek the meaning of life?"

"Not exactly. I'm not really looking for the answer to that question. I'm looking for the experience of being alive, so that my physical encounters resonate with what's here." He tapped his heart. "With what's real. So I can actually feel the joy of being alive."

She stared wordlessly up at him for several heartbeats. "That's a very eloquent way of putting it," she murmured. They walked for a bit in silence.

"Have you ridden down the road?"

"No, I haven't. I'm not all that keen on extreme sports. I enjoy the work here in the office more than the trip, to be honest. But the scenery is breathtaking, and I completely love it when I'm not driving."

"What brings you to Bolivia?" he asked.

She shrugged, her eyes going to the cobblestone. "A change of pace. I took a year off to—"

"Eat, pray, love?"

She smiled softly at his humor. "Something like that."

"So, you're trying to find yourself?"

"No. Not exactly. Let's just say Bolivia has interesting hidden secrets."

They came abreast of the van, and the tourist group from yesterday was assembling near the front door.

"I've got to get going and ready everything for the trip.

Have a great ride if I don't get a chance to tell you after we get on the road."

"I will."

He headed toward the van, greeting people when a booming voice said from behind him, "You've got to be Pete Wilder's kid."

Kid stopped and turned around.

"You're the spitting image of the guy." He reached out his hand. "Bryant Anderson."

A pained sigh escaped him, echoing the ache in his chest. "Ashe, and, yes, Pete Wilder was my dad." Kid shook his hand, Anderson's grip crushing. Dropping the contact almost immediately, Kid turned to enter the van. Anderson followed.

"I knew it. I was there when he was killed in action. I remember the funeral and you. Your dad was one tough son of a bitch."

For two heartbeats, Kid just stood there, the crashing memory of the day he'd lost his father washing over him like ocean foam and heavy water. If he'd been at the funeral, Ashe couldn't remember him or place him, except for a vague familiar look about him, but that could be the shaved haircut, the honed and muscled body and the look in his deep blue eyes that screamed warrior. Grief, hard, heavy, and aching, hit him like a ton of bricks. It'd been so long since that beautiful sunny day when through fanfare, a twenty-one-gun salute, and heartbreaking tears they had buried his father.

Kid's gut churned, and he nodded toward the big man. "I've heard," Kid said, his tone abrupt and unwelcoming, a funny feeling going up his spine, getting sharper, even more intense. He didn't really want to rehash the day he'd lost his father, a day lost in time.

Paige slipped past Anderson and entered the van. He met her eyes and then looked away. The wealth of her compassion was overshadowed by her apparent dislike of Bryant Anderson. The look she gave him was piercing and reprimanding. She had known loss, too. It drew him as much as made him want to push away.

Sweat beaded on his upper lip, and he wiped his hand across his mouth. He'd never talked about his dad's death, not to anyone. Not his mom, his sister, his teammates. His face suddenly felt hot. He'd been obsessed with his dad's homecoming only days away. They were going on a family trip—camping and fishing. God, he'd loved fishing with his dad.

The memories piled up on him. The man with shaggy black hair and a shit-eating grin, strongly built, ripped and lean through the waist, a man who resembled Kid in every line of his face, the same brows, the same cheekbones, and the same color in his eyes.

But that man hadn't come home. Instead there had been a knock at the door, and a man that wasn't his dad stood there dressed in an impeccable blue uniform with a white brimmed cap on his head. The minute his mom opened the door and saw him, she'd clutched her blouse over her heart and burst into tears. The man leaned forward and embraced her, his hand patting her back.

The heat in his face spread, running down his neck and onto his shoulders, sliding like water down his chest to his stomach and down to his legs and to his feet, his heart squeezing so tight. It was beating hard and slow, feeling like a half-ton weight.

Anderson shouldered past him to take a seat. He smiled like this was the greatest thing ever. "Maybe before you leave, we can sit down, and I'll give you the lowdown on him."

Not damn likely, Kid thought. He gave the man a tight smile and turned his back, settling in a seat in front of Anderson, one that gave him a vantage point, not only to the scenery out of the front window, but to Paige. She waited until the others were tucked away in their seats before she put the vehicle in gear and headed out.

His dad wasn't a subject for conversation—any conversation. He drew in a long breath, fighting the pain, waiting for everything to go back to the status quo. Back to where he was unbreakable.

Back to where he needed to be.

4

Anderson was such a jerk. A brutal, Mack truck-like jerk. Either he hadn't clued into Ashe's physical cues or he had ignored them.

She was betting on the latter.

Ashe's reaction had been subtle, molded in the curves and angles of his face. It was written in the sudden tightening of his sexy mouth, in the breadth of his stiff shoulders and the clenching of his jaw, in the way he shifted.

Gone was the teasing, cute man who had eaten breakfast with her. Gone was the twinkle in his blue eyes, and gone was the calm, easy-going demeanor.

In its place was someone who was wound very tight, locked and loaded and ready to explode into action. She got a twinge of concern about the now imminent ride down Death's Road. Ashe looked way too reckless.

Pain gathered in her gut like a stone. The kind of pain that was associated with losing a parent, only in Paige's case, her mother had left them. Her, her three brothers, and her wonderful father. Mixed in there was anger and resentment and, Paige only acknowledged the pain on rare occasions when she witnessed someone else's.

It seemed to trigger hers like a tripwire she couldn't see or avoid.

When she glanced into the rearview, his eyes met hers with an unnerving intensity, her still pained gaze holding his. Looking back out the windshield, she tightened her hands on the wheel as the van shifted up into a higher gear to counteract the steep incline.

The road connected La Paz with the low-lying region of Yungas in the Amazonian rainforest. To do this, the road had to be cut into the mighty Cordillera Oriental mountain chain. Beginning at La Paz, the road climbed to La Cumbre Pass, then made a steep descent to the village of Yolosa, the end of the trip. That was a drop of about twelve thousand feet.

Ashe switched seats to the one right behind her. "How long to the Pass?" he asked.

"An hour." She smiled at him in the rearview. "I bet you're excited."

He smiled back at her. "Yeah, I'm stoked."

"What other extreme destinations have you done in the past?"

"I've been to a few beautiful and stirring places. Gokyo Ri, a peak in the Khumbu region of the Himalayas was gorgeous. The valley was filled with stone houses, walled pastures, and amazing lakes. Life was easy and peaceful there. We stayed at either tea houses or local lodges in the communities. The highlight was watching the sun rise behind Everest."

"Sounds amazing." Paige hadn't ever thought about anything but work. She'd thrown herself into advancing her career every day. Here Ashe was her age, and he'd done so much more while holding down a job. Made her wonder at the possibilities.

He talked on about rock climbing in Morocco and dog sledding in the Yukon. "On this trip to Kilimanjaro, we started off from this little village called Nale Moru where the maize filled farmland merges into the Rongai pine forests. Then after making it to First Cave, a camp at twenty-six thousand feet, the landscape changed from open moorlands that led up to Mawenzi, the second volcanic peak to the moon-like desert area known as the "Saddle" between Mawenzi and Kibo cones. We started the final climb in the dark by torchlight to the rim of the crater with the goal to get there before sunrise. Once I reached the summit, it was like being on top of the world."

She had always been about getting ahead with many payoffs, something her dad had taught her, but now she wondered at how hard it would be to juggle some downtime to experience something as personal as what Ashe was describing.

Once there, he was the first one out of the van. Bryant and Cris exited right behind him, climbing up to the roof to pass down the anchored mountain bikes.

She exited after all the passengers and headed to the storage unit in the side of the van. Opening it, she began to pass out helmets and orange vests. The cold wind howled across them, plastering their clothes to their bodies. She wanted to talk to him as he checked over the bike and donned the helmet and vest. But he looked so...remote. She barely knew him, yet there was something so compelling, it was hard to keep her eyes away from him. And it was more than his drop-dead looks.

Anderson was looking at her looking at Ashe, and she went back to her tasks, her shoulders tight. What was she doing? She took a deep breath, realizing that she had a job to do. Getting justice for the two men who were killed and retrieving the guns should be her number one priorities here, not a man she'd just met. The added pressure of her promotion made this an opportune time to keep her head in the game and not on distractions. So far, her non-existent personal life had served her well. She really had no time to be engaging in...anything with him. No matter how much she wanted to get to know him, and she did. Maybe she could fit in some personal time somewhere as long as it didn't interfere with her job. Ashe wasn't going to be here that long.

She sighed, slammed the storage compartment cover closed, and stood waiting while Anderson and Cris outlined the rules and guidelines for the ride.

Once the blessing of the ride by a local guru was over, she got back in the van and slowly followed after the descending riders.

She worked at keeping her mind on her investigation, thinking it might be a good idea to check out the warehouse she'd only just discovered after snooping through Anderson's office. It was located close to the office and apparently was a storage place for supplies and bikes when not in use or waiting for repair. It might be a prime spot for concealing the smuggled guns.

When they reached halfway, they stopped for a snack. This was the beginning of the most challenging part of the ride—the narrow dirt road cut precariously into the side of the mountain.

～

Kɪᴅ ʙɪᴛ into the power bar and chewed, downing almost half the water as he walked to the edge of the road where they had stopped for a break. The wind eddied and flowed around him, bringing with it the fragrant scent of vegetation, a warm, almost humid breeze from the valley below where the Amazonian rain forest spread out in a lush sprawl.

The ride was everything he was hoping it would be, exhilarating, challenging, and scenic. Although he had to keep his eyes on the road in front of him, the sheer drop-off to the left, and the towering rock walls to the right, his mind was busy thinking once again about Paige.

He looked over at her. The wind was whipping her hair around, and she gathered it, holding it back off her face in an intrinsically feminine pose, the soft curve of her arm limned by the sun. Her eyes, hazel and intense, turned toward him.

Reacting to her as a woman was making it difficult to keep his distance. Without even trying to fight it, he walked toward her.

Anderson cut across his path, slapping him on the back. "Enjoying the ride?" he asked with a smile. Kid bristled at the guy's interruption, but it was more than that. Anderson had rubbed him the wrong way almost from the moment he laid eyes on him. The familiarity with him was also grating.

Kid stepped away and said, "It's one of the best experiences I've had so far this year." He went to go around him, but Anderson either was dense or was blocking his way on purpose. "So, it's a small world, huh?"

He sighed, and Paige gave him a sympathetic look. "It is." His thirst for information about his dad warred with the image he had already built. He was a war hero, and Kid worked every day to be like him. He didn't need this guy telling him who his dad was.

When he didn't initiate any more conversation, Anderson asked, "It's been how many years now that your dad died?"

"Eighteen," Kid ground out. When Anderson opened his mouth again, Kid interrupted. "I'm sure you knew him, and that's good for you, but I don't talk about my dad. With anyone."

Anderson held up his hands at Kid's brittle tone. "Hey, okay. I get it. But if you ever want to know anything, I'm your man."

"Sure. Now if you'll excuse me."

He brushed past the big man who had probably forty pounds of muscle on Kid. He might be lean, but he was fast and lethal. He figured the bigger they were, the harder they fell. Not that he was going to get into a dustup with Anderson. As long as the guy heeded his wish regarding his dad, they really had nothing to talk about. Anderson reminded Kid of the mercs he'd seen while deployed. Ruthless, unscrupulous, and out for one thing only—themselves. Anderson had that merc air about him, and Kid wasn't fond of mercenaries, even ones who looked like they were running a legit business.

He wondered briefly how someone as personable and easy-going as Cris, Paige's boss, had hooked up and partnered with this guy. They seemed worlds apart.

Enough about Anderson as he got closer to his original destination—Paige.

She'd pulled off the hoodie and had it tied around her waist. The white tank top she wore curved around her breasts, and white lace peeked out from under one of the shoulder straps.

Lace bra.

He was definitely a lace kind of guy. The delicate fabric scalloped around the edges, disappearing under the white cotton was tantalizing.

Initially, after Mia, Kid had gone on a sex spree, not proud of his drunken prowling. That had lasted about a month, then he'd been deployed again, and it had been some time since he'd kissed a woman. Since he'd gotten one buck-assed naked and soft against him.

He took an uneven breath. He hadn't thought about it much lately, which was telling. He sure as hell hadn't thought about it since Mia had dumped him. At first, he'd been too busted up. Then his head had to be in the SEAL game or he wouldn't last a minute in the field. He'd pushed everything into a box and closed it tight.

"Everything okay?" she asked as he came up to her.

Damn, she was beautiful.

"Yeah, he's persistent. I'll give him that."

She glanced over at Anderson who was now talking with one of the other riders. She crinkled up her face. "Was he acting like he's your best friend again?"

Kid nodded because she hit so close to home there. "Yeah."

"I'm sorry."

"About what?"

"Your dad. That must have been so hard."

"It was." He shifted and looked out over the valley below. "The truth of the matter is—it had been hard, and I was proud of my dad. Who wouldn't be? He died a hero. But I would have rather had the flesh and blood man all these years, not a piece of metal and the memory of him." His voice hitched, and he had to swallow down the bitterness and feeling of being cheated of something many people took for granted. "All those father and son things, even the inevitable teenage angst and arguments from 'how the hell do you shave your face' to 'how to be the kind of man he would be proud of' was something I had to muddle through without him."

She closed her eyes, and he was shocked at how easy it was to talk to her, this woman he barely knew, about something that was so personal, so intimate. It made him want to get closer to her, feel her skin, breathe her in. Tell her more about how he felt. It was freaking crazy, but since batshit crazy was in his arsenal, he was pretty sure that just normal, everyday crazy wasn't any stretch of the imagination.

She didn't answer, and after a moment, he realized she couldn't. She was trying too hard to control whatever emotion had caused her to pull in on herself. She turned to look at him, and the softness in her eyes, the compassion for him, was something that went deep inside her, hit her hard at the very core of her. He was sorry for her pain, but damn he loved that she cared about what had happened with his dad. Things he could tell her, this stranger, that he couldn't say to his mom or sister. Things that had been trapped inside for too many years. Truthfully, things he had internalized and used to propel him not only in his career, but his life. A deep-seated need to know him, really know his father, the man who had lived and died in the short ten years of his life. Her gaze slid away from him, looking out over the valley, too. What was she seeing? The view of what was right in front of her, or nothing but her own internal landscape?

She heaved a big sigh and brushed at the hair at her temple, then folded her arms across her chest. "My mom left when I was twelve, so I know a little about an absent parent." Her uneven voice was low and strained.

"I'm sorry about your mom," he said, realizing the

missing influence on his life was the masculine energy that would have come from his dad, and for her, it had been the feminine. He'd been nurtured by his mom, and she'd tried hard to be both mother and father, but no one could really pull that off. "My dad didn't leave voluntarily."

"No, of course not. I was just saying—"

"I know what you were saying, and I appreciate it," he said. "But she chose to leave, so that's fucked up, Paige. Really fucked up."

She turned to him, startled, the look on her face registering every word he said, and they stared at each other for a couple of heartbeats. Whatever he'd been about to say was lost in the rumble, like the crack of thunder in the distance. He stiffened and went to turn around, but the rumble became a snapping and popping.

Falling rock!

He whipped around to see small boulders heading right for them, pounding down onto the road, rolling death.

He hit Paige hard, pushing them both out of the path of the rockslide. They slammed to the ground, the impact felt in every muscle of his body. But they were too close to the edge of the chasm, and she went over, dropping toward the abyss in the blink of an eye, her scream lost in the roar and cascade of broken earth.

In a lightning streak of movement, he grabbed onto her hand and held tight. For a moment she dangled in mid-air; her only anchor was his grip. Her face contorted in terror, her eyes frantic, but he felt nothing but calm. He didn't think about them both going over; he didn't think about dropping her. No freaking way was he letting go of her. Everything, his breathing, his timing, his thought process all slowed down into milliseconds as he fought to brace himself. Using his legs as if they were spring-loaded, he heaved backward, jettisoning her like a rocket as he fell onto his back and she collided against him from chest to groin.

This wasn't how he pictured full body contact with her, pulling her from certain death off the side of a cliff. Yeah, last night he'd had this fleeting fantasy of her plastered against him, her long legs tangled with his, her generous breasts pressed against his chest, her beautiful, astounding face so close he could have kissed her.

He had his arm around her waist, and he was painfully aware of exactly how recklessly he was holding her, how recklessly he needed to hold her.

Split-second timing, a little slower off the mark, and he would have lost her before he'd even had a chance to know her. That made him sick.

Her heart was racing, her breath coming fast and shallow, and she was shaking, an all-out quaking.

"Ashe," she whispered his name and he gave a short nod, letting her know he'd heard her and was ready to receive any information she was ready to say to him.

"Ashe." A short sob escaped her, and every cell in his body went on instant alert. She was breaking down.

When she sobbed again and wrapped her arms around his neck, his arms tightened around her reflexively as he went into pure caveman mode, protecting what was his, pulling her in close, lamination-level close, and holding her even tighter.

Fuck. That drop was...too damn real.

"It's okay, babe. You're safe now," he whispered, a promise he could keep. "I'm here. I've got you."

She crumpled against him, holding him like she wasn't ever going to let him go. Which suited him just fine. He was so into this sweet babe.

He waited until he felt her begin to relax; then he

eased his hold. After a heartbeat, she raised her head. Her black lashes matted, her mouth not quite steady, she looked at him, her eyes so dilated there was hardly any color. Their connection sizzled between them. In the depths of her eyes was her thanks and something else that made his heartbeat speed up, something more potent and immediate that not even a rockslide and the possibility of plunging to his death could do. The air felt thick between them, heavy and filled with a texture that was so fine and arousing, he almost forgot where he was. Her gaze softened, her mouth relaxed. He lifted his head, homing in on her lips.

"*Dios mío!* Are you two all right?" Cris Oyola shouted as he approached them. Anderson was right behind him, looking just as concerned, but in a detached way like he was calculating how much this would cost him in liability.

Hands reached down to help her up and off him, and even though he knew it was coming, he'd been lost in the moment. He was disappointed, and he wanted to be alone with her. He wanted that damn sexy mouth. Even better yet, she'd wanted his.

She was dirty, and she'd lost her hoodie, the tights torn at the thigh. She had a small gash on her forehead, but other than that, she looked pretty damn good.

He saw her get control like a general moving all her troops into formation: the tightening of her jaw, the squaring of her shoulders, and the lifting of her chin. Wow. He was blown away by her.

She wrapped her arms around herself and shivered, and he unzipped and took off his own hoodie, wrapping it around her.

They cleared the slide and found the others and the van all intact, nothing but a few rocks and debris in the road.

Anderson was on the phone, most likely reporting it. Cris touched Paige's shoulder. "Are you all right to drive?"

She nodded, but Cris looked skeptical. He walked to the van and dug around inside, pulling out a first aid kit. "I got this," Kid said and took the kit. "Attend to the other riders. I can drive the van."

"That's not necessary." Her mouth tightened, her eyes going stormy.

Cris nodded and said, "You will miss the rest of the ride."

Anderson chimed in. "Aren't you a hero?"

Kid ignored him. "No problem. You'll owe me another trip," Kid said.

Paige stood by, not looking as grateful as he expected. Cris took her shoulders in his hands, staring into her eyes with affection, then embraced her. "Dios, I am so glad you are all right." She hugged him back. Then he pulled away and looked sternly in her eyes until she relented. "You will let him drive the van. You've been through enough for one day. I want you to take it easy for a few days, and they will be free days for you with pay." He held up his hand when she went to open her mouth. "No arguments."

Anderson looked sour for a moment, as if Cris was too coddling. Kid wanted to deck the guy right there. Just haul off and cold-cock him. Kid's whole body went tight when Anderson tried to do the same thing as Cris, but Paige stiffened and sidestepped his attempt to embrace her. It turned into an awkward pat on her shoulder, and he marched away, calling out that the break and show were over.

When she didn't move, Kid took her arm and then made her sit down on the van steps. He opened the box, took out an alcohol pad, and swiped at her cut. She flinched and bit her lip, but that was all she did.

"Anderson is a piece of work," he said softly. Her eyes hardened, and she nodded.

"That he is. To think we have the same kind of relationship Cris and I share. What a jerk."

"Agreed," Kid said, even though there was pique still in her eyes. "Sometimes you have to be the bigger person and walk away, but then, sometimes you have to throat-punch a fucker to get your point across."

She burst into laughter and he pressed a bandage over her cut.

"Sometimes," she said, her laughter fading as she met his eyes, and he saw that she was quite aware that he had saved her life. Most of the time he was toting a gun and doing something crazy—saving hostages, protecting the US, and safeguarding the civilian population in many different countries, all for people he didn't know. But in Paige's case, he knew her, wanted to get to know her more, even against his better judgment. He was only going to be here for a week. He wasn't really interested in doing something long distance. It was hard enough to be deployed without having to handle someone else's location. He'd had his heart stomped on and kicked to the curb by a petite, ninety-pound package. Paige looked tougher and more solid than Mia.

She watched him, and the longer he was with her, the more intrigued he became with the change and the curious but undeniable fact that she still had a powerful effect on him. He was so aware of her, of the way the sunlight and the wind played with her hair, of her whole body, her breath, of the intensity of her gaze and her barely hidden distress.

Her brow furrowed, and she tucked her chin, and her hand slid up to cover her eyes. A soft curse left her mouth.

"Hey," he said, moving a step closer and bending his head to better see her face. "Are you okay?"

"Yeah." The lie was barely a whisper. A tremor went through her. He saw it in the brief trembling of her shoulders, in the way she leaned her weight into the side of the van. She sighed and looked away, her eyes moist. "Thank you," she murmured. "Thank you so much, Ashe."

She stood and turned toward the steps, her shoulder brushing his, and the contact brought her to a sudden halt. Her head came up, and their eyes met.

She was close, very close, her fragrance coming to him on the air, all thankful woman and soft sweet.

Powerful.

He found himself breathing deeper just to have more of her. Crazy, crazy, so batshit crazy, the word went through his mind. He was a lunatic, trying to breathe her in—but, God, he loved the way she smelled. He didn't know how to read the shadowed expression in her eyes.

"Everything's fine now. You're safe."

"Thanks to you."

He reached out and gently took hold of her upper arm.

Gratitude. It was a hell of a lot better than wariness, but it wasn't even close to what he really wanted from her.

He moved his hand down her arm and slid his thumb along the edge of her wrist, feeling the silken softness of her skin and took another step closer.

"Ashe," she said his name half as a protest and half as a plea.

Her hand came up to cover her face again, and he couldn't help it. His fingers smoothed along the curve of her jaw.

"Come on! Let's get this show on the road," Anderson yelled.

Paige jerked, and then they just looked at each other. Kid

wanted to throat-punch the fucker, that was for sure. Instead, he followed her up into the van.

Cowboy crouched low in the cover of the jungle. "No sign of anyone," Hollywood said into the mic, delivering his low-worded message straight into Cowboy's ear. They were currently in one of North Korea's many lowlands between mountain ranges where flyboy Captain Shawn Martin had gone down while doing top-secret surveillance in his Dragon Lady, an American single-jet engine, ultra-high-altitude reconnaissance aircraft—in other words, a freaking spy plane.

"Any sign of the downed wreckage?" Cowboy asked.

"Negative," Hollywood answered.

Cowboy looked to Ruckus, who said, "Bring them back, and we'll go at this from a different angle."

"Yes, sir," Cowboy responded, but just before he keyed his mic, he was interrupted.

"We're on deadline," Scarecrow said in his soft Southern accent. "Just got the intel that Korean troops are on the move."

"Copy that. Come back to base. We'll regroup and search the next grid."

"Roger," Hollywood said. He was with Wicked, Blue, Tank, and Echo, searching for any clue as to where Captain Martin might have crashed after he was downed by a surface-to-air-missile.

"Wait, Echo has picked up something. Standby."

Petty Officer Ryuu "Dragon" Shannon, their sniper stand-in for Kid, shifted next to Cowboy. His dark eyes never left the field in front of them. Even though Cowboy knew most of the guys on Team Seven, Dragon was enigmatic and quiet. He had a baby face, lean, ripped body, and shock of dark hair like Kid's, but he wore it cropped close on the sides and thicker on top. With a slight New York borough accent that leaned more toward Brooklyn, he spoke only when necessary. His mixed heritage of Japanese and American clear in his features, Dragon was as mysterious and myriad as the orient Easily as intense as their preferred point man, but more darkly so. Where Kid cracked jokes, Dragon was silent and deadly. Cowboy wondered how Kid was doing in Bolivia. He'd kept his eye on the boy wonder, who showed no signs of his melt down six months ago, but Cowboy wasn't quite sure that Kid was exactly okay.

"Hollywood?" Scarecrow said.

"Patience," Hollywood murmured. "The dog can't exactly say what's got him agitated."

"Copy that, but patience is only important when there are no witnesses," Scarecrow drawled.

"Haha, man, that's funny. You're giving my finger a boner."

"Your girl tells me that's the only way you can get one," Scarecrow countered.

"Yours tells me my dick is bigger, and I'm better looking."

There were several chuckles over the mic. "Echo has found the flyboy, but there are several tangos between us and him," Hollywood said, his voice hushed.

"What's his status?" Cowboy asked.

"Looks like he's not mobile. He's nicely concealed, but if they start beating the bushes, they're going to find him. LT?"

"Lay low until the sun goes down, then go get him under their noses."

Cowboy and the four SEALs bided their time until the sun dropped into the horizon. Egress wasn't for another hour, but they had to get Captain Martin and hightail it to the LZ.

"LT, we're moving in," Hollywood said.

There was tense silence until Blue said, "He's in bad shape, LT. Broken leg, banged up good. I'll need to set it before we can move him. He's conscious, though, and wants me to tell you he's glad to see us, even if we're SEALs."

Ruckus laughed and said, "Roger that. The plane?"

"Five klicks from here. He said he's been in and out and can't say for sure if he destroyed the intel."

"Hollywood and Wicked, get to the plane and make sure no one is going to get any use out of it. Then head to the LZ."

"Roger," Wicked said.

"Blue and Tank, we're headed your way." Ruckus rose, and Cowboy, Scarecrow, and Dragon rose with him. They started moving to the coordinates Scarecrow was tracking on his computer. Once they reached them, they crouched down, Dragon taking up a position to handle any surprises from the Koreans.

"We're ready to blow the plane, LT," Wicked said, his voice hushed.

"Give us five more minutes, then light it up. That's going to get their attention. Make sure you're headed to the LZ."

"Copy that."

"Blue, let's move."

He picked up Captain Martin and headed toward the LZ. Moments after that, an explosion lit up the night. There was some chatter, but they were headed away from Cowboy and the rapidly moving SEALs. Suddenly there was a muffled shout, and all of them turned to find Dragon pulling a knife out of a guy's throat. With a nod, LT gestured them into motion. Once they hit the LZ, the chopper landed, and they rendezvoused with Wicked and Hollywood.

Once they secured the pilot in the Blackhawk, it took off, and the North Koreans, except for one unlucky dude, didn't even know they'd been there.

The perfect op. Again, Cowboy wondered about Kid. Dragon was cool, but Kid belonged to their team. He'd be glad when he was back.

5

A day later as he tied up his running shoes at his hotel, Ashe couldn't quite figure out why he'd kept his distance and why Paige had given him a chilly goodbye at the end of the trip. It was as if nothing of their heat and intensity had survived the rest of the drive down the mountain. Maybe she was angry with the way he'd taken over for her. Competent women didn't want to look bad in their boss's eyes. But geez, she'd just been through a harrowing experience. What the hell could he have done? Let her drive, trembling and handling the aftershocks of almost getting plowed by falling rock, hanging off the edge of a cliff, anchored by a guy she just met?

Sure, she didn't know him. But he had a hard time dealing with his own indecision. An uncertain SEAL was a dead SEAL. Yet he couldn't seem to figure out what to do about this particular choice.

He headed out of the hotel and soon found himself running on the outskirts of town as night settled over the mountains. The air was chilly, and he'd only donned his gray hoodie, the hood now over his wet and perspiring head. Maybe he could sweat the babe right out of his system and avoid the whole morning-after routine completely.

Okay, so one-night stands weren't his modus operandi. He liked a committed relationship. So, sue him. He wanted to know a woman was his, exclusively.

He'd been totally blindsided that he would end up halfway across the world, completely lost in the wilds of Bolivia with a woman who broke his heart just from looking at her. It made him feel uncomfortably exposed, vulnerable.

Edgy.

The thin mountain air didn't slow him down one bit. He hadn't been affected by the altitude at all. The terrain was uneven and challenging, just the way he liked it. It got his muscles working and made the workout more grueling. He couldn't slack ever, vacation or no vacation.

He was on a ridge overlooking some warehouses, the moon rising and the stars brightening his way. He was drenched now, perspiration running down his torso, soaking into the waistband of his running pants.

He saw someone crouching, but the figure rose abruptly and pointed a gun at him. "Stop right there."

THE DARK FIGURE sneaking up on her in the night unnerved her. She was still on edge after what had happened yesterday, and only part of that was the whole plunging-to-her-death thing. The other part was what had happened afterward at the van with Ashe being so darn sweet and protective. God, she'd wanted to kiss him in the worst way, inhale him whole, but she couldn't get past her obligation to NCIS. Her job here was crucial to two families who were waiting for justice and the imperative recovery of those weapons.

She didn't have time for pleasure. And after one look at Ashe Wilder, there was no doubt the man could deliver on pleasure tenfold.

Her eyes never left the dark silhouette. She hadn't heard him, and her snooping outside the warehouse had given her some valuable intel. It was guarded. Why would a warehouse that stored old bikes and other equipment need this level of security?

"Are you armed?" she asked in her don't-mess-with-me agent's growl.

"No," he said, his voice low and hard.

"Let me see." When he reached for the zipper of his hoodie, she cautioned, "Slow and easy."

"That's the way I roll," he murmured.

Her grip on the Glock 9mm was firm and strong, her finger along the trigger guard poised for violence. One wrong move, a quick squeeze and he would go down.

He slowly unzipped the hoodie and grasped each side in his fingers to reveal...a ripped and lean torso. Her gaze slid down the length of him, every muscle delineated, a work of art, each curve a union of strength and testosterone, of conviction and the iron will to survive.

He turned slowly around and everything about him was intriguing, the aura of him...so familiar. The tight, fine butt, the long, strong legs. She tilted her head, her eyes squinting. "Come to where I can see you."

He stepped forward so that the security light from the warehouse illuminated him. She gasped and whispered harshly, "Ashe."

"Yes, ma'am," he said firmly.

They'd had breakfast together while he took every pleasure he could in vexing Marco, her would-be suitor, told her intimate things about his dad that she was quite sure he'd never told anyone in his life, and saved her from crushing boulders and a sheer drop in a matter of seconds. Here he was still calling her *ma'am*.

"What are you doing out here?" Immediately, she was wary. She realized she didn't know him at all. Wasn't sure about his "tourist" classification. From the beginning, he looked more like a warrior than he did anything else. Who, exactly, was he?

"Running."

"Running?"

He stepped closer to her. She couldn't seem to lower the weapon, feeling threatened by him. She'd never met a man who looked so dangerous but was so darn sweet. Sweetly fierce like he'd been when he was saving her, sweetly sincere with his confession about his dad, and so sweetly beautiful, it hurt.

He didn't stop moving until the gun's barrel was just under his chin. His eyes were deep pools of blue that she could drown in, and there was a recklessness about him that set off sizzling, daunting vibes. Something inside her told her to flee—that she would never be the same if she tangled with him—but she couldn't move.

He was lethally irresistible.

And so, so on edge. She pushed him there to the edge; the knowledge flashed through her like a heartbeat.

Oh, man, she liked him off-balance for sure. She liked him unsteady, because he rattled the hell out of her. His dark hair was covered with the gray hood. Only his bangs were visible, hanging like wet, black silk over his forehead and into his eyes, catching on his thick, dark lashes. A trace of beard stubble darkened his jaw and upper lip. The gray cotton was soaked through, still open over his bare chest and all that rippled muscle. But he was still distracting, with cheekbones she wanted to slide her fingers over and a mouth she wanted to kiss—thoughts even more disconcerting now than they'd been yesterday when he'd grappled her out of thin air and onto his hard, hot body.

"Have you ever pulled the trigger while looking a man in the eyes?" His voice was low, seductive, and cold as the night air around them.

She took a shallow breath. She had no words, no response, waiting for what he had to say, her body quivering, the gun nothing but a flimsy barrier under his chin.

His head tilted, his mouth lowering toward hers and stopping a hair's breadth away. "In that instant before you pull the trigger, death is personal, to you, to your target. Three and a half pounds is all it takes." His gaze was now hot, an incandescent blue. An infinity of snowflakes floated onto his shoulders, into his hair, onto his face, melting when they came into contact with his hot skin.

More long seconds of silence passed. "You're going to live; he's going to die. That's the way it's orchestrated. You're never closer to life right there in one breath to the next. It's silent and quick and ruthless—a perfect cold zero."

This brought them to the inevitable moment, a moment that she knew was coming at her like a freight train, but when his mouth covered hers, nudging the gun down, it wasn't with the force of a freight train, but like that of a feather, soft, gentle. The sweet, tantalizing warmth enfolded her as his arm tightened around her, pulling her closer to his body, closer to his heat. His breath was so alive, the faint touch of his lips a seduction on a primal level, the culmination of a kiss that had been coming forever.

One that she could not have dodged or avoided, as certain as death and as dangerous as hell.

He brushed her lips again, lingering longer, and all she

could think was that they were both crazy. She still had the gun under his chin. She had the upper hand. But she was the one trembling—and he was pushing her too far.

Right out of her comfort zone where she realized there had never been any comfort at all. Just hard work, lonely, hastily consumed meals, and even lonelier nights. Before this kiss, she thought it was a necessity to get ahead, be all that she could be. Show her dad that she had the same work ethic as him, learning it the hard way all those years of his absence and her raising three hellion brothers. But now it was about hard, velvet muscles, lethal looks, and heat so hot she swore the night was filled with steam instead of snow.

But this new zone, this, this...Ashe Zone was almost more than she could bear, and something she couldn't get enough of, no matter how hard she thought about it. But there she was thinking when everything about this encounter was tactile, rousing and astounding.

Before she realized it, the gun was out of her hand and in his. Disarming her seemed to be this man's specialty, and if his motives were hostile, she wouldn't even see it coming. She'd have her eyes closed kissing him.

The sound was barely perceptible, a scuff of a boot, a soft disturbance in the night, but Ashe shoved the gun in her hand, turned her shoulders and whispered in her ear, his breath hot against the delicate shell. "Hide," he hissed.

She reacted, her agent instincts finally kicking in. She bolted for cover and the shadows. When she threw a quick glance over her shoulder, he was gone...simply vanished as if he had blended into shadow. She heard a scuffle and headed toward it. No way was she leaving the man who had saved her life out here to deal with something she'd stirred up. Not when she had the gun, the training, and the deter- mination. My God, Ashe was a lone wolf distraction that she couldn't afford. If she blew her cover...her boss would have her head. So much was riding on this assignment.

Down the hill, toward the warehouse she'd been watching, a man stood, alert, searching the night. Paige crouched down, looking for Ashe. Then darkness moved at her peripheral vision. The guard was a brute. Much, much bigger than Ashe, but with several graceful, powerful, lightning-like moves, the huge man let out a gasp and a grunt, then was down and out. A shot echoed, whizzing past her, the *zing* like the twang of a bow, displacing the air.

Ashe burst into action. He disarmed the second man who never saw him coming, and after brief hand-to-hand combat, the guy was down. Without breaking stride, he pelted up the hill as if the incline was flat ground, his feet throwing dirt and debris behind him. He caught her by the arm and growled, "Move."

Below them, several shouts sounded. Swearing and pounding feet filled the previously silent night. He picked up his pace.

"Is he dead?" she asked in the thin air.

"Nope. But he won't remember either one of us," he said, spurring her on across a hill and down toward the city at a breakneck pace.

As she ran beside him, growing more breathless and wondering how long she could keep up—and what he'd do when she couldn't—it occurred to her, ridiculously, that he was some kind of elite operator, which made her blood go ice cold. Was he connected with Anderson? Had she missed something?

Lungs burning, heart pounding, she grabbed the rail of the stairs they were going down, Ashe's hand still firmly around her upper arm. He wasn't even breathing hard, and she could hardly breathe at all. His hoodie was still unzipped, flapping in the wind, giving her tantalizing glimpses of his six pack and wide, gorgeous chest.

So help her God, who was he? She had to find out once this was over and they were safely away from the current threat of exposure. If Anderson got wind that someone was snooping around the warehouse and he discovered it was a woman...well, he wasn't an idiot, just a jerk.

But no, her thinking was muddled. If Ashe was mixed up in this somehow, he wouldn't be helping her at all, definitely not kissing the hell out of her in the snow in the dark during her clandestine recon.

Behind them on the stairs she could hear someone struggling to keep up. He was big and brawny, like the last gorilla Ashe had flattened. Anderson was big, too, but he was all muscle and horrendous strength and smart as a whip. If it was him behind them, she couldn't afford to get caught.

"Faster," Ashe commanded, doing his best to single-handedly carry her down more than one stair at a time.

They hit the cobblestones, and she stumbled. He caught her against him and kept moving, all steel and speed. He vaulted a concrete wall as she did the same. It was attached to a small church, blocking in a small cemetery. His eyes shone in the meager light from the chapel. He tugged left, and she tugged right, "No, this way," she insisted.

Without argument, he trusted her, and they changed direction. The men chasing them had momentarily lost them, and she could hear shouting. Lights came on in an apartment building as they rushed past.

She'd been here long enough to understand La Paz was all about the geography and the fact that its identity was closely tied to the culture here. The mountains were everywhere, infused by the indigenous people with spirits. She relied on them now, watching over them as they ran.

They hustled down a steep cobblestone street that cascaded down to the main avenue known as the Prado, hoping to get as far away from the pursuit as possible. There were more people here, too. Easier to get lost in the crowd. Traffic was heavy as they passed a small green square, highrises to the left and shops to the right. As they got deeper into the area, they passed singers and street performers, the aroma of food making her stomach grumble.

She was jerked off her feet, and before she knew what was happening, Ashe had her in a shadowed doorway, his body pressed up against hers so tight, she could barely catch her breath. Her hands went to his bare waist, his skin slick and scorching, the muscles beneath like iron.

In a split second, his mouth slammed into hers. Her body was humming. His lips, damn, were so hot, so soft. He slid his fingers along the back of her neck, beneath her hair, sending a delicious cascade of shivers all the way down her spine.

He lifted his gaze just enough to look into her eyes, his shell-shocked and aroused, his face tight. She held his gaze for what felt like all eternity, then slowly lowered her eyelids as she closed the distance between them and kissed him back. Their pursuers went by, three of them. And one of them *was* Anderson.

His fingers twitched against the back of her neck when she opened her mouth on his, then pressed a bit harder as he accepted the invitation and devoured her. This man was a first-class kisser, and she had the melted body to prove it.

He groaned and raised his head again before taking the kiss deeper.

He was a natural at kissing. She had no doubt about it,

and her entire body thrilled at the knowledge that he'd be even better in bed.

He broke the kiss. "*Fuck* me," he said softly.

And all she could think was, *Oh, God, yes. Over and over again.*

~

Ashe took two quick breaths, made sure the coast was clear, and grabbed her hand. They crossed the street and were on the run again, but this time there were no footfalls behind them. As they exited the Prado, she tugged him toward the outskirts of the city.

When she reached a small stucco cottage, she went up the path. Baby blue paint with a darker blue trim set the house apart on the street. The windows were funky, each covered with an iron grate worked with circles across the top, lacy hearts in the middle, and stars beneath and painted in the same baby blue. The multilayer gardens surrounding the place turned it into a gem hidden in a jungle of trees, bushes, and clumps of vegetation.

"Who does this place belong to?"

She grinned and produced the key. Unlocking the door, they hurried inside. As she flicked on the light, he headed toward the kitchen and opened the fridge. Pulling out bottles of water, he threw one to her, then drank three in a row while she polished off one. He threw her another one.

The place smelled wonderful, earthy and sweet—Paige. He could hear a fountain bubbling and splashing from somewhere around back.

She went to the fireplace and started it burning. It was white, square stucco, and as she set logs on the beginning spark, it was soon blazing. He was still drenched after that run. He couldn't keep his eyes off her.

The house was as quaint and well-kept as the outside, with colorful striped rugs on the concrete floor. The couch and chairs were all upholstered in a deep red with an abundance of striped throw pillows dotting them. The coffee table was a rich, dark wood and looked handmade.

This is the kind of home Paige made, and he had to admit he liked it a lot. It was clear from the delicious aroma in the kitchen she cooked, too. Something about that set him on edge—in a good way.

The quiet warmth and security of her place settled in him like hot cocoa.

"So, what were you doing up there?" The hoodie was soaked, and he slipped it off his shoulders. She went to a small cabinet and came out with a towel. She tossed it to him, and he wiped off his face and chest, then sent it through his hair.

Her face changed, her eyes caressing him as if he'd somehow distracted her. For the life of him, he couldn't figure out how drying his hair made her look at him like that. "Walking," she said, her voice uneven.

"With a gun?" he countered and prowled toward her. That's how he felt right now, aroused, heat suffusing him inside and out, primal. The fire felt good on his damp skin.

Her chin came up, her eyes flashing. "For protection. You never know when you'll need to shove a gun under a crazy guy's chin."

"Touché." He gave her a sly grin.

She shook her head. He couldn't disagree with her.

"Yeah, a Glock nine millimeter, the kind of gun government agents carry."

"I think you really need to mind your own business," she said.

"I was never really good at that."

"Just because you saved my life doesn't mean I have to tell you anything." She folded her arms across her chest.

"I could eat a bowl of alphabet soup and crap a better argument than that."

She narrowed her eyes. "Tell me how you downed that big guy. I don't think the *government* job you have is pushing papers."

He looked away his jaw flexing. "I'm a Navy SEAL."

Her jaw dropped open, and she just stared at him. "Seriously? A Navy SEAL? Got the trident and everything?"

He took a breath at her skeptical look. "Yeah, I got the trident and the call name, too."

Her hands went to her hips. "A call name?"

"Kid Chaos."

She closed her eyes as if she was remembering every moment he'd spent kissing her. "That I believe," she whispered. She sighed heavily and look worried. "You're an active SEAL?" At his nod, she went and folded down on the couch and dropped her head into her hands.

"Yeah, I'm on leave. Why is this a problem?" Damn, was she doing something illegal? He didn't want to bust her, he wanted to jump her bones.

"It's not a problem," she said, but it was clear to him that she was lying.

He strode across the room, his anger and sexual frustration pumping through him. "I don't appreciate being lied to, Paige. What is going on here?"

She stood up and said, "I have to make a phone call." She left the room, and he just stood there wondering what the hell was going on.

6

She dialed her boss, Mike, and as soon as he answered, she said, "We have a problem."

"What kind of problem?"

"There's a guy here claiming to be a Navy SEAL. He saw me doing surveillance on the warehouse."

"Dammit, Paige."

"I know. It's not ideal, but if he's an active SEAL, I can at least read him in on what is going on." She sighed. "As you can imagine, he's very pushy and insistent."

"What's his name," her boss said.

"Ashe with an e Wilder."

"Just a minute."

After a few minutes he said, "Yeah, Petty Officer First Class Ashe Wilder. He's a SEAL all right. Sniper. Highly-decorated badass. Black ops stuff because most of his file is classified." He sighed. "This might not be too bad. I'll call you back."

She waited until fifteen minutes went past and she heard the shower come on. He was bathing? She could use a shower herself.

Her cell rang, and she answered. "I just talked to the Director and Wilder's commanding officer. Put him on the phone."

"Now," she squeaked.

"Yes, Paige. Now."

She walked over to her closet and dug around inside. There were guy's clothes the previous owner had left. Jeans, underwear, shirts, mostly T-shirts, socks and a nice pair of hiking boots. He must have left in a hurry. She gathered up a set of clothes and took a deep breath. She couldn't keep her boss and the Director of NCIS waiting. She slipped out of her bedroom and into the hall, the bathroom right in front of her. The door was ajar. She had to take a big, huge breath. Ashe—Kid Chaos—for God's sake was in her shower—naked. *Buck-assed naked. Oh, happy day. Right, Paige, that was so professional.* She tamped down her randy thoughts that had sunk down into dirtymindland.

She pushed the door open and said, "Ashe, my boss wants to talk to you."

He slid the curtain aside, and she almost swallowed her tongue. Wet, Wilder, and wonderful, he stood there, the curtain barely covering him, so tantalizingly male, she had to work to keep her mind on the professional...business... murdered MP's and their families...her promotion...missing military grade weapons.

That helped, but didn't exactly diminish him one iota. Talk about chaos. He should have been called Master of Chaos. She pressed the speaker icon before she held it out.

"Your boss?"

"He'll explain."

He frowned, but then stiffened and immediately went to attention. "Kid, can't you even go on vacation when you go on vacation?"

"LT? What the hell..."

"It seems you've fallen into an NCIS undercover operation. Agent Paige Sinclair is working a suspect who is under investigation for the murder of two MP's and a boatload of weapons and ammunition. She's going to fill you in on the details, but as of now, you're working with her."

"Copy that, sir." His eyes went to hers and stayed there.

"Kid...don't get into anything you can't get out of...is that understood, sailor?"

"Understood, LT."

Her boss's voice came back on the line. "The circumstances aren't ideal, Wilder, and you've just been dropped into this mission, but Paige is one of my best and she'll fill you in. You have my agent's back."

He agreed, and his voice was all business, but his eyes... Oh, his eyes gave her a very different message, like he'd have her back, front—every inch of her.

"Give me regular updates, Paige."

"Yes, sir," she murmured.

She disconnected the call.

"So we're working together," he said.

"Looks that way?"

"A you wash my back, and I'll wash yours kinda thing?"

Had she thought he'd dominated her house when he'd walked in? His presence was so much bigger than life it felt as though he'd been in it far longer than that. But now that he was standing in her tub, the flimsy shower curtain all that was covering him, she realized she had sorely underestimated just how big a presence he truly was.

"Ashe..." She ached to lose herself in his sensual kisses, the knowing stroke of his hands, and the heat of his mouth tempting her beyond thought or reason. And judging by the dark desire smoldering in his gaze, he had already been thinking those thoughts.

He let go of the shower curtain. "You want to come in here with me."

She gasped. It wasn't a question, and he wasn't at all arrogant. It was confidence, and that made him all the more attractive to her, a strong man who knew what he wanted and had no compunction about saying so. The honesty in his words made her tremble. That and he was just so damn beautiful, the full glorious view of him completely naked was just as gorgeous and magnificent as the man himself.

"We both know it." He was already hard and thick, his erection curving up from his body as if begging for her touch.

She glanced up the length of his ripped torso, watched the rapid rise and fall of his ches, and finally met his gaze. His eyes were dark and intense, hypnotic.

"We both feel it. We both want it."

Her body went fluid at his words. She was very aroused. She did want him. But now everything was a freaking complicated mess. He was now entwined with her job. "Maybe we should heed your commanding officer's order."

"Babe, if I heeded all his orders, they wouldn't call me Kid Chaos, would they?"

His eyes were so dark, so fathomless, it was like drowning in velvet blue, and she wanted to drown, suck in deep lungfuls of him and say to hell with reality, work, common sense, and sanity.

She forced herself to take a step backward, and he looked down as if he was composing himself. When he looked back up, the fire was banked in his eyes. "Okay, I get it. I'll back off, but, babe, the invitation is open-ended. Whenever you want me, come get me."

He flicked the curtain closed over all that tantalizing skin and hard body. She swallowed and clutched her phone in her hand, her determination wavering.

He started to sing, and she jumped. His voice was deep and melodic as he ripped out Earth, Wind & Fire's "September," hitting the high notes just perfectly. Unexpectedly, she laughed. He pulled the shower curtain open and said, "What? You need to sing "September" in the shower at least once a week. When I sing it in the locker room, I get applause." He sang the ba-de-das into the upside-down end of her back scrubber as a makeshift mic, all while keeping a straight face, rocking his body to the rhythm of his voice. He flicked the curtain closed again, then transitioned to "Purple Rain." Then when it opened, he was wailing on an air guitar, once again using her back scrubber. She'd never be able to use it again without thinking about this. About him and his antics.

"You need some purple lighting in here to make that one work," she offered. He grinned and nodded. She laughed again. "I didn't know I was going to get a show here."

"I am entertaining and take the er off shower and what do you have? Am I right?" When she laughed, he flashed her a wicked and debilitating smile, his wet hair so dark and tousled. "Now it's time to get sultry." His grin faded, and he went all moody and broody male. "Are you ready for the ballads?"

She nodded, then leaned against the door for support.

He tilted his head in an adorable little boy way. "No, you're not." He flashed her another grin. "Are you sure? Maybe."

He closed the curtain and started with Sam Smith's, "Stay with Me." Then segued into "Best Thing I Never Had," which tugged at her heart. The tone to his voice said he'd been hurt before. Paige shifted. There was nothing funny about him getting his heart broken. She couldn't imagine why any sane woman would let him go once she had him. He was sweet, funny, tough, and now that she knew he was a SEAL, lethal fit him as well. The way he took down that big guy had been...lethal. She was well aware that if things hadn't changed between them, and if he had just been a tourist, she'd be in there with him or tangled in the sheets on her bed. The wanting tugged at her so hard, she wanted to just strip and wrap herself around him. He'd been so understanding, damn him.

He poked his head out again. "You're still here? I should have sold tickets. So, Beyoncé, right? Girl power to the max?"

He reached out his fist. She shook her head and took the steps required to reach him, thinking this might be a big mistake. She fist-bumped him, then he grabbed her around the back of her neck and gave her a wet, lips-so-soft kiss, lingering just at the end as he tasted her. Letting her go, he disappeared back inside the tub.

When he started on Celine Dion's "The Power of Love," she thought her knees were going to give out. Wow, he could really sing, but his rich voice singing those wonderful lyrics every woman wants to hear had the most impact.

"Hurry up. I need to get in there, too, and I'm starving," she groused.

He popped out one more time, his voice so smooth and liquid. His expression was so sexy, his eyes a bit narrowed, his mouth curving up at the corner so provocatively. When he got to the 'lady and man' lyrics he didn't reverse them, his eyes dancing. The air trapped in her chest burst out into laughter, and he said, "Hey, it's not funny. That goes over big in the transport. I get standing o's."

She had to go or she was going to lose it. "Just what a serious deployment needs." She had to take a deep breath as their eyes met again and the laughter faded from his face. She read people for a living, and Ashe "Kid Chaos" Wilder was more than larger than life. He was wonderful with a soothing voice and incredibly beautiful eyes—something she'd noticed more and more tonight. They were thick-lashed and filled with a fierce intensity. So very easy to get lost.

"Yeah, dropping into danger and all that needs some levity." She felt the weight of his gaze. "It's just so quiet in there, I can't resist, and the acoustics are almost as good as a shower. Me and Celine. We know how to break hearts. Every man in there wants to be mine."

He gave her a wink and then started up with "I will Survive." She closed the bathroom door and leaned against it. "I left you some clothes."

He broke long enough to say "Thanks," then was back to Gloria Gaynor. But the words of "The Power of Love" kept going around in her head. Here she was, almost thirty, and she had never been in love. Sure, lust a few times but never love. She'd never really had the time to invest in finding the right man. What did that even mean—the right man? She grew up in a household of men with her three brothers and her dad. She was still living at home, even with her dad being retired. She didn't have time to do all the girly things teenagers learn from their moms. In fact, she'd had to nurse her little brother Atticus on prom night because he was sick with a fever. When he graduated from high school, he had his sights set on becoming a SEAL. He would be pretty excited right now to know that his big sister was in the same room with one.

She went into her bedroom and grabbed her own

clothes. As he finished up in there, she tried to keep herself under control. She glanced at her bed and took a deep breath, almost able to picture him there looking hard and aroused, sleepy and sated, warm and compassionate. She swore softly, and he said, "Who do these clothes belong to?"

She whirled to find him at her doorway, a towel around that amazing waist. The white was a contrast to his dark skin, the stubble on his face accentuating his strong jaw and fine mouth. "Some guy."

He chuckled. "Oh, okay. Just a random guy, huh?" He wiggled his brows.

"No, not someone I slept with...I don't do that. I mean...I do sleep with men, but not like that."

He leaned his shoulder into the doorframe. Giving her a deadpan look, he said. "Now, I'm getting a show. Stand-up comedy?"

"Very funny."

"You'd sleep with me, but not like that? How exactly do you go about sleeping with a guy?" His voice was pitched low.

She took a breath. "Shut up. He was the previous tenant."

"Oh, I see."

She wanted to go past him, but he was blocking the way. "Your turn for a shower." He also had no intention of moving. She was an NCIS agent. She'd looked bad guys in the eyes and taken them down. She could do this. He was just a man. *Yeah, right. A beautiful, funny, amazing singer man.*

She lifted her chin and snatched up her clothes.

"I think the jeans will fit and the T-shirt, but no way am I wearing some guy's skivvies."

"What?"

"I'm not wearing his underwear whether you slept with him or not."

Exasperated, she said through clenched teeth, "I didn't sleep with him. I don't even know him." She looked at the briefs in his hand. "Well, then what are you going to..." The smirk on his face said it all. She had to take a breath. "Oh."

"Yeah, commando, babe." He still didn't move.

She squared her shoulders and went to the doorway. He conceded to turn sideways, but otherwise, he didn't give an inch. The minute she was sliding past him, plastered to him, he set his arms on either side of her. Pressing into the doorway made his biceps bulge. He smelled so good, clean and fresh. She wanted to bury her nose in the crook of his neck and breathe deeply. "I heard if you go commando, you never go back."

His close proximity was making it really difficult to concentrate on what he was saying. Her body was getting the message loud and clear, but it had nothing to do with underwear or lack of it. He was a freaking tease. Well, two could play at that game.

"Is that so? It could be hard getting that zipper up over the merchandise, so be careful there." She straightened and deftly moved under his arm, but before she stepped too far away, she flicked at the tuck of his towel, and it unraveled. She walked calmly down the hall and into the bathroom. Pressured to look back to see how he'd reacted, she peeked around the jamb. He was standing there looking amused and bested. The hard curve of his hip, the thick ridge of his abdominal V—hip-things is what she called them—as sexy as the rest of him. She wanted to trace them with her tongue.

He turned his head and grinned, looking even more

boyish than she thought possible. He was incorrigible. She giggled and shut the door on his sigh.

After she was finished, she left the bathroom. She glanced in her bedroom, but the only sign he had been there was the towel draped over her door and the pair of underwear. She went looking for him, but he wasn't in the living room, either. Then she saw his silhouette outside. She went to the patio doors and slipped through. "Hey, what are you doing out here? It's cold."

He was wearing an edgy motorcycle-inspired leather jacket with buckles and zippers that was also orphaned from the tenant. It made him look rebel-bad. He smiled, his hair still damp. "It's beautiful here. Different from Tibet and Tanzania. The mountains are just as big and jagged, but the landscape is so different. The people, though, are the same. Tough, resourceful, and warm."

"Have you found that in most places you go? You know, other than the ones where people are shooting at you?"

He turned to her. "As a matter of fact, yeah. I was just in a place like that. Ended up at a cantina and got food and drinks just like we were hanging out. Local populations have really, on the whole, treated us pretty well. We are, after all, human and want the same things in life."

She nodded. "True." She looked back out to the mountains. "I've only been here for two weeks, and most of that I've been working, but I agree, the people are very good and kind."

She heard her stomach growl, and he gave her another one of those boyish looks that made her insides melt. "Someone's hungry."

"Starved." His stomach was just as noisy. "Let's go inside, and I'll cook us up something."

"Cook?"

She turned and narrowed her eyes at him. "What is that supposed to mean?"

"Nothing," he said, halting and holding up his hands. "It's just that I've dated a lot of women and most of them just don't."

He'd dated a lot of women. Why did that make her more irritated than the fact that he just lumped her in with his harem? "I'm not most women," she groused as she went inside.

"Oh, geez, I didn't mean to piss you off." He caught her in the living room. "Wait," he said as he grasped her arm. "I'm sorry. I just love the idea of a home-cooked meal. It's been a long time since I've had one. I've got some time set aside to visit my mom, sister, and nieces before my leave is up, but it made me a bit homesick there for a minute."

"If this is a ploy to save your behind—" One look in his eyes, and she realized that those words held no weight. "You are a charmer, aren't you?"

"Am I?" he asked, those blue eyes of his open and sincere. "I just am finding it really difficult to keep my hands to myself, even though you asked me to. I've never dogged a woman in my life. I'd like to think I had more sense than that, was classier than some hound dog."

Was she being too much of a tight-ass? Worrying about her job when, in reality, she deserved a life, too? Had she grown boring and predictable over the years while she raised her brothers, dedicated to their well-being, to her father's needs and simply out of necessity, ignoring her own? When had she ever let go? Never. That's when.

"There's a lot riding on this assignment, not the least of which are two men who lost their lives and a promotion I've worked very hard for."

She was thinking distance was something she wasn't

liking too much with Ashe. For a few minutes, she took him in, and God, she liked what she saw, what she felt, what this man had already offered and proved. She was grateful for his patience, for his intensity. It made her want to lower her guard with him. Made her want to believe that engaging him in a little harmless flirtation was natural and normal between two people who were attracted to each other. Except he was trouble. And there was nothing harmless about him.

"You call the shots, babe. I'll follow orders."

"All right," she said, breaking away from him and lobbing two throw pillows at him. "You can help with dinner."

With lightning reflexes, he caught the pillows and sent them back at her with a grin. "You're going to make me work for my dinner, huh?"

She caught one, and the other one glanced off her shoulder. She didn't have those big hands of his to catch both.

Her mouth went a little dry thinking about those strong, sure hands on her. She didn't have to imagine how they felt; warm, pushy, and fast. Somehow her life had turned much more complicated when she wasn't looking. And the leading man was Ashe "Kid Chaos" Wilder.

"So, boss, how do you want me to help?"

She turned toward the kitchen. "We have this little thing called a stove."

He chuckled.

She opened the refrigerator door and hid her smile. Her life was going topsy-turvy...and here she was, grinning like a fool over a little banter with an attractive man. So what if it had been a little while? Okay, a long while. And so what if it was a man she'd just met, a sexy and exciting man who had just burst into her ordinary world? A little professionalism at the moment would go a long way.

But then she felt him at her back, and before she could close the door and move, he was peering over her shoulder at the contents of her fridge.

"So, PB and J? I can spread the peanut butter," he said, his breath warm on the side of her neck. "Got any chips to go with?"

She grabbed the fresh vegetables and a bottle of salad dressing from the rack in the door. "You can spread more than that," she said, elbowing him out of the way. His amused grunt made her fight her smile.

God, he was so damn cute.

"Grab the chicken, wiseass. It's in that white dish."

"It's in some kind of sauce, and it smells damn good."

"It's a mango and lime marinade. You'll love it." She set down the salad fixings on a cutting board and turned to the stove. Preheating the oven, she took the dish and set it on the stovetop. "You can make the salad." Reaching into a cupboard, she pulled out a serving bowl, two little bowls, and a box of croutons.

She went back to the fridge and grabbed the sack of pea pods. Dumping them in the sink, she went to a cupboard, and, of course, she had to lean into him to reach the bowl she wanted. He stopped chopping and fixed his eyes on her as she pressed her upper body against his. Her skin tingled from the close contact with all that muscle. Back at the sink, she started to shuck the peas into the bowl. Out of the corner of her eye, he just stared at her for a moment, and then shook his head as if coming out of a daze, focusing back to chopping. When the oven beeped, he said, "I've got it." He slipped the chicken onto the rack.

"These are generous portions for one person," he said, putting the salad together with ease.

"It's habit. I raised my brothers after my mother left, so that left four hungry guys to cook for if you include my six-two dad." She thrust her chin to a cupboard near one broad shoulder. "There are dishes in there, silverware in the drawer just below."

"Set the table. That sounds familiar."

"Why?"

"My mom always had me doing that chore. But I will admit, I use a lot of paper plates."

"And eat a lot of pizza?"

He stacked silverware on top of the dishes, grabbed a few napkins, and moved over to the table. "Guilty." He sent her a sideways look that was anything but innocent.

She tried not to be affected by his devilish charms, really, she did. "Men," she said, shaking her head. Picking up the last pod, she used her thumb to knock the sweet, green peas into the bowl.

"Hey, we're not all clueless. My teammate, Wicked, can whip up a gourmet meal. Man, he can cook."

"Wicked?" She reached down and grabbed a pot, dumping in the peas and adding water. She set it on the stove and turned on the burner.

"Yeah, call names. When we're in the field, it keeps us incognito and sometimes guys have the same first name, so we wouldn't want any mix-ups going on, so call names are safer. There's Cowboy, big Texan, used to be a real cowboy, he's my best friend; Tank and Echo, SEAL dog handler, built like a tank and puts together these great models as a hobby; Scarecrow, Southern badass from Louisiana, his folks own a farm; Hollywood, looks like a movie star, is the biggest skirt chaser on the team; Blue is our medic and delivers profound statements like pearls before swine; and Ruckus, tough as all get out, met his fiancée during one of our missions, a reporter. He's our LT, which stands for lieutenant."

"And you're Kid Chaos." She broke apart the freshly baked rolls she'd bought at the market this morning and closed them up in tinfoil and popped them into the oven to warm.

"Yeah, most people call me Kid. I'm unruly, daring, and mad. But who says batshit crazy is wrong?"

"I'm sure combat is crazy, but some form of self-preservation is a good idea." On that note, she moved around the table in the opposite direction, setting down the salad dressing and trivets. Protecting herself seemed like the prudent idea right about now. Those quicksilver eyes of his created chaos for sure.

She went back for the salad when he came up to her. He took it out of her hands, and she was edging up against her limits. Bracing herself, she looked at him. Up close like this, almost as close as they'd been in her bedroom doorway when it was obvious he wanted to kiss her, it was impossible not to fall into the blue of his eyes, caught in the waves of intensity as effortlessly as breathing. He didn't have to try hard and working those eyes and his looks to his advantage was as easy to him as walking. But there was that lethal quality, and anyone with an ounce of smarts could tell he wasn't just a pretty face.

"That's quite a list of co-workers. I work with two other agents, Patty and Sam. Both are very good. And my boss, Michael Donovan. He was a former marine, blunt and outspoken and suffers fools even less."

"And your family?"

"My dad is a retired NCIS agent, former marine like Mike. My brothers' names are Leo, Knox, and Atticus. Leo is in the navy, much to my dad's disapproval, Knox is an EMT, and Atticus is graduating from high school next year. He wants to become a Navy SEAL. Surprisingly, my dad's okay with that."

"No kidding. I could give him some pointers."

"He would be ecstatic."

They stood there for a minute. "And you raised these guys after your mom left?"

"Yes, through school, fevers, and sports—a lot of sports."

He chuckled. "You managed to become an NCIS agent in between all that?"

"And go to college."

"Tell me something," he said, holding her gaze with a direct look.

Anything, she thought. *I want you to know me. I so want to get to know you.* To hell with logic and reasoning. A girl got this lucky only a few times in an entire lifetime. If that.

"Do your family and boss realize how much you've sacrificed? Does your dad?"

She blinked. What the hell did her family and job have to do with Ashe seducing her? "What?"

She took the bowl out of his hands, still thrown. Okay, she let herself get carried away, thinking that he was going to kiss her again. It wasn't a stretch. Who was she kidding? Since she'd come face-to-face with him in the Going Down office, it was all she could do to not think about how badly she wanted him. She shrugged. "I'm not sure I know."

She set the bowl down, and when he hadn't answered, she looked over at him. He folded his arms onto the counter and stared at her. With a look that sent shivers down her spine, he said, "Yeah, that doesn't surprise me."

No, not a stretch at all. She let her gaze slide along that stubbled jaw, down to his strong throat and those broad shoulders, the play of muscles beneath his T-shirt so tantalizing.

It was scary thinking about how much she already wanted him. How hard was it going to be when they really started working together day-in and day-out?

7

Christ on a cracker, he was still hard beneath the zipper of his borrowed jeans. They were a little snug as it was and getting snugger by the minute.

He stood at the counter and watched her pussy-foot around the table and him. Damn, he'd wanted a little R&R, and sex would even him out right about now, especially with his dick in a knot over this scrumptious woman.

But LT had given him an order, and it complicated this thing between them. He might be in her bed right now if things hadn't gone off the rails. In the shower, he'd imagined her sucking him with that soft, sexy mouth of hers, then climbing on top of him and riding his dick while he watched her caress her breasts and make herself come while he was fucking her. It wasn't a surprise that he'd jacked all over himself.

Yet that release hadn't been enough, as evidenced by his erection straining his zipper.

The surprise was that she wasn't anything like Caitlin or Mia. Both of those women had been fragile and innocent. Soft. Not that Paige wasn't soft. She was, but she had...backbone...sass, and he liked it more than he'd thought he would. Whenever he remembered Caitlin, it hurt too much to recall how she had left him. Then Mia. Both of them unable to really handle his deployments. Maybe, just maybe that's what he had been going for? Women who weren't strong enough, women who wouldn't want to move forward with him, start a family, then if he was killed in battle, he wouldn't leave anyone behind to mourn him like his mom, sister, and he had mourned his dad.

He swallowed hard, rising up at the thought. He pushed it away, not wanting to delve in too deep at their separate betrayals. Caitlin had gone back home, and Mia had found someone easier.

He wondered what his dad would do in this situation if Paige were his mom. His dad knew he wanted to marry her from the moment he laid eyes on her. He wouldn't have given in or given an inch. But Kid barely knew Paige, and really, he insisted, he just wanted to have an uncomplicated fling with her. Sex could often be so simple.

But then, he knew, also, that sex could be one colossal mistake as evidenced by his train wreck relationships. Except, he had to think again, Paige wasn't like either Caitlin or Mia.

The oven's timer went off, and she came back into the kitchen. He straightened to let her pass but couldn't help watching her take the amazing smelling chicken out of the oven and set it on the cooktop. She checked the peas and, obviously satisfied with their tenderness, removed them from the burner and twisted the knob to off.

"Anything I can do?"

She shook her head. "Just have a seat, and I'll bring everything over."

He did as she asked, removing himself from temptation,

the thoughts of his exes crowding his mind and curbing his usual exuberant recklessness. Frankly, it was much easier to stealth in the darkness and take down enemies or fall off a cliff and use his skill and reflexes to not only recover but get a win out of a clumsy mistake.

He didn't want to make a clumsy mistake here. Maybe women like Paige were much too hard to handle, too strong for him.

He scowled at that thought and didn't like that he'd even entertained it.

He wasn't used to acknowledging any kind of weakness in himself. It was counterproductive to getting the job done, to winning. It wasn't his mindset, too deep and serious. He rejected it completely.

She brought over a basket of rolls, then went back for the serving plate with the chicken, decorated with mangos and orange slices, and peas, the butter still melting on top.

"Looks great," he murmured, the scent of food making his mouth water.

"Dig in," she offered and sat down across from him.

He reached for a roll, helped himself to the chicken, salad, and peas while she did the same.

"So, you have details about this assignment."

"Yes." She popped up. "I forgot the wine." She went to the fridge, emerging with a bottle of white and then grabbed two goblets. Coming back to the table, she set one down in front of him. "About three weeks ago, the main armory at NAB Coronado was robbed, and two MPs were killed during the attempt. By the time security and NCIS showed up, the plane with the weapons had already taken off."

"Plane?"

"This was a well-executed, precision robbery. We believe

that the weapons were already on the transport when the MPs caught and wounded the pilot."

"And you used the DNA to find out his identity. Who?" She set a glass in front of her own plate, then one in front of him. The creamy white wine smelled like juicy grapes as it filled his glass. When she went around the table and sat down, pouring her own glass, he picked up his and took a sip. The full-body pinot grigio was crisp and refreshing with the flavors of citrus, melon and pear.

"David Duffield, a former marine. But we believe he didn't act alone."

"What makes you think that?" He forked up a bite of salad, the taste of the dressing exploding on his tongue. He could put together a mean salad.

"There were too many weapons stolen for this to be a solo gig, and the security cameras were tampered with."

"Hacked?"

"Yeah, and that person was very, very good at hiding both presence and identity. My best guys say it's untraceable."

He nodded. "Why do you think Anderson is involved?"

She finished chewing her forkful of chicken. "How do you know it's Anderson I'm investigating?"

"That's easy. Cris wouldn't hurt a fly, and I can tell when a guy is legit. But Anderson is cagey, and I flat-out don't like him. He gives me bad vibes."

"Ex-CIA."

"Figures. Those guys know how to get things done under the radar. A heist of government weapons would be like taking candy from a baby." Everything was tasty, the chicken tender, the peas sweet and buttery, and the rolls flaky and delicious. "I'm sure it's not the first operation he's been involved in. Let me guess, he's an international gun for hire and dabbles in arms."

"Yes, to all of that. I don't like him either, but I'm here to find out who was behind it and to recover government property."

"With a promotion riding on it."

She put her fork down and leaned forward. "What is that supposed to mean?"

"Nothing. You have something personal at stake."

She gave him a quelling look. "For you, this is just something you're being forced into doing because you got in my way out there at the warehouse, and I knew you weren't going to let it go, so I had to read you in so you didn't blow my cover. So, yes, it's personal in more than just my promotion. For me, it's my whole life."

She rose and pushed her chair back.

"Paige—"

She raised a hand to stall him. "I need some air. You finish eating. We'll continue when I get back. All of it about business." She grabbed her coat off the back of the sofa and went out the patio doors.

Kid sat there for a moment realizing that he'd hit one hell of a hot button. He'd only mentioned it because it was part and parcel of this mission of hers. It wasn't an accusation or a way to subvert her.

He did finish eating, then cleaned up, put everything away, and washed the dishes. When she hadn't come in, he grabbed the leather jacket and headed for the back. Stepping out, he saw the moon had risen and the snow-covered peaks of the mountains glowed in the soft light. Back in Coronado, it was summer, San Diego warm and sunny, as was the whole of the US. But here, it was winter, and it felt like it with Paige's obvious cold shoulder. She sat in one of the chairs with her back to him, looking out at the light-drenched landscape.

She was tense, reading her like he would anyone coming as second nature. Her hands were balled into fists on her thighs.

"Paige—"

"Don't Paige me. I want you to read over the reports, see the crime scene photos, and you can draw your own conclusions, see if anything triggers something I might have missed."

"I doubt you miss much."

"Don't try to charm me."

"Tell me about the marines, the MPs."

She took a breath and turned her head to look at him, held his gaze for what felt like forever, and he thought she was going to argue. This...this was the soft spot. She cared about those men, and his mention of the promotion diminished it. Damn if he didn't like her compassion. This woman was the full package. And, hoo-yah, that made him want her more.

"Corporal Ronald Miller. His mom kept calling him Rusty. Played baseball, volunteered at a soup kitchen in downtown San Diego for the homeless. His dad was a vet who went off the radar. He wanted to serve in the worst way. He had a shock of carrot-colored hair and a laugh that would light up the room. He loved building model sailboats and sailing them in competitions. He was twenty-eight."

Kid's exact age. It shocked through him that the guy was as young as he was, still a full life ahead of him. He came around the chair and crouched down, bringing his face closer to eye level. In the moonlight and dark shadows, her eyes gleamed like a tiger's, fierce and primal. That's how he felt around her, as if she boiled him down to basics.

"And the other man?"

She bit her lip and looked down. "David Hong. Father of little twin girls, Alice and Ariel. They had his beautiful eyes and dark hair, very adorable. Big softie, fan of Disney movies obviously. His wife was devastated, so much so, she couldn't even talk to me. Her mom had flown out to visit and it was lucky she was there. He was getting out after this tour. They were moving back home to Indiana, closer to their parents. She was so excited that he'd be finally home and out of danger. He was thirty-two."

He reached out. Her hands were icy. "Come on. Let's go back inside. Show me what you want me to see. I have more questions."

She nodded and rose. "It's not about my promotion. I want it. I do. I feel guilty every time I think about it, but it's just part of my reality."

"I get that. I can see that. You don't have to justify what you want for yourself to me. I understand. They're not just dead marines to you. They're a murdered son and husband. If we can't feel the pain of the people we help, then why are we doing what we do? It's not a sin to work hard and expect to get ahead."

"I know that. But, thank you. I'm sorry I got snippy."

"It's okay. I can handle it. I'm a SEAL, and we're tough both inside and out."

She pushed his shoulder and slid around him, walking toward the house. He wanted to put his arm around her in the worst way. He didn't know where the tenderness came from; it was just there and felt more real to him than any emotion he'd ever felt.

She stopped and then turned back around. He saw the look on her face and he simply opened his arms. She closed the gap between them. This tough, sweet woman needed a hug, and that's what he was going to give her.

Realizing he was stepping across a very dangerous line, and sharply aware of how hard his heart was pounding, he held her body against him, his jaw clenching. Those stark words about the marines touched on his own pain, and his eyes burned.

He gave her a reassuring squeeze.

"So, the marine is hit, worse than he thought and he what...crash lands? How do you know it was here and not in the ocean?" he murmured against her hair, breathing in her scent.

"We don't. That's the problem. But we have to make sure those guns don't fall into the wrong hands and that our MPs and their families get the justice they deserve."

He was totally on board now, thinking about his dad, thinking about his mom and sister, thinking about Paige.

Yeah, thinking about her was the most dangerous thought of all.

CRIS OYOLA HAD GOTTEN MARRIED LATER in life at a time he figured he was going to be out of luck in finding a family, something he'd wanted for so long. His days of looking for adventure were behind him after a harrowing tumble from one of his mountain bikes woke him up to what was missing in his life. But just when he had given up hope, Ariane had walked into his office looking for a job. She was ten years his junior, but that hadn't stopped her from showing him that she was attracted to him. She'd been young, but there hadn't been a moment of time that had passed that she hadn't shown him her maturity. Not in managing the books, helping him with decisions in expansion of their company, or having and raising Ricardo, who they all called Riky, and Jhosselin, their two children. She...they were everything to him.

Cris was shaved, showered, and dressed in blue jeans and a cream, short-sleeved silk shirt. He was standing in front of the stove frying *buñuelos*, balls of yeast dough flavored with anise, when he heard Ariane enter.

He turned and gave her a thorough look from head to toe. His beautiful wife had long, dark hair that tended to curl when she didn't have time to tame it, something he thoroughly approved. She was delicate and slender, her skin smooth and creamy, the color of light brown sugar, dark brows over a set of almond eyes, the irises so brown they almost looked black. She had a lively sense of humor, and the love she had for him shone from those expressive eyes. She returned his gaze. The intimacy they had shared this morning had turned him inside out, and he was still lost in the wonder of her. As if attuned to him, she gave him a small half smile that spoke absolute volumes. He said, his voice husky, "Good morning."

Ariane wet her lips. "Good morning."

The devil glinted in her eyes, and he smiled. "I think you must have been completely distracted, my love," he said, indicating her shirt with the lift of his spoon. The glint intensified. "Your shirt is inside out."

Riky chortled and smacked the table. "He's right, Mama." She blushed, which only made her more appealing. "You can't take me to school like that. I would be embarrassed."

"Hey, no disrespect. Your mama is always beautiful, even with her shirt inside out."

"Thank you," she said, kissing him on the cheek.

She poured herself a cup of coffee and sat down next to their son, ruffling his hair. He had the same coloring as Ariane, but his features were purely his papa's. Breakfast proceeded along until their seven-year-old daughter Jhosselin appeared, looking just a little cranky, a bedraggled llama clasped under her arm. Jhosselin wasn't like her sunny mama in the morning. You couldn't expect her to rise and shine until you fed her first.

Ariane got up to fix Jhosselin a *buñuelo*, drizzling a generous portion of melted *miel* or honey on the dough ball. Jhosselin plopped down in her mama's vacated seat. He looked at his daughter, a smile for her on his lips. "Good morning, *bambino*."

She grunted and gave him a grumpy look. "Morning is yucky."

"I guess they are at first, but then they get better."

She gave him a look that made both him and Ariane laugh.

Fifteen minutes later, he had to maneuver around a few police cars, wondering what had initiated the increased police presence in the Prada. He was opening the doors of Going Down when he was greeted. "Good morning, Mr. Oyola," his employee Juan said.

"Why are the police at the Prada?"

"There was some shooting going on last night. They are worried about tourists as you can imagine. Started near a bunch of warehouses just behind our office."

Cris stiffened. That was where Bryant had insisted they needed warehouse space. His increasing anxiety about Bryant Anderson, his so-called partner, jumped up a notch. When he'd met the man, he'd been overjoyed to have the kind of partner with Bryant's skills. The fact that he was an American also was attractive. He was sure he could increase the traffic to their business. He also had a nice offer of cash to sweeten the deal. But over the years, Cris had become... concerned with his secrecy and his aggressive behavior. Not only on the mountain bike treks, but with employees as well.

"Juan, you get things going. I have to do an errand I forgot about."

"Yes, sir. Got you covered, Mr. O."

He drove over to the warehouse district. There were armed guards at the door, but they let him pass when they recognized him. As he approached the office, he could hear Bryant's voice and another man's voice, one of his "employees," a shady-looking, rough character named Dean Norris. Cris didn't like him or trust him.

"Did you get a look at them?" Bryant was agitated, his voice filled with anger.

"No, sir. The guy was too fast, and I was out like a light. He was good. I'd say special ops. But it was too dark to see his face."

"And the other one?"

"Small, slender and fast. If I had to guess, I'd say a woman. But I can't be certain. They could have been drug runners, maybe. Got caught with a deal going down."

"It's possible, Bry." The other male voice in the room was a booming, deep baritone. Bryant's other shadow, Reggie Monroe. An even scarier guy. Cris was thinking he'd let vipers into his beautiful, ordered world, and he wasn't quite sure how to get them out. Apprehension slithered down his spine.

"I can't afford to ignore any breaches in security. Duffield messed up big time. After all that planning. Son of a bitch is dead and the plane in pieces."

"No one's onto us, though. We're scot-free," Dean said.

"If they are...well, we'll make sure they keep quiet." His tone was ominous.

"I don't like what happened last night. My gut is telling me it ain't good," Reggie piped in."

"We're just about ready to search the area. It's slow going with just the two of us. We'll get them all."

Cris had heard enough. He knocked, and the room went silent. "Come in," Bryant said. Cris pushed the door open. Reggie rose from the edge of Bryant's desk. He was a huge man, black, his eyes cool and confrontational—all the time. Reggie's head was completely shaved, and he looked to be far more comfortable in a combat zone rather than a city that wasn't under fire. He was the bigger of the two, a muscled, expressionless warrior wearing camo cargo pants and a long-sleeved Corps T-shirt with an unbuttoned olive shirt over the top.

Dean was blond and lean, but all muscle. His eyes were mean and hooded, devoid of any expression. His boots were pure military issue, flat black and lace-up. He wore a T-shirt with the sleeves torn out showing the tattoos on his fore-arms that went up to both shoulders, full sleeves filled with skulls and crossbones and other symbols of death. Cris's apprehension doubled.

"I need to talk to you." He glanced at the two men who didn't move a muscle. "Alone," he emphasized. His shadows looked to him, and Anderson gave them a quick nod.

Dean bumped his shoulder as he passed. "Oh, excuse me," he said, but it was clear both the bump and the apology were nothing more than intimidation.

When the door closed behind them, Cris said, "What the hell happened last night? We have a business to run and protect, Bryant. I don't like that there was gunfire around our warehouse."

"It was nothing. The police are investigating, but probably just drug dealers." Bryant's tone was conciliatory, but after the overheard conversation, Cris knew there was something going on, something that involved a dead man and a plane. He didn't know what, but Bryant wasn't going to involve him in anything illegal. He would be ruined. He had to think about his family's welfare.

"Look, I know we've had our differences, but you've been an asset to the company. I feel it might be time for us to dissolve our partnership. I think you might be interested in going in a different direction with expanding, but I've decided the three offices are enough for me and Ariane to manage. I can buy you out."

Bryant's gaze narrowed. "No, Cris. I think we do well together. I am staying."

Cris moved forward and said, "It's not going to work. We have different visions."

"Don't come in here and dictate to me. I saved you and this company. I'm not talking about this anymore."

"Bryant—"

Cris backed up, his words cut off when Bryant lifted his arm and pointed a gun at him. "Don't push me. I say what goes, and you're going to follow in line like a good little partner." He rounded the desk and shoved the gun against Cris's forehead. "I've got things going on, so you and that sweet little family of yours better keep your noses out of it." He nudged the gun for emphasis, the barrel cold against Cris's sweaty brow. "We wouldn't want anything to happen to you...or to them." His platitudes couldn't hide the ominous threat in his words. Bryant was giving Cris an ultimatum. "You understand," he continued in a caring tone, but his eyes were hard and cold. "It's safer."

Cris swallowed hard, the fear for his family escalating

just as Bryant had intended. Anger was mixed in as well. Bryant was a barbarian, and there was no telling what he would do to protect whatever illegal and dangerous thing he was doing. Cris's mouth went dry...the thought that Ariane, Riky, or his precious little Jhosselin would be harmed made his gut tighten, every protective instinct surface.

Cris held up his hands. "All right!" he bit out. "I'll back down. I don't want to be involved in any of your messes."

"You won't be if you fucking mind your own business. This meeting is over." He stared at Cris until he backed away from the gun's threat. His heart pounded, and he felt trapped in Bryant's threat. Outside the door, he almost ran into Reggie and Dean. They regarded him with hostility, but this time it wasn't hidden. He left the warehouse, shaken and afraid. There wasn't anything he wouldn't do for his family. Not anything.

~

BRYANT ANDERSON CLENCHED his jaw and tucked the gun back into his waistband. Reggie and Dean walked in and closed the door.

"Why didn't you just kill him? He could be trouble," Dean said. "Hell, I'll do it in some dark alley, make it look like a robbery."

Bryant shook his head. "We can't afford any heat right now. We'll finish this operation, and Cris and his family can find another way to make a living." He was well aware what Cris would do. Not a goddamned thing. He had his family to protect, and they meant everything to him. He knew now that if he stepped out of line, Bryant would put a bullet in each of them.

No one was going to mess up this operation. He had

buyers for those weapons, buyers who were breathing down his neck. Kirikhan rebels from Kirikhanistan, filled with radical Islamists and rebel fighters who wanted independence from the now post-Soviet states, the former Soviet Union. When a vast amount of oil had been detected in the small state tucked against Uzbekistan, Tajikistan, and Afghanistan, there was an attempt to overtake it that led to unrest and civil war. Now, there were always bottom feeders in every society, but the leaders of the Kirikhan rebels were some of the finest. Boris and Natasha Golovkin. The only funny thing about them was their connection to Rocky and Bullwinkle. Those two didn't give a damn about complications or stupid former marines who couldn't assess whether they had a mortal wound or not. A former marine who had died just on the other side of La Paz close to the town of Colomi. The stupid, incompetent bastard. Bryant had practically tied everything up with a bow before he, Reggie, and Dean had left Coronado. All Duffield had to do was fly the damn plane.

He mulled over what Dean had said. The guy who'd attacked him had seemed like he'd been special forces. Hmmm, Pete Wilder's kid? Ashe. Bryant wondered if he had followed in his old man's footsteps. "Get on the horn to one of our contacts. Find out what Ashe Wilder is doing when he's not skirt chasing and extreme sporting."

"Roger that," Dean said, pulling out his cell.

If that kid was anything like his bleeding-heart father, then they would have something else to handle. Wilder had been a tough, fearless bastard, but in the end, he had died, and he'd never seen it coming. Medal of Honor winner, ha! The CIA never got recognition for their deeds. Bryant was okay with that. He'd screwed over the agency as easily as he'd screwed everyone else he'd come into contact with. It was survival of the fittest, and Bryant was at the top of the food chain.

Except for the Kirikhans. They were animals and had no patience for people who screwed up. That was a scary duo, and he had no intention of missing his second deadline with their arms dealer, Anatoly Makarov. He seemed like a jovial Russian bear, but his claws would rend and tear Bryant apart.

It didn't matter who was involved, he was going to recover everything, or his life wouldn't be worth a plug nickel.

The Kirikhans would see to that.

———

8

Kid woke up, momentarily disoriented and confused about where he was until his sleepy vision and mind cleared and his surroundings came into focus. This wasn't his hotel room...no, the scent of smoke in the air, the fact that he wasn't lying down and his body felt heavy clued him in to that. The scent of this place stirred his senses, feminine, delicate, delicious. With a low exhale, he turned his head and glanced to his side.

Paige was fast asleep, snuggled up against him like he was her favorite pillow. Her silky black hair was tousled over his shoulder and down his arm, her hands curled against her face. Even in sleep, she was a paradox. While she'd been confident and assertive last night, now she looked vulnerable and sweet.

He wondered at her independence, at how she seemed to like to be alone. Was that how she'd felt when she was growing up? Was she afraid of relying on one particular person too much, even for something as simple as tenderness and a warm, secure embrace? Or was he reading too much into her actions?

She had three brothers whom she raised to be men. As he continued to watch her sleep, he wondered if he'd ever figure her out. All those facets and layers that showed him that the person she presented to the outside world wasn't necessarily who she was inside.

That kinda hit him in the heart.

The usual male occurrence in the morning was tight against the zipper of his jeans, and waking to Paige didn't help it one bit. She twitched, then stirred, gradually coming awake. She blinked slowly, her lashes still weighing heavily with sleep.

"Morning," he murmured. She looked up at him and sighed.

"Kid Chaos," she whispered softly. Then she slid up, closing the barely there, intimate space between them. Settling her mouth over his, she ambushed him, took him down with nothing but her hot mouth.

He made a low, indistinguishable sound as he kissed her back. She clutched at him, and he grabbed her around the waist and pulled her across his hips. When she straddled him, intimately and fully aligning her body against his, he groaned, soft and deep, his dick thickening and pressing hard against the jeans. He caught her jaw, his hand sliding around the back of her neck, over her soft, satiny nape, his fingers tunneling up into her hair, holding her, his tongue sliding into the warm, honeyed depths of her mouth.

And sliding again, exploring, taking her with a kiss again and again while she moved those beautiful hips against him. He held her tighter, kissed her harder, his heart starting to pound—because she let him. She more than let him. Damn, for such a solitary little thing, she was so sweet, turning into him, her lips so soft, her tongue sliding over his. She made a sound deep in her throat, and he knew he was in trouble, hands down, no holds barred—and he loved it, the heated thrill of it, the chase, anticipating the hot, hot sex of discovering a woman for the first time, the excitement of taking her clothes off—the way he wanted to take Paige's clothes off and just get into her.

Yeah.

He slanted his mouth over hers more fully, taking more of her, taking everything he could get, all the sweet surrender and every soft sigh.

She rocked against him, and his eyes almost crossed. The torture of it ached all the way down to his tight, engorged balls.

Her cell phone went off, and they both froze as if cold water had been thrown on them. He swore, viciously. She stopped kissing him and lifted her head, her mouth swollen, her face burned by his beard.

He was pinned to the sofa, his body rigid with the need for her aching through him. She gasped softly, her breath hot against his mouth. He closed his eyes to gain control.

They both trembled, the need rippling out, hers vibrating against his body. "Fuck it. Just fuck the whole damn world," he growled.

He held her as she reached for the damn instrument of his sexual destruction and frustration.

"Hello." She listened, the need draining from her face. "Is he all right? I'll be there in fifteen minutes." She disconnected the call and threw it to the sofa. "Oh, Ashe," she murmured, softening against him and running her fingers up through his hair. "I think we're in trouble here."

He tightened his arms around her and buried his face in her neck, breathing her in, filling himself with the warm and lovely scent of her skin. "You feel so damn good."

"You do, too." She sighed. "I guess this is going to be an issue."

He nodded. "Yeah, babe, from where I'm sitting, I don't think it's something easily ignored. We can talk about it later. You need to go?"

"Yes, that was Juan from work. He said Cris came back from an errand looking really upset. I want to make sure he's okay. Also, I could possibly get you a job as a guide since Juan dislocated his shoulder from his last trip down, and Cris has him on office duties."

"That's a good idea. Get me into the fold."

He groaned softly when she moved. He couldn't help it. She came back down on him. Which was both wonderful and torturous. She looked so upset. "I'm sorry. Should I..." She moved again, and he bit back a curse.

"Wait," he gritted out and grabbed her around the waist, standing. He held her against him.

"Oh, this is so much better."

"No, what would be better is if you were riding me right now." She had her arms around his neck. He loved the way she met his eyes.

"I'd like that, too. I'm sorry about your..."

"Hard-on? No need to be sorry there, ma'am. It's working as intended."

"I can vouch for that."

"It's all because of you." He tortured himself by letting her slip down his body.

She stepped back. "I should get a shower." She was looking at his mouth.

Sweet Jesus, his eyes closed on a silent prayer. And the answer was...yes. He wasn't sure he wanted it to be no when he felt her hand on his face, tracing his jaw to his bottom lip.

Could this be the biggest mistake of his life? And if he stopped running from commitment, might he find it?

His eyes opened, and he felt as if his chest was too tight. What? He hadn't run from commitment. Where the hell had that thought come from? He was committed to the navy and to both women he'd loved. Fuck that. What?

He had no doubt where he and Paige were going to end up—hot and naked and all over each other. He didn't see any way around it.

His gaze was riveted to her eyes that roamed over his face. She was well aware of it, too.

He was so doomed.

He brought his hand up to her face and gently cupped her cheek, then leaned sideways and pressed his mouth to her temple, just to feel the softness of her skin—and she was soft, incredibly, seductively soft. He slid his mouth lower, closer to her ear. Her hair tickled his skin. He breathed her in again, her scent was a deeper, unnamable essence that was simply, irrevocably her. He was taking her into himself, fill himself up with her spirit, her sweetness and toughness. He needed that because this woman was grounded, feet firmly planted, and she was a contrast to his chaos.

He breathed her in, letting his mouth roam even lower, down to the delicate angle of her jaw and the tender skin of her throat. Moving back up, he nuzzled his face into the curve of her neck and his satisfaction deepened. She was trembling, her pulse fluttering, and she was cupping his face tenderly in her hand, her palm brushing lightly against his just-there beard.

He'd won her last night, through strength and cunning and skill. Fought for her and won.

He was completely in chaos, not here in this place, not

like he'd been in other places, at other times—but he'd still won her, and he wanted to claim what he'd won.

He lowered his mouth to hers and gave himself up to the biggest risk of his life. It was the sweetest thing he'd ever done—to sink into her kiss, to feel the texture of her mouth beneath his, absorb her. The feel of her was like a balm to his soul, soft, warm skin, sweet woman sighing in his mouth and firing him all the way up. He pulled her close, loving the feel of her, the life of her.

It had been too long since he'd done this, lost himself in a woman.

With a soft exhalation, he gave her a nudge toward the bathroom. "We'd better go, now, babe, or we won't be going for some time."

"Ashe," was all she said, and he liked that there was regret there.

"Shower, now," he whispered. "I'm going to run to the hotel. I'll meet you at the office."

She nodded.

And he was already gone. Out the door, down the cute path between the palm trees, and to the street. The boots he wore were quite nice, and unlike the borrowed clothes, he decided he would keep them. He made it back to his hotel room in record time, stripped, showered, and ran an electric razor over his face.

He donned cargo pants, a T-shirt, and an open shirt over the top, then a light jacket. He wished he had his nine mil. Then he was back out the door to the street. He eyed the church where they had cut through the cemetery to get to her little cottage.

As he reached Going Down Wilderness Excursions, he saw her coming down the street. He waved to her. She looked good in her jeans, boots, a light jacket over a deep brown sweater that only made her tiger-eyes pop.

She handed him some fruit and a doughy cake. "I stopped at the market," she said. Her eyes went over him before he opened the door for her.

They stepped inside and Juan, his arm in a sling said, "He's in his office. He hasn't come out." When he spied Kid he said, "Hey man, Juan."

"Ashe," Kid responded with a smile and a handshake.

"This way," Paige said. "Thanks for calling me."

When she got to Cris's office, she knocked. "Come in," he said. She pushed the door open and Kid walked in behind her.

"Paige, I told you to take a couple days off," he scolded. "You had quite a scare yesterday. I wanted you to have the opportunity to rest. What brings you into the office against my orders?"

"You. I heard you were upset. Are you okay?"

"Never better," he said in a forced cheerful voice, but Kid could see he was lying. He could smell the fear on the guy.

"Cris, you can always count on me," she said, and he could see that she was completely sincere. Cris's features softened, and he smiled, but it didn't reach his eyes. He was spooked, royally spooked.

"Of course, I know that, Paige, but everything is fine." He looked at Kid. "How are you, Ashe? You had just as much of a scare. This was supposed to be your vacation. I thought you'd be doing some sightseeing."

"No, I heard that you were looking for a guide. I can do the job for a bit if that will help you out."

He mulled it over, giving Ashe a scrutinizing look. "We can talk about it. I want to make sure you know the drill and can handle the job."

"Of course."

He talked with Cris while Paige went out to the front office to do some work. When they were finished, Cris was happy to have him on board. "So, Ashe, what do you do for a living?"

"I'm in the navy."

Cris's brows rose, but it wasn't because he was surprised. It was almost as if he knew Kid would say that.

"Special Operations?"

"Why do you ask?"

"The way you handled yourself with Paige, your reflexes. A split second too late, and she wouldn't be here."

That made his gut tighten. "I'm in the teams. I'm glad I was there to save her. She's special."

"That she is. Thank you for helping us out."

Kid nodded and rose. "I will see you tomorrow."

Cris nodded, looking preoccupied. "You have family, young man?"

"Yes."

"They are precious."

"Yes, they are."

Cris nodded once more, then turned back to his computer.

Kid exited the office and when Paige saw him she came around the counter. "I'll see you later, Juan."

He waved with his good arm.

"Why don't we get a bite at the hotel? Then we can discuss your reports."

"All right," she said as she followed him down the cobblestone street. "About last night and this morning."

"Intense," he said, giving her a side glance. Her hair caught the breeze and fluttered. He wanted to touch her.

"I don't really have time for relationships in my life, but I could make room for something temporary while you're here."

"Yeah, I get it. Distance is a bitch."

"Don't get me wrong. I live in San Diego, so that's not a problem. I just need to focus on my job, even more so when I get the promotion."

He nodded. "Totally get it." He felt the need to say, "I'm gone a lot, Paige. It's not an easy time for anyone who's waiting for me at home. I'm focused one-hundred percent on what I do. It's primary in my life. I don't apologize for that ever. You always have to suck it up and do what needs to be done. It goes double for my private life."

"Just as long as we're clear, Ashe."

"You know, my friends call me Kid."

"Do they?"

"Well," he shrugged, "my guy friends."

"Are you uncomfortable with me calling you by your first name, too personal?"

"No."

"All right, it's interchangeable then."

They went into the hotel bar, and Kid ordered them each a meal once they were seated. A beer for each of them after asking her preference. He raised the bottle. "To keeping it simple," he said.

She nodded and clinked his bottle.

"You have some baggage then?"

"I think it's a good idea we're keeping this casual. I've had some breakups that have been pretty tough." He told her about Caitlin, the memory old but his emotions a little rawer since Mia gave him the boot.

Paige leaned forward. "I'm so sorry. Man, that must have been so hard."

"It was, but it's old news. I just don't want to be one of

those guys who doesn't give you an honest answer to a question."

"Well, isn't this cozy."

Anderson's snide voice cut across the conversation. "Bryant," Paige said by way of greeting and Kid fully expected him to move on, but instead, he pulled up a chair.

"So, we haven't had much time to converse, my young friend."

Kid took a sip of his beer, his jaw clenching. "I'm not your friend," he said succinctly. "This is a private party," he added.

"Yeah, I bet it is," he said giving Paige a suggestive look, making Kid's irrational anger at this guy form into a ball in his gut. Anderson sat back. "Had a little trouble at the warehouse last night. Two drug dealers stirring things up. Cris was pissed, but I calmed him down."

Paige glanced at Kid. "Drug dealers?"

"Yeah, put the moves on Dean and took both him and Reggie down. Pretty slick moves for a street rat, huh?"

Kid gave nothing away. His deadpan was iron clad.

"So, what are you doing with your life, Ashe?"

"This and that," he said. "I help people for a living."

"Do you? And what does that entail?"

"Long hours and dedication."

Anderson smirked. "You didn't follow in your old man's footsteps? You know, being a hero for a living, like a SEAL maybe?"

"Why don't you go outside and play hide and go fuck yourself. I'll stay here and count to infinity."

Paige reached out and put her hand on his forearm. This guy was an asshole, and he was fishing. Ashe flashed him a grin and took a sip of his beer. He set his bottle down and looked at Paige. "Let's go."

"I'm sure all you've heard about your dad were great things. Maybe you should live in the real world. I can tell you who he really was and his lack of total commitment."

Kid stood and grabbed Bryant by his shirtfront and got into his face. "I don't give a flying fuck what you have to say about my father. I'm not interested." He shoved the guy back into his chair.

But before he could take a step, Bryant threw a punch that knocked Kid back against the table, cracking his back against the chair behind him. He ducked the next one and came up swinging, punching Anderson so hard in the jaw, he reeled back. The man had forty pounds on him, but when he came charging back toward Kid, he pushed off with his legs and planted his feet in his chest, drop-kicking Anderson hard enough for Kid to end up on his back, dazed. From his position on the floor, Kid saw a blur and did a quick, powerful kick-up using his hands and lower body, landing firmly on his feet, then backflipped to avoid the first blow by Anderson's lackey. He turned to engage the blond man, immediately remembering him from last night. He took some punishing blows to his face and mid-section. Without hesitating, Kid got under his guard with lightning quick moves and, with one shot to the temple, he went down as Anderson recovered and came at him again.

That's when the bartender got a hold of Anderson and the manager of the hotel screamed at them to stop. Well, he was screaming the whole time, but Kid was getting double-teamed and couldn't exactly respond. Bryant held up his hands and pulled out his wallet, shoving money into the manager's hand, apologizing left and right, stating it was just a little misunderstanding. Kid didn't let his guard down until Anderson helped Blondie up from the floor and they exited the bar.

The manager came up to Kid and said, "I'm sorry, Mr. Wilder, but you must vacate the premises. We can't tolerate this kind of behavior from our guests."

"Damn, I'm sorry. I'll clear out."

~

OUTSIDE, BRYANT TURNED TO DEAN. "WELL?"

"It's him. Same moves, same agility and lightning speed. This guy is trouble, Bry."

"That means the woman who was there was most likely Paige," Anderson bit out. "Look into them both. I want to know everything about them down to the brand of their underwear. Use our contact in DC."

"You got it." They took a few steps, and Dean halted Bryant with a hand to his shoulder. "Can I have her when the time comes?" He licked his lips. Dean was one of his former colleagues, but he was one sick son of a bitch. That's why he kept him around.

"As long as she dies."

"Oh, she will. I promise." He wheezed out a soft, maniacal laugh. "How about the SEAL?"

"No, leave him to me. Ashe Wilder needs to be schooled about who his father really was, and what reality is all about." Bryant smirked. No one, not that pathetic girl or Pete Wilder's wet behind the ears kid was going to stop him from saving his ass from the Golovkins.

9

Paige gave him a worried look on the way up to his room. Once inside, he just stood there, face stinging and throbbing from the blows, clenching his jaw, the intensity of his emotions threatening to overtake what he knew, what he damn well knew to be true about his dad. His mind and heart reeled. Anderson and Blondie tried their best. Both of them were former CIA and they fought like pansies.

But the CIA's strength was always their mindfucks. He didn't want to let Anderson get into his head. He knew who his father was, and he didn't have to listen to some asshole trying his best to get at him through his connection with his father. He closed his eyes and took a deep breath. The pain of his father's death, the loss Kid had felt in every aspect of his life, spun on its axis and came back at him with even more pain. Commitment. Was that all tied up in this somehow? Was he not committed to the people in his life? To the SEALs? His gut tightened.

He reached for his duffel, but Paige's hand clasped his wrist. "Sit down," she murmured.

He turned to look at her, and it struck him right in the

solar plexus that Mia would never have done this. She would have been passive, following his lead. Caitlin as well. They didn't challenge him, ever.

But Paige did. Every step she had a mind of her own. He didn't like to think he ever felt fear, but if there was fear, and he wasn't admitting to it, it came from clashing with a strong woman who would make him look harder and deeper.

Hell, this woman scared the crap out of him. But with that and the doubts, he still wanted her.

Maybe all this time, all this damn time he'd never been committed, fully committed. His recklessness was his way of flipping his finger at the world that had taken his father, and he dared it to take him. Did he have a secret death wish? Was his military service nothing but a means to an end? Did he want to go out in a blaze of glory like his father so that, deep down, he would feel worthy of his sacrifice, his service, him as a man? Did he have to die for it to matter?

Did he pick weak women like Caitlin, superficial women like Mia on purpose? Did he even know what to do with a strong woman like Paige?

If he didn't face these fears, these truths, would he die inside? Die on the battlefield? Was it possible to have a life after this was over, this turmoil and pain? Anger and fear trapped with nowhere to go. He would have to forge a path if he was strong enough.

As these thoughts streaked through his head, she tugged on his wrist. "Come on. Sit down."

He let her lead him over to the chair in the room. He sat down, lost in his thoughts again. Next thing he knew, she was pressing a cold, wet washcloth against his bruised face, wiping away the blood and soothing the pain.

With every tender touch, she quieted the ache in his core.

Slipping her fingers along his jaw to his chin, she lifted it, so he would look at her. "Are you okay?"

He stared up at her, then wordlessly, he reached out and pulled her down to the chair. She curled onto his lap, wrapping an arm around his neck.

His chest contracted when she smoothed his hair off his forehead, caressing him, supporting him. He inhaled unevenly and turned his face against her soft neck, his body heavy, his muscles slow to respond. Sensation wrenched loose in his chest, and he closed his eyes and rested against her.

"Don't listen to what Bryant said. He's such a jerk. Really, Ashe. He was just trying to get at you."

He swallowed. "I'm okay, Paige."

She let out a breath that told him she was disappointed with his answer. He owed her more, he knew he did, but right now he was much too raw to open up about it. He needed time to get his shit together. He squeezed his eyes closed. He didn't want to act like a fool in front of her. Dealing with fear was a new element, something he hadn't done before.

"Is this macho shit you're shoveling at me?"

"A man needs to deal with macho shit in his own way."

"Oh, for the love of God. All right, keep everything bottled up inside. That'll help."

"Paige—"

She cut him off. "Don't Paige me, Ashe. It helps to talk about it."

"Maybe, but I'm not ready."

Her voice lost its edge, her expression softening. "I'm sorry. I'm pushing you just like my dad always pushes me. That's not fair to you. He's always worked so hard, been so hard on himself. I guess I got that from him."

She leaned down and softly kissed his mouth. Kid experienced a rush of throat-clogging emotion. Grasping the back of her head, holding her to his lips while his other arm crushed her to him, he kissed her back.

That's when everything changed, and the tenderness turned into something else, something that coalesced into a thick, heavy feeling in his groin, that condensed in the air between them. An out-of-control, batshit crazy attraction that wouldn't stay controlled or tame.

His heart jumped into overdrive, pounding so hard that it felt as if it would come through his ribs. With his mind teetering on meltdown, he shouldn't want this. But he did. It was basic and primal.

Determined.

He already knew how this was going to end from the moment he set eyes on her. He knew they would be naked together. Struggling with the thick surge of desire, he clenched his jaw and rested his forehead against hers, his body painfully engorged. With a catch to her breathing, she rose and dragged him up and to the bed, pulling his shirt out of the waistband of his cargo pants as he toed out of his boots.

This time there would be no brakes, no banter, no stopping.

Paige was already half undressed, going between pulling on his button and zipper to shimmying out of her pants. When she pulled her top over her head, exposing her bra, soft and see-through over her breasts, it was more than he could handle.

He reached for her, pulling at the rest of her clothes as she freed him of his pants and underwear.

She choked out his name and came into his arms. His heart laboring against the frenzy in his chest, he caught her against him and carried her down onto the bed. Heat to heat. Skin to skin. And it was too much. Dragging in a ragged breath, he closed his eyes in a grimace of raw pleasure as she shifted beneath him and opened to him. When he touched her with his fingers, she was hot and wet, so ready. In moments, she was gasping, her cry spurring him on. He wasn't usually so turned on he couldn't wait. He was definitely a foreplay man, but at her response, the need to seat himself inside her now was too powerful.

On a ragged groan, he settled himself in the hot cradle of her thighs. And lost himself in her tight, wet heat.

He could feel her tension, the delicious mounting moment when a woman let go. He shifted his hips, and her breath caught on an agonized groan as she clutched him tighter. Kid reveled in the way his dick fit to her, too perfectly, gloved in her slick heat. He moved his hips again, maximizing body contact, and her sharp intake was his reward.

He slowed it down, flexing his hips with slow, deep thrusts. She arched her neck and closed her eyes, the pulse point in her throat beating erratically.

Watching her lovely face, he moved again, and he could feel the surrender in her, her acceptance of him. He was so tuned into this woman. She was once again in Kid Chaos sensory overload, and it would take nothing—nothing—to push her over the edge.

Tangling his fingers in her hair, he whispered, "Stay with me babe." Then moved again. His gaze locked on hers like a heat seeking missile, grateful for his honed instincts and his hard, muscled body that he could give her so much pleasure. She clutched his arms, her hands palming his biceps, her eyes glazing even more, and she drew up her knees grazing his hips, her body arching with tension. His breathing turning erratic, he continued to move, watching her respond, her tightness driving him on. She gripped his biceps, nails digging, a desperate look turning her eyes dark and feral. On a fragmented moan, she twisted her head, and he felt her contract hard around him, her release shuddering through her. Feeling as if something wild and unbearably beautiful had been set loose, he closed his eyes and gathered her up in a fierce embrace, experiencing feelings that went far beyond sexual.

It took several moments for her to come back down to earth, and he grasped her by the back of the neck, holding her tight and secure. Finally, she shifted under him, letting go a long shaky breath.

Her hands travelled to his shoulders as she turned her face against his neck, licking, biting, and kissing him until he gathered her hair in his hand and wrapped it around his wrist, pulling gently.

Paige whispered, "Ashe," as she locked her legs around him, her movements urging him on, and Kid crushed her against him, white-hot desire rolling over him. Angling his arm across her back, he drove into her again and again, pressure building and building. A low guttural sound tore from him, and his release came in a blinding rush that went on and on, so powerful he felt as if he was being turned inside out. He wanted to let it wash over him, but he forced himself to keep moving in her, knowing she was on the verge again. She cried out and clutched at his back, then went rigid in his arms, and she finally convulsed around him, the gripping spasms wringing him dry.

His heart hammering, his breathing so labored he felt almost dizzy, he weakly rested his head against hers, his whole body quivering. The thin air hadn't messed with his equilibrium, but this sweet babe was spinning him on his axis. He felt as if he had been wrenched in two.

He didn't know how long he clutched her, breathing around the pleasure she'd given him and the aftermath of having her.

He was aware of her toying with his hair at his nape, then periodically running her palms up and down his back. Sex was always good, even bad sex was good, but this... He couldn't really catalog this into anything but fantastic. He buried his face in her neck, kissing her collarbone, nuzzling her, getting her scent all over him. A feeling of over-whelming protectiveness rose up in him. He couldn't let her go. Not yet.

Fuck, not yet.

He didn't know how long they lay like that. Hauling in an unstable breath, he turned his head and kissed her on the mouth, her face flushed, her eyes sated. "We'd better get out of here before they come banging on the door."

She nodded and tightened her arms around him. Sharply aware of her body so warm and slender under-neath him, he cursed the fact he had to move at all. He wanted to lose himself in her again. This was...different from all the other times he'd been with a woman, any woman. It threw him, but he fought his instinct to with-draw. This wasn't meaningless sex; he knew what that was. He'd engaged in it enough the last few...fuck. He popped up, his heart pounding. *Protection*. He hadn't even *thought* about it.

"Paige, fuck." He raised his head. "What a cluster."

"What?" Her body stiffened at what must be an alarmed look on his face.

"I didn't use anything to...protect you."

"Oh, God. We...you...I...you're right, but I'm on the pill."

He breathed a sigh of relief. "I just wanted in. I wasn't thinking."

"I wanted you in and neither was I."

"I'm clean. Damn, I always take precautions. We have to take tests in the military all the time."

She nodded. "I don't doubt that. You wouldn't ever compromise me in any way."

"I wouldn't." Hit with a rush of affection for this beautiful woman, he nestled her tighter against him, stroking along her body, needing the feel of her against his hand. When he felt her shiver again and melt around him, his heart rolled over.

After a long moment, he pushed up. "We'd better go," he said, his voice low.

This time he went to his knees and backed off the bed. He reached out his hand, and she clasped it. He pulled her up and hugged her against him. She took a deep breath, then withdrew from his hold, reaching for her clothes. He wanted to watch her, but he looked away and got dressed in silence. He stuffed his shirt into his cargo pants, then went over to her, silently brushing her hands aside. He finished doing up the buttons on her shirt, then helped her into her jacket. Tucking her hair behind her ear, he tipped her face up and met her eyes, caressing her cheek. She smiled. Then he grabbed his duffel and packed up.

He wasn't quite sure where he was going to go. This was a nice central location, and he wished he could shove his fist into Anderson's face again for getting him kicked out.

Before they left the room, he crowded her against the door, trying to sort through all these pesky feelings. With the rawness that Anderson rubbed open, he covered her mouth with a soft, searching kiss, trying to find a way to close up a wound he'd thought had healed a long time ago.

"I thought we had to go. So get going, Wilder."

He tightened his hold on her jaw, his tone commanding as he whispered against her mouth, "Don't tell me what to do unless you're naked."

Her breath caught, but she yielded to the pressure of his thumb, and Kid adjusted the alignment of his mouth against hers, deepening the kiss with slow, lazy thoroughness. Working his mouth softly, slowly against hers, he enjoyed her, savoring the taste of her. Her breath caught again, her response as unrestrained as his, and he grasped the back of her head, her hair tangling like silk around his fingers. His chest tightening, he massaged the small of her back, and he felt her muscles go slack as if he had released the rigid tension inside her.

When he let her go, she said huskily, "Come stay with me."

Kid just couldn't argue.

~

PAIGE COULDN'T SEEM to get her head around what had happened between them. As they walked toward her house, he reached out and clasped her hand. Not exactly what she thought a temporary boyfriend would do. She bit her lip and tightened her grasp. Damn, but she liked him so very much. The sex they'd shared, mindless and out of control, was something that she had never experienced before. Ashe was...special, and she knew it. She just wasn't sure how everything would work out.

Anderson had hurt him, and she wasn't referring to the physical. He'd just tarnished Ashe's hero. He was processing. She'd worked with men long enough, lived with them long enough to know when they were in denial. She wanted him to open up to her in the worst way, showing her that he was getting as lost in this thing between them as she was.

But she had her own demons, and they were tied to her own dad. Something she could easily deny and hide her head in the sand, but Ashe's struggle with his own pain made her feel small and petty for not facing up to her own internal musings.

Her life had revolved around work for so long, she couldn't really see where she fit in a future that included something different. But when Atticus graduated from high school, he was going into the navy...into BUD/S. Ashe would be such a great role model for him.

She bit her lip again. What the hell was she thinking? She was getting ahead of herself. Ashe was a SEAL, and he had told her he wasn't good with relationships, had said he was gone almost all the time. She didn't think she would like that. She glanced over at him, so handsome, charming, and freaking adorable.

All she wanted to do was kiss him again, losing sight of the future or the past. Right now seemed so damn important.

"Do you know where I can get a knife around here."

She turned to look at him. "I guess it would be prudent to have you armed. There are always ways to get anything you want."

"You have a permit to carry that Glock?"

"Yes, it's already been sanctioned by the government. They know I'm here and only that I'm searching for suspects in the MP murders. The navy doesn't want to broadcast information about the arms. We might be able to procure you a sidearm."

He gave her a half-smile, a slight up-turn of his mouth. "All I need is the knife. Usually when the shooting starts, there's plenty of weapons to be had. I'll just *procure* one of those."

Okay, more shivers, and was it kinky that she was so turned on by his badass, boy wonder confidence?

She took him to the market, and they bought a wicked looking tactical piece of steel that was nothing but a killing tool. He paid extra for the sheath. When they reached her house and they stepped in the foyer, she knew her way around her cozy little place in the dark. But she dropped her key on the foyer table, the *ping* of it barely registering.

She could feel him in every pore of her body as he closed and locked the door, dropped the duffel. She'd never lived with a man like him. It had only been her father and brothers. It galled her that she still lived with them.

He pressed her up against the wall as she shrugged out of her jacket, as if he was trying to climb inside her, the crazy sexual tension that had been brewing between them since she'd laid eyes on him ratcheting up. She'd forgotten about the danger of exposure, about the fact that this was one complicated mess, about...what the hell was she thinking about...her train of thought just derailed—crashed, twisted metal, chaos.

Her hand slid up his amazing torso, up his heated, strong-muscled back to the nape of his neck and burrowed into all those thick, dark waves, so soft, so the opposite of him. He pressed his hips into hers, growling just a little as she tightened her fist and pulled his hair.

He fit perfectly between her legs. She pushed back, cradling the hard bulge pressing there as she clutched at his head to keep his mouth on hers. She knew what that hard part of him felt like deep inside her.

He pulled her shirt over her head as he dueled with her tongue, controlling the kiss as he drew his thumbs along her jawline, before sliding his fingertips down the length of her neck to her collarbone. Now it was her turn to groan as he efficiently popped the clasp to her bra, his palm following so fast, the tactile feel of him cupping her breast making her moan. He broke the kiss and started to leave a trail of kisses and nips along her jaw, around to the skin below her ear, setting off fireworks popping all over her body.

The memory of what he had done when he'd saved her from going over that cliff made her want to get closer to him. The strength of him was overwhelming; the power in his upper body and his legs turned her on. She'd drawn herself closer to him, all but laminating herself to the length of his body, pure, unadulterated reaction to the anchor who had pulled her from the jaws of death by sheer physicality and mental determination. The closer she'd gotten to him, the tighter he'd held on to her, but whether that was for her sake or his, she didn't know. He'd felt like he'd been falling apart, and she hadn't been in any better shape. If he hadn't been there, she would have no future to contemplate, and it had weighed on her ever since. How much time had she wasted? Working herself to death—was that any way to live? But how disappointed would her dad be in her if she lost this promotion over being stupid when it came to a man, letting Ashe derail her from her duty? She was undercover and on the job. This wasn't her vacation.

But there was so much Ashe, so much Kid Chaos piling up on her, over her, around her. The way he had so fearlessly walked right into her weapon and kissed her turned her on even more. She was melting, her sex tingling where his fingers had only been just a short walk ago. Lifting his free hand up to her face, he gently brushed the backs of his knuckles against her flushed cheek before threading his fingers through her hair and curling them around the nape of her neck. He drew her face closer to his, and the last thing she caught was the blue fire in his eyes. His lips grazed along her jaw, all the way up to her ear.

He pressed his cheek against hers, the electric scrape of his stubble on her soft skin a stirring sensation that heightened the heady danger he posed.

"I want to put my mouth on you. Kissing you with long, slow, deep kisses. Hard, sucking kisses against that place that makes you cry out my name. Then, when you're wet and soft and ready for me, I'd slide deep, deep inside you," he murmured, his breath warm and damp against her ear. "I want to fuck you slowly, make it last so I can savor everything about how you feel, inside and out...how hot and tight you are, the way you moan when I thrust high and hard, and the way your soft breasts and hard nipples feel rubbing against my chest. But there's nothing more exquisite than the way you feel gripping my dick as I come."

She'd never been with a man who was like this...a dirty-talker. Most of them did the deed with the lights out and in one position. But she had a feeling, Ashe "Kid Chaos" Wilder was much more creative, much wilder than that.

She'd been in tough places before, and this most definitely didn't count.

Hell, who was she kidding? She was in so much danger right now.

She shivered, and with his fingers tangled through her hair, he gently tugged her head back so their gazes met once more and their lips were mere inches apart. There was something strangely exciting about being at this man's mercy, as she currently was. God, she wanted him, with a fierce, powerful kind of need she'd never experienced before.

If she couldn't get past this thing...this conviction that

work was what got her attention, recognition, everything she craved, then she was looking at one lonely, empty life... like her dad who had never moved on after her mother left.

With her own mouth poised so close to his, she issued a challenge to get exactly what she desired. "That's some great talk. Let's see some action."

"Paige," he whispered, his voice husky with what she already knew as he roughly took her mouth with his. How could they want each other so much after just having each other less than half an hour ago? "Your bedroom. I want to get naked and tell you what to do."

SECURITY WAS tight at the warehouse, but Cris knew the code. It seemed that Bryant and his two lackeys had left. Cris had to know what he was dealing with here and how bad it was. Closing the door softly behind him, he carefully avoided the guard they'd left behind. He slipped into the cavernous warehouse, the silhouette of bikes in a row in need of various repair was stark against the light streaming in from the long windows alongside each wall. He wended his way through metal shelves until he came out to an open area. Two big double doors at the end of the storage area were closed, but they were big enough to drive a semi through.

His heart lurched in his chest when he saw the crates, hundreds of them stacked everywhere, but what caught his eye were the ones set on a table that looked like they were brand new. One lid was off the container closest to him. His heart in his throat, he looked over his shoulder to make sure the coast was clear. He walked quickly over to the table. He peered inside, and his gut clenched.

Reaching into the box, he pulled out a rifle. The stock was collapsible. He wasn't any kind of soldier, had never served, but he knew a military grade rifle when he saw one. Looking over his shoulder, he took a picture of it, then the boxes around him.

"Slow down, man," Bryant's booming voice echoed through the warehouse. Cris ran and ducked behind a large stack of boxes. He knelt down, his heart in his throat.

"Wait. I need to put you on speaker." He peered out of the shadows and saw Bryant with Dean and Reggie. He set the top on the box and nodded to one of them. "So what is so important?"

A hushed male voice on the other end of the line said, "Plenty. I couldn't find shit on the girl."

"What do you mean?"

"The file was too clean. I'm looking into it, but Paige Sinclair is more than what's in her file."

"Dig deeper. I need to know what I'm up against."

"If you were a better judge of character, we wouldn't be in this mess, Anderson."

"Yeah, Duffield made a fatal error."

"I handed that job to you on a silver platter. Easy in and out. Instead, you *kill* two MPs. You think the navy is going to look the other way? This is turning into a royal cluster fuck and you're the architect. Clean up this goddamned mess."

"What about Ashe Wilder?"

"More good news. He's a fucking Navy SEAL, decorated, lethal, and black ops primed. And Anderson, he's a sniper. If you don't want a target on your back or a cold zero in your forehead, eliminate him asap. Those guys don't stop, and if he finds out we were behind that Coronado job—"

"I can't do that right now. There are weapons all over the Incachaca and the Tunari mountain range and I'm still salvaging them. We didn't go to all this trouble for millions in profits for nothing. Not to mention, if someone else discovers those weapons, we're screwed. There are only the three of us. I can't get help and jeopardize this op with locals. If Wilder disappears, there will be an investigation."

"You're in the Andes, for Christ's sake, Anderson. Push him off a cliff. Make it look like an accident, take care of the girl, too, just in case. How you've survived all these years both in the CIA and out is beyond me. Get it done or I'm washing my hands." There was an audible *beep*. "Stand by."

In the ensuing silence, Cris watched as Anderson wiped his face with his hand. He looked stressed, the scowl on his face intimidating.

"I have a solution for your manpower problem."

"What?"

"I contacted our buyer. He's already got boots on the ground. We all will be in the crosshairs if this deal doesn't go down."

"I guarantee you I'm not going to be the fall guy for this."

There was nothing but an ominous click.

Anderson swore just as the grinding sound of the galvanized doors split. Silhouetted in the glow from the sun were several SUVs with tinted windows. This was like something out of a movie. But his worst fears realized, Cris was certain he didn't really know Bryant Anderson and that his partner, his friend, would carry out his threat to his family. Cris couldn't let that happen.

10

Cowboy stretched and got off the very uncomfortable transport. He was dead tired, all of them were. They had been going for seventy-two hours straight. They'd gotten the flyboy out but then had been called into another op to rescue two aid workers from some overzealous warlord in Africa. They had been going for three days with combat naps when they could get them. He was looking forward to sleeping for eight hours. He'd made it in time to get on a plane next week and head off to Galveston, Texas, for his cousin's wedding. He wondered if Kia Silverbrook had been invited. His cousin knew her in high school. His leave had been approved, but he wasn't sure he'd make it in time.

He couldn't figure out if he had a burr under his saddle because he was going home or because he was getting a feeling that Kid was getting himself in some danger.

"Have you heard from Kid?" LT asked.

Cowboy shook his head. "No. Dragon's a good dude, though. He knows his stuff."

"He sure does, but he's—"

"Not Kid," Tank said. Echo, panting, his pink tongue

lolling, looked just as tired as the rest of them as he trotted alongside the big SEAL.

"Leave it to Kid to go on vacay, meet a hot babe, and get in an undercover operation," Hollywood said. "He's stealing my mojo, that thief."

The rest of them laughed. "He does go to cool places for leave," Scarecrow said. "I would be heading for family, but then, I don't have much of a choice. The folks are getting up in years and the farm is getting almost too much for them. Tough decisions coming," he said, his accent soft and his words thoughtful.

Blue nodded. "It's a tough and complicated thing to watch our parents age. We get protective like they were protective of us. Just be patient, man, and answer the same question again as if it wasn't answered a moment ago. There'll be a time you wished you could answer that same question again."

Cowboy smiled when he saw Dana waiting for Ruckus.

"When you call him, Cowboy, let me know how he's doing." Ruckus took off at a run for her the moment she spotted him. Cowboy didn't get a chance to even answer. He thought about what that must be like to have a woman waiting for him when he came home. He smiled again, envious when he swung her around and then kissed her soundly.

The memory of Kia surfaced, and since he was heading home, he wondered about her all over again. Once he got to his apartment, he laid down on the bed. He called Kid.

"How's your vacation/op going? I swear you never do things by half. Is the NCIS agent a babe?"

"Yeah, and I'm knee deep in trouble with her, man." He talked about her, and Cowboy started to hope that Kid had finally come to his senses and found himself a woman who was going to stick. Now it was up to him to follow through. Something Kid had always been good at, except the women he chose just weren't strong enough for him. But Cowboy held his tongue. This was for Kid to figure out. After they finished their conversation, Cowboy hung up.

Going home next week wouldn't be at the top of his list. It always, always made him dang angry and ashamed.

PAIGE WOKE up but wasn't sure why. It was dark, and they had been at each other for the rest of the afternoon and had fallen asleep. She realized that Ashe wasn't beside her, and she looked at the digital readout on the clock by the bed. Two-thirty. Where was he?

She rose and grabbed the closest thing to her hand. It happened to be his blue T-shirt with Navy in white letters across the back. It caught her at mid-thigh.

She left the bedroom and came out into the living room. She looked toward the glass French doors. Moonlight cast long, faint shadows through the trees, and off in the distance, a lone coyote yipped. The call was answered, then answered again, until a discordant yodel resonated along the length of the valley, the sounds carrying for miles on the cool, clear air.

"I hope I didn't wake you."

As if her thoughts had conjured him, Ashe's deep, husky voice sounded from somewhere behind her. Turning around, she found him across the kitchen, standing near the counter, the moonlight streaming through the window illuminating him like a dark, fallen angel. He looked as lonely as that coyote sounded. Leaning casually against the granite, his corded arms were crossed over his bare chest, and he wore a pair of gray sweat pants that rode precariously low on his hips and revealed a good amount of his taut, rigid belly and tantalizing V. Lower, the soft cotton emphasized everything that made him so heart-stoppingly virile.

Her mouth went dry, and she swallowed hard as she slowly, leisurely dragged her gaze back up the length of his gorgeous, well-built body, until she finally reached his face. That stubble was thicker, looking dark and rough against his jaw, warring with the boyish cast to his features, and his bangs were over his forehead again, accentuating that sexy, bad boy image of his.

He'd never looked so Kid Chaos to her as he did right now.

"Hey, no," she said, her voice soft and low. "I missed your snoring."

He stiffened, then said wryly, "I don't snore."

His eyes were as blue as the shirt she wore, and as she walked across the concrete floor, the dying embers of the fire he must have started now glowing red, she saw that he was hurting and hurting bad.

Usually when her brothers or dad were wrestling with something, they would go and lick their wounds. It wasn't good to give advice to men when they didn't want it. If they were upset and needed solace, they asked for it. But a man like Ashe, he was a SEAL, bred and trained to be tough and strong. Never to let anything get to him, but she knew the truth. They might be tough and strong, but things got to them. They were flesh and blood men, and she knew it was true.

She knew no matter the training and no matter the mental acuity and toughness, everyone had doubts.

Ashe held her gaze for a split second then stared at the floor. There was something about the set of his shoulders, about the tight lines around his mouth that made her want to cry. An ache sharp and searing cut through her at the memory of her mother walking out and leaving them, leaving her with her devastated father and three boys under the age of six. She knew the kind of pain he was dealing with, but Anderson had added another layer. He had tried to shatter Ashe's memory and image of his heroic father. She looked up at the ceiling and swallowed hard.

The ache finally eased.

"I'm here, Ashe, to listen."

His face contorted in a fury of pent-up feelings, and he hit the counter with the side of his fist, then abruptly turned away. He raised his hand for a second blow, but Paige was across the room before he could act. Shaken by the uncharacteristic display of anger, she seized him by the wrist, then slid her free arm around his rigid shoulders. Grasping him by the back of the neck, she used all her strength to hold him against her.

"Don't," she whispered brokenly. "Please don't." He tried to pull away, but she refused to let him go. Closing her eyes against the feelings that washed through her, she tried to soothe him with the sound of her voice. "Shh, shh," she crooned softly. "It's okay. It's okay."

He shuddered and turned his face against her neck, then dragged in a deep, ragged breath and caught her in a crushing embrace. Cradling the back of his head, Paige pressed her whole body tight against him, trying to physically give comfort, trying to wordlessly let him know that it was okay. His hand tangled in her hair as he shifted his hold, locking her flush against him. He inhaled raggedly and turned his face against her neck.

"What if what Anderson said is true? It makes me sick to think my dad"—his voice caught—"wasn't what everyone thought he was, including me. It makes me feel like a disloyal asshole. He was awarded the Medal of Honor, Paige. That means something. That's not just a freaking happenstance. It *means* something."

"I know."

"I've been in battle; it gets so out of control. But I always have the mission in mind. Save the hostages, tag and bag the terrorist, criminal, rebel, warlord. But if he was..." His voice trailed off as if he couldn't even say *dirty*.

Letting go of his head, Paige blinked rapidly, the sound of his voice breaking her heart.

"I can't stop thinking about commitment. Why I went into the navy; why I became a SEAL. I rush into danger all the time, not thinking, not worrying. Now I wonder if I have a death wish, if the only way I can be like him, worthy of him is to die in battle." He closed his eyes. "Sometimes I think I crave it. That kills me inside. I'm part of a team, a damn fine team. If you'd met them you would know. Damn, LT is like a father to me. I love those guys. I swear I'm committed to them."

He finally ran out of steam, and she just held him. Hugging him hard.

"I think sometimes we put people up on a pedestal that they can't possibly live up to." She closed her eyes and thought immediately of her dad and how she had followed in his footsteps, each triumph looking for his attention. "I know this is painful and it's not fair because you really don't know what happened. Bryant can make up anything he likes. If your dad didn't make the right choices for the right reasons, it only shows one thing about him."

"What?"

"He was human, Ashe." Her voice softly chastising. "Flawed, contradictory, complex. For all you know, he was building a case against Bryant, waiting for the right moment to turn him in, making it look like he was playing along." She brushed at those thick bangs, then rubbed the back of his neck. "Whatever it was. You can be sure that he deserved that medal. Like you said, they don't just hand those out." She continued to caress him, giving him time to think about it. "They mean something important, and anyone who hears that someone in the military has received such a high honor, they know that it's true. Just like they know the trident means something important."

She took a breath, and her heart tightened. There was so much truth in her statement, and in helping him realize that his dad was only human, Paige realized that not only was her own dad human, but she was, too.

After a while, he released a heavy sigh, and Paige raised her head and looked at him. His expression drawn and sober, he touched her cheek. "I can concede that. I know my mom loved him and my sister." He looked away his voice strained. "And I did, too."

"Then accept that you're doing what you're meant to do, just your way. Being your own man is something that is all your own. You don't have to live under his shadow."

He took an unsteady breath.

"Because there's no brightness there, and you have a right to discover your own light and let it illuminate just who you are." Smiling, she reached up and touched the tips of her fingers to his unshaven cheek, watching as his gaze darkened with awareness. "There's also another truth."

"What's that, smarty pants?"

"You're human, too, Ashe," she whispered. "I've never met anyone like you, and I think you're pretty damned amazing." Now it was time for her voice to be unsteady.

"We'll have to talk more about that death wish you seem to think you have."

Ashe kept his intense gaze on her. "Oh, yeah?" he asked gruffly.

"Yeah," she whispered.

Ashe caressed her hip, then eased his hold. "I need a shower; then can we get something to eat? I'm starving."

Paige placed her hands along his jaw and began stroking his mouth with her thumb, rising up on tiptoe. "Men and their stomachs. You'll have to sing for your supper."

His pulse leapt beneath her touch, and his breath caught sharply. "Hey, no fair to—"

Tightening her hold on his face, she closed her eyes and brushed her mouth against his. "Shut up, Kid Chaos," she murmured against his lips. "You're singing."

"Okay." He started to belt out the "Wheels on the Bus" song. She pinched his side, and he laughed and jerked away from her.

She chased him to the bathroom, catching him just inside the doorway. She wrapped her arms around his lean waist from behind, pressing her hand flat against his ripped abdomen. Pushing at the waistband of his sweatpants, the dropped off him and he kicked them aside. She slid her palm down over his hard-on, brushing the heavy sacks beneath his shaft, until her hand was wrapped snugly around the base of his heated flesh.

Kissing his heavily muscled back, the rapid rise and fall of his chest expanding and contracting against her arm, she stroked him all the way to the tip of his cock, then glided her thumb over the swollen head. He shuddered and jolted against her sensuous glide.

Then he whispered her name and turned, gathering her up against him. Holding her fast, he shifted against her, and

Paige gave a soft cry and opened her mouth against his. It was like an exploding ordnance, and a fury of want, a frenzy of need ignited between them. Paige made a helpless sound against his mouth. Angling his arm across her back, he lifted her higher and caught her behind one knee, dragging her leg around him. Then he continued, sliding his hand up her thigh, his breath fracturing when he encountered nothing but bare skin. Securing both legs around him, Paige tipped her head back and rolled her pelvis against his groin, and Ashe grasped her by the hips and held her still. "Paige, babe, my knees are going to give out." As if unable to control himself, he thrust up against her, then locked her against him in a savage hold.

His gaze was dark and intense, hypnotic as he tightened his arms around her, his breathing hard and labored. "Just hold on." He hauled in a deep, jagged breath, then turned toward the doorway. "And for fuck's sake, don't move."

Paige woke up the next morning, naked, boneless, weighted with a delicious heaviness. God, but she felt wonderful. She felt Ashe's influence in every aspect of her life, physical, personal, professional, mental, and intimate. He was, once again, gone.

She heard the back door slam, and she sighed. Rolling over onto her back, she glanced at the clock. "Yeesh, six-thirty," she groused to her really soft and wonderful pillow. Part and parcel of getting involved with a SEAL. She didn't even start her workout until seven.

She got up and put on a pair of shorts, her running bra, and a couple of layers. She went out into the living room and stopped dead. Ashe was using one of the iron bars that braced her ceiling for chin ups...one-armed chin ups in just a pair of black shorts. He was drenched in sweat, barely straining as his biceps bulged, and he made it look so damn easy. He grasped the bar with his free hand and then did a few more, switching finally to his other arm.

"Wow." He was so spectacular. He continued his workout with a few more. "I take it you've already finished running?"

"Just sprints, not long distance. I finished my sit-ups and push-ups. I'll go with you." With that, he dropped easily from the bar.

"So, Atlas, got tired of holding up the world?" She was in shape, but he was...ridiculous. He gave her that adorable half-smile. "Let's go," she said.

After an hour-long run through the crisp mountain air, her thighs burning on the inclines, they came back to her place, showered, and fooled around until Ashe had enough and made her come three times before he finally joined with her.

As Ashe got dressed, she came out into the living room and into the kitchen. She preheated the oven. She filled the reservoir on the coffeemaker and put fresh grounds in the basket, her movements automatic and detached. Flipping the switch to start it brewing, she then reached into the fridge and got out eggs and tortillas. She put the tortillas on a baking sheet and slipped them in the oven, then scrambled the eggs.

Ashe came out of the bedroom, his hair combed off his face, with a few strands fringing his temples giving him a rebel look, accentuating his cheekbones and the strong arch of his dark brows.

"I've been thinking."

She added salt and pepper to the eggs, sprinkling cheese over them and adding a dollop of salsa. The stove beeped, and she pulled out the warmed tortillas. "About what?"

"What if Duffield overflew La Paz? Then you would have been looking in the wrong direction."

She stilled. "That did cross my mind, but really, it's a needle in a haystack. I guess it's possible." She mulled it over. "You know, Cris has been bothering me to take a look for possible bike routes around the Incachaca, a transition zone between the extension of the Tunari mountain range and the cloud forest of the Yungas of Chaparé. It's a hike to Cochabamba, a small town about two and a half hours from here, then another hour to Colomi. We can map routes around there. It would be scenic, and you'd get a nice tour of the countryside. We could stay overnight and come back the next day."

"And we could look for the wreckage." He crossed his arms over his chest, which only made him look more devastatingly male. More masculine. Sexier.

"Bingo." She set the breakfast burritos on the plates and pulled a container of mangos and assorted fruit out of the fridge, scooping out a generous portion for each of them. Grabbing the OJ, she poured him a tall glass. By this time, the coffee was brewed. Fixing herself a cup, she added half and half, sliding his glass and plate across the counter. "Let's go talk to Cris about it. I'm sure he'll agree."

11

Kid followed Paige's beautiful butt up the cottage's path to Cris's front door. He hadn't been in the office, and not wanting to wait until he got in, she'd decided to come to his home. She knocked, and Ashe could hear the laughter inside. It made him smile. He was still mulling over Anderson's snide words and Paige's soothing ones, his body and mind remembering how she had supported him last night. His heart was still twisted, and his mind still fucked, but she had helped him to see it in a better light.

He couldn't imagine after all these years the image of his dad could be tested this way. He'd never challenged what had happened to earn him the medal. Now, feeling like the disloyal asshole he'd mentioned to Paige last night, he couldn't stop running scenarios in his head. He had always wondered about the people his dad had saved. Wondered how they fared now. The kids would be his age.

She smiled at him as they waited for someone to answer the door. Damn, but he liked being with her. Every moment was interesting, and he loved the way she challenged him and kept up with him...mostly. He couldn't help, once again, comparing her to Caitlin and Mia.

He had to admit to himself, grudgingly, that all the signs for both of them had been right in front of his eyes. But he'd loved Caitlin, thought he'd loved Mia. But he now realized Mia was shallow, selfish, and simply didn't have the strength to handle him. She was seduced by his physicality and his looks. She responded to his SEAL persona, not deep down to his core. Caitlin wasn't shallow or selfish; she had been unable to handle his choice of profession.

Paige was courageous, driven, strong, and did have the strength to handle him in both demanding an equal partnership and in being his true match. She didn't just see the hero, she saw him, Ashe, the whole man. She challenged him to be a better man, to look deep for his answers, to overcome the blows to his heart and soul, to his very values, where Mia didn't and never would have, taking the easy way out with her banker.

A little girl opened the door. She was adorable and reminded him instantly of his nieces. She faced them with direct eye contact and said, "We're not buying," in Spanish.

Paige crouched down and tickled her under the chin. "Don't you recognize me Jhosselin? It's Paige."

She giggled and hugged her around the neck. "I did. It was a joke."

"A good one," he said. She shifted to look up at him from under a thick set of eyelashes, her curly dark hair an unruly mess.

"Jhosselin? I need to do your hair..." A woman's voice trailed off, then she smiled broadly. "Paige, come on in. We're just finishing up breakfast. Can I offer you a plate?"

"No, we've eaten." She touched his arm and said, "Ariane, this is Ashe Wilder. Ashe, Ariane, Cris's wife."

Wow. What a beauty. She was also younger than Cris, and the daughter resembled her right down to the cute nose. She looked harried, but with a nice sense of taking it all in stride like his mom had when they had gotten a bit out of hand. "Of course, Cris has mentioned you. You're filling in for poor Juan. Thank you for that. I do the books, so I usually get filled in on everything." She reached out her hand in a graceful gesture.

Two hair ties fell to the floor, and he bent down to pick them up. Something sounded in the kitchen and she said, "Oh my goodness. What now? I'm sorry. Please excuse me."

Paige gave him an amused look, "I'll go help her."

He was left with Jhosselin, two hair ties, and the brush her mom had set down on the foyer table. "How about we help your mom out here, and I brush and braid your hair. That sound good?"

"You're pretty handsome," she said, tilting her head. "I bet the girls really like you."

He chuckled. "I do okay, ma'am. Do you mind?" He held up one of the hair ties. He wasn't exactly sure what her mom had planned for her hair, but he was a pro at braids.

"No, sir. I'm a girl, too." She was all adorable and bubbly and had a dimpled smile that would turn granite to mush. He never really stood a chance.

He laughed again. Going to his knees, he grabbed the brush, and she turned around. "You're pretty outspoken."

"That's what Mr. Cassadia says about me. He says I'm..." She tightened her shoulders. "prekow...precowcious."

"Precocious is the word you're looking for, and I'd say that fits." He sent the brush through her thick, dark, curly hair as Paige came back into the hall. She smiled softly, and he gave her a roll of his eyes. Gathering up her hair from her temples, he focused on winding it into a French braid. Once he was done, he twined the elastic around the end and said, "There you go."

She went to the hall mirror. "Hold me up so I can see."

"Please," her mother said coming back into the hall and giving Paige a thank you smile.

"It wasn't me. Ashe has many skills it seems."

"I have nieces," he said with a smile, now looking forward to seeing them even more now than he did before this Bolivian vacation had gone off the rails.

"*Please* hold me up so I can see." She gave him a gap-toothed grin, and his heart melted. He grasped her around the waist and lifted her. "It's as pretty as you are, Ashe," she cooed. "Thank you."

Her mother gave her a stern look and opened her mouth to scold her, but Ashe intervened. "You're much too young to be a flirt," he said, somehow managing not to laugh when she gave him a dimpled smile.

He gave Ariane a raised brow and said," Heartbreaker."

Her mother nodded.

A boy not much older than Jhosselin came into the hall, his coat on and a backpack on his back, a bundle of energy who was, unquestionably, all boy. He greeted Paige with open affection. "Hi, Paige! You look real pretty today." He flashed her a smile that was pure charm. He regarded Kid with unveiled curiosity. "Hello," he said. "I'm Riky." He offered his hand, his grin deepening to reveal a big dimple in his left cheek.

Ashe nodded and said, "Nice to meet you, too. I'm Ashe."

His brow furrowed. "Like the boy in Pokémon?"

His mother ruffled his hair affectionately. "Another heartbreaker."

"Yeah, competition." Kid noticed he had the same steady

hazel gaze as his father's. "Yes, just like the kid in Pokémon, but I have an 'e' at the end of my name."

"Oh, that's different." He shrugged.

"Yeah, and I don't have a Pikachu on my shoulder."

The boy giggled. "True. Too bad. Pikachu is my favorite."

Ariane was reaching for a small pink coat on the rack in the hall. She walked to her daughter and slipped it on her. "Come on, you two. Let's get you to school. It was a pleasure to meet you, Ashe with an 'e,' even if you don't have a Pikachu." She smiled.

He chuckled. "Same."

"Bye, Paige. Keep that man in line."

"I will. Have a great day."

They piled out the door after Ariane donned her own stylish coat.

"Was she talking about me?"

"No, she was talking about Cris, but I guess it could apply to you," she chided with a nudge to his shoulder.

"Hey," he said, pulling a lock of her hair.

She gave him a sidelong look. "Pokémon and Pikachu. You really are impressing me."

"I told you. I have nieces and, for your information, I'm their favorite uncle."

"You're their only uncle." There was an undertone of amusement in her tone. "Cris is in the kitchen."

"Semantics." Ashe followed her through the well-kept, cozy cottage to the warm kitchen. The smells would have made his mouth water if he hadn't already eaten.

The smile on his face faded when he walked into the room. There was a subtle tension in the man who was working on buttoning his cuff. His hands weren't steady. Maybe he'd had a fight with his wife, but Ariane hadn't looked at all hassled except for the usual mommy chaos. There was a feeling he got when he would meet one of the Team's in-country escorts for an op. A sixth sense that had been honed over his years on the teams. Fidgety, tension lines around the mouth, anxiety in the eyes.

"Here, let me help you with that," Paige said softly, affection in her voice as she took the cuff out of his hand and did up the button. She might be a seasoned agent, but she had taken care of her father and brothers and some of that nurturing responsibility spilled over here. She glanced at Kid, concern in the depths of her eyes. Cris looked up at them and forced a smile, but it didn't rise all the way to his eyes like Ashe had seen in the past. There were now dark circles under his eyes and a darkening bruise on his jaw.

It looked like Cris had been mugged. "What happened?" she asked, nodding to his jaw.

"Just clumsy," he said, waving away her concern.

Keeping his voice relaxed, and capturing Cris's eyes, Kid said, "You doing okay, *compadre*?" In the bright cheery light in the kitchen, Cris's hair had the same sheen as polished pewter, the silver shade contrasting sharply with his weathered tan and the dark fabric of his shirt. Cris nodded and turned away from them, pouring a cup of coffee from the carafe, his hands still unsteady.

Working to school his features, Cris quickly asked, "What brings you here?"

They told him their idea. Something like desperate hope blossomed in his eyes. "I think that's an excellent plan! I have been nagging you to take the trip, Paige." He went to a board filled with keys. "Take the Range Rover. I won't need it." He tossed the keys toward Paige.

She deftly caught them and said, "Are you sure?"

He nodded vigorously. "Yeah, it's got a hitch for the

trailer for the all-terrain vehicles. Stop by the office and grab a couple ATVs and some camping gear, just in case. Make sure you bring a first aid kit. There's a rack on the vehicle."

"Will do."

"I think you'd find the Incachaca and Tunari mountain range very interesting. Just watch your backs, predators out there. I'll see you both tomorrow."

They drove for half an hour before he finally asked, "You know him better than I do, but did Cris seem...off to you?"

"What do you mean?" Her casual tone was belied by a quick swallow and the way her hands flexed on the steering wheel.

"I have this sixth sense. When we hook up with in-country guides, I get a vibe off them. If it's edgy and anxious, we're more on guard. Could be a sign of someone who's only pretending to be okay with working with Navy SEALs when they're exactly the opposite."

She tensed further, and he could see her wage her own internal battle "And you feel Cris is only pretending to be okay?"

"I got a vibe off him. He was agitated, his hands were shaking. It couldn't have been a fight with his wife, she didn't have that pinchy, disapproving woman look on her face."

"That what...pinchy?" She glanced at him, then shifted her gaze firmly back to the winding mountain road.

"Yeah, you've got it down pat."

It took a moment for his words to register, then she snorted. "Ooh, you should be glad I'm driving right now. Go on."

He grinned, then sobered. "He seemed eager for us to go on this trip."

"I told you. It's a possible new route. He would be excited."

"Maybe. But he wasn't excited. He was tired, worried, and I just think we should be more vigilant."

She didn't respond at first, keeping her gaze on the road. "All right." She glanced at him again. "This is how you think all the time, looking for danger?"

"Mostly when I'm deployed. It's weird. One day you're home and you go grocery shopping, play b-ball with the guys, go to the gym, do your routine. Then you get that phone call and the next thing you know, you're jumping out of an airplane at thirty thousand feet, oxygen mask, black jumpsuit. You're stealthing into enemy territory, and guys are shooting at you."

"How do you deal with that when you're stateside?"

He sighed. "The honest truth?"

"Of course."

"Lots of sex, pumping iron, and more...ah...sex. Sometimes mixed with alcohol."

"Wow. That is honest."

"I'm kidding."

She punched him in the arm. "Ashe, c'mon."

"My day is usually decided by assholes."

"What does that mean?"

"No two days are alike. Every day and every week of every year varies according to the current world situation—hence, assholes who decide to do something that pisses us off. When we get pissed off, we go over to where they are and do something about it. Every day I get out of bed, I put on my ass-kicking boots and kick ass. The trick is being able to ramp up aggression or cool your jets. It's clear cut."

"And you love it. I can hear it in your voice."

"I love it, hoo-yah. It's all about the cycle a particular team is in—for example, deployed on a mission, pre-deployment, post deployment, team training, Special Skills training, or leave. Right now, I am supposed to be on leave, but some gorgeous NCIS agent roped me into her undercover op and enticed me into her bed."

"And you're okay with that, aren't you?"

After emerging from one particularly long curve, they were about halfway up a high mountain with wave after wave of soaring peaks, some of them dusted with glistening snow and dotted with sparse vegetation. She smiled.

"One-hundred percent. I do the jobs that need to be done when they need to be done. Period."

"And with the stuff with your dad? How are you doing with that? You seemed pretty upset last night."

He stiffened, then relaxed. After waking up with Paige against him, his face still sore, he'd gone to the kitchen to apply ice to it and search for a painkiller. But the tablets he found might have taken care of his physical pain, but it couldn't touch the pain that always revolved around his father. He'd taken to heart what Paige had said about being under his dad's shadow. Maybe he hadn't realized how in the dark he'd been, that stepping into the light was his right and the last vestiges of the fear he'd kept concealed deep down inside him were unfounded. Every step of the way he knew he was going to make it through the SEALs because he came from the same stock. The shame of not making it would have been too much to bear, so determination was baked into his bones, into every inch of his body, sunk deep into his heart.

He realized he'd chosen women in his life who didn't challenge him for a reason. He didn't have to be vulnerable with them. They wouldn't ask the tough questions or give him the kind of tough butt-whooping that he needed. But Paige was what he needed. He knew they wouldn't stick around, and he didn't have to feel guilty about loving what he did for a living, knowing the pain, the havoc it played with the people that were left behind to handle the deployments, the danger he dealt with as easily as breathing, and who would mourn his loss hard if something were to happen.

His throat got a little tight, and he looked out at the landscape, trying to hold it back, but then realized that he was safe with her. She would catch him if he stumbled. If he fell, she would pick him up. "I had to look a little deeper because you challenged me to. I had a lot of guilt deciding to do what my father died doing, especially when it came to my family, especially my mom and sister. My sister was pretty mad at me for a while."

"That doesn't diminish the courage you had to go the path you wanted to follow."

That's just it, he thought. *Was I the one to choose the path or had the path already been chosen for me just by virtue of my father's legacy?*

"And your mom?"

"She's a rock. She was worried, but she supported me. So, I'm still working through all that stuff, but better," he said, taking her hand and holding it. "You were pretty great last night."

"You were, too."

This conversation had gotten much too serious. He set his hand on her thigh and smoothed his palm to her knee. "Twice last night and twice this morning, if my count is accurate."

"It's right on the money." She glanced down at his hand

as it traveled back up her leg. "If you don't want to end up in a ditch or even worse off the edge of a cliff, you'd better rethink that hand, Kid."

A frisson of heat crawled up his spine. "Hmmm." He scooched over and nuzzled her neck. "I like it when you call me Kid."

"Kid...Ashe. Driving here."

He went back over to his side of the car and whined. "Are we there yet?" Just as she slowed down, he glanced out the windshield to find—llamas and sheep. A ton of them were crossing the road driven by a young boy.

"Don't look now, but you have a friend over there."

Kid turned his head to find a pure white llama looking curiously at him through the glass. On impulse, he rolled the window down and reached out. The animal didn't shy away from him, but sniffed him. "Hey, buddy." He slowly petted his neck. The boy did a clicking call to it, and it turned its head. Looking back at him, it made a soft humming noise, then trotted off after the herd.

"You even charm llamas, it seems. They might be curious about strangers, but petting one and getting it to hum at you? Yeah, that takes chemistry."

"I got it in spades, babe." He flashed her a grin. She put the Rover in park and scooted across the seat.

She grabbed his jaw and planted one hard, knee-melting kiss on him. She leaned back and said, "Yeah, you do."

A half an hour after they encountered the llama and sheep herd, the Rover whined at its struggle up a steep hill, and when they descended, wisps of white smoke engulfed them. They had reached the cloud forest. Shortly after, the fog cleared to reveal moss-strewn jungle lowlands. The forest around them was a blanket of green so dense he could barely see a few feet beyond the road. They'd passed a small village a few miles back and had stopped to stretch their legs and answer the call of nature. Kid was used to roughing it, so he didn't bat an eyelash when they were told to go out back. The ladies went to the right and the gentlemen to the left. "Talk about answering the call of nature in nature," she'd groused, then walked to the right. He, nothing like a gentleman at all, laughed.

The rest of the trip to Colomi was a study in driving over some paved and some rutted roads. Then they went farther until they came into another small village. Paige parked the Range Rover behind some houses and they unloaded the ATVs and grabbed their packs.

Paige pulled out a map that Cris had drawn for her. She looked off in the distance. "The Incachaca is in this direction." She tucked the map into her jacket pocket, then shed the garment as he did the same. It was easily fifteen degrees warmer down here and heading toward noon.

They took off and entered the jungle along a worn walking path empty of tourists or locals. After driving for about half an hour, they came upon a village even smaller than the one where they'd parked the Rover.

His gaze went over the village, and he recognized the sudden tension in the air, most of it from a young boy about ten curled in the doorway of a house, barefoot and dirty. His big eyes watched him as he and Paige sat on the outskirts. Once, Kid had a boy like this in his scope. He'd been toting a weapon, and he'd done what was necessary to protect his team. But this one was unarmed and scared.

He touched Paige's arm when she went to get off the vehicle. Following the kid's gaze, he noticed the street was empty. His attention flashed to the homes, a couple of people he could see. They peered from behind curtains, taking cover in flimsy homes. Then he heard the rowdy

Russian voices before he saw several men walk into the thoroughfare with automatic weapons. He knew that dialect, and his blood ran cold. Kirikhan rebels in Bolivia? What The Fuck? What kind of hornet's nest had they just walked into?

12

"What is going on?" Paige whispered.

"A royal cluster fuck from where I'm sitting. Those are Kirikhan rebels."

"How do you know that?"

"The Russian dialect."

"You speak Russian?"

"Yeah, and several other languages." He grinned. He couldn't help it. "Don't tell me you only speak Spanish?"

"Yeah, that's it," she bit out. "What do you think they're doing here?"

"I haven't a clue, but if they're here, you can bet it's in support of the revolution. They work for a really bad duo. In fact, they're on our list of HVTs."

"High-value targets," she said, nodding.

"Boris and Natasha Golovkin."

"Boris and Natasha? Like, 'How do we kill moose and squirrel' villains? Is that a joke?"

"Believe me, it's not a joke, Rocky and Bullwinkle aside."

"I'm sorry, but they're not on my radar or NCIS as far as I

know." She reached back for her weapon. "What do you want to do about this?"

"My gut says that it might have something to do with the guns, but I don't know for sure. It couldn't be a coincidence that Cris sent us here, Paige."

"I was thinking the same thing."

"Why would he knowingly send us into danger blind?"

"I don't know, but it's not like him at all. If you're right and he is under stress, it probably has to do with Anderson."

"Then does Anderson know who you are?"

"You think my cover is blown?"

"Yeah, I'm thinking they got tipped off the night at the warehouse and are, at the very least, suspicious of us. Let's push these further down the road and hide them in the cover of the jungle. We're going to need to do some recon."

"Is that what you do on the team?"

"Yeah, point man, sniper, sneaky bastard."

The thick jungle closed around him, blocking sunlight, and the cooler temperatures created a thick rolling mist over the forest floor. The beauty of it escaped him, his steps slower because he couldn't see the ground well.

They were about thirty yards into the forest when the first shot came.

He went still and sighed. His inclination was to head toward it. It didn't matter that he was only toting a knife. She put her hand on his arm. "Ashe, we can't."

"Sure we can."

She shook her head. "It's better if we check it out first before we start killing people pell-mell."

"It would be controlled chaos," he said, completely serious.

They found a good place to stash the vehicles just as they heard someone running through the forest, shifting debris and displacing foliage. When he peered out, he saw it was the kid from the village. The boy would never outrun whoever was behind him, and Kid caught up with him, snatching him off the ground and covering his mouth with his hand as he backed into a darkened area off the path. The boy squirmed, and Kid kept him tight in his arms, grunting when the kid bit him.

He forced the boy to look him in the eyes and gave him a stare he reserved for terrorists. For a second, he thought the kid would faint. Then his frightened eyes went to Paige, and her projected calm soothed him. He nodded, relaxed, and Kid released his hand. The boy opened his mouth to speak, and Kid covered it.

"Not a word," he warned in Spanish.

He released him, and the skinny kid folded to the ground. Kid motioned him to hide behind him in a burrow of vines, and the boy quickly obeyed. Kid slid forward, his knife drawn as he watched the rebels strut along the path. They were overconfident, laughing about scaring the villagers, and while Kid wanted to teach them a lesson about being bullies, he couldn't afford to reveal their location. The trio moved deeper into the valley, and he let them pass, then motioned to Paige and the boy.

"What's your name?"

"Jorge."

"Nice to meet you." He didn't offer their names.

"They were looking for you two."

Most likely not, Kid thought. "Why are they here?"

"They don't say. They just keep going into the jungle and at night we hear helicopters. They don't like strangers here."

That Kid could believe. Clear out the untrustworthy, threaten the locals and you've got your bases covered since it the police were scattered thinly in these outlying parts.

The reason they were here had to be tied to those weapons. Had they somehow gotten wind of the mishap?

Then he saw him, striding confidently with two more rebels. Dean Norris. Anderson's shadow, his tattoos visible down his arms. He nudged Paige, who was looking the boy over for injuries. She turned to look, and her mouth tightened.

He bent down and whispered to the boy once Norris was safely past. "Get your butt back home."

"I can show you where they go," he said with a sheepish grin. "I followed them, but it was too dark to see what they were doing."

"Show me." Kid followed the boy, watching his back while Paige, her weapon drawn, watched his. With a finger to his lips, Jorge smiled devilishly, then pointed through the underbrush. There were crates stacked everywhere, new construction, bits and pieces of old shattered wood scattered over the ground. Those three he'd seen previously and the two with Norris were standing around until one of them pulled out a two-way radio and spoke into it. Then Kid heard the *whop, whop, whop* of the chopper rotors. Transport for the recovered guns.

This didn't bode well for those weapons. If the Kirikhan rebels were involved in the salvage, they were either part of this deal or the buyers who had come to claim their merchandise. Kid was not going to stand by while these weapons fell into their hands to be used against NATO.

He pulled out his cell phone, but when he activated it, there was no service. "We're either too far out or they're jamming the signal." He slipped the phone into his back pocket. For a moment, he considered capturing one of the five for a little interrogation, but nixed it. It was a better plan to pick up intel. Then they would hightail it back to La Paz to report to LT and NCIS so that they could send a force in here and to the La Paz warehouse to recover the navy's weapons.

The men started to argue, and finally two of them grabbed a crate as the chopper materialized in the sky, flying directly toward them.

Arguing heatedly, they lost their hold on the crate, and it hit the ground. The lid cracked, and for a moment they all just stared at the spilled contents.

Kid's gut clenched hard and alarm tightened every cell in his body. Paige gripped his shoulder as she also registered the crated cargo—warheads. Ballistic missile warheads.

Holy fucking shit!

Someone wasn't forthcoming on the intel about the warheads, and with the threat of them now in the rebels' hands, this was dire. American weapons being used against their own was bad enough, but the Golovkins with ballistic missile warheads? That would mean many NATO deaths, including Americans.

Suddenly out of the jungle, three uniformed Bolivian police emerged, guns drawn and trained on the three rebels. "What is going on here?" the lead police officer demanded in rapid Spanish.

The rebels looked unconcerned and none of them said anything. The police moved in, and one of them pulled his radio. Before he could bring it to his mouth, his chest exploded, taking his lungs out his back. Kid pushed Jorge down, and his gaze went to the direction of the shot. He couldn't see a thing. A second later, another shot came, knocking the second guy backward off his feet, a clean hole in his forehead even before the report echoed. Kid was admiring the precision hit as the third officer turned to run. The shot cracked a couple of seconds later.

The sniper was about six hundred yards away, Kid thought, in the hills. No noise suppressor, but a scope. That meant the shooter was unconcerned about being hidden.

He turned to look at Paige, her face drawn and solemn. He'd almost forgotten about the boy. Kid motioned Jorge toward the village as he eased back, careful not to disturb the bushes and give the sniper more targets.

When they were a reasonably safe distance away, Kid said. "Jorge, did you see a plane go down around here?"

The boy frowned. "There was the sound of a plane a while back, maybe two weeks ago, but I didn't hear any crash."

Back at the ATVs, Kid said, "Jorge, get back to your mom and keep quiet."

He nodded. "Good luck," he said before he ran off.

"The plane can't be far from here."

She nodded. "I need to see it and document it before I call my boss. We find it, get some pictures, get back to the car and La Paz. We need a signal to call NCIS."

He nodded. "I'd like to see how many of these rebels we have milling around as well. Give your team and mine a better idea of what they'll be up against when they storm in here."

"Okay, let's go find us a plane."

They set off in the direction of the rebels and the downed Bolivian cops. Skirting around them, they came upon a green SUV with *Policia Bolivia* stenciled on the side in white. Kid leaned inside and grabbed the radio, but when he tried to use it, he got nothing but static. "Yeah, they're jamming communications."

She blew out a breath. They left the vehicle, and that's when Kid saw it. Broken branches. A lot of broken branches. Paige pulled out her phone and started snapping pictures. He started tracking the distinctive path until he came out to a clearing and a lot of chewed up ground. There was a long scar of disturbed earth, broken vines, and displaced brush, and at the end, the nose of the plane sat at an angle against a copse of trees, wedged into the branches. The fuselage was gone, broken off and had flown into a tangled mass of metal and wires across the field.

"He crashed landed," Paige said, framing and capturing the scene. "He must have been out of it and totally missed the airport, then when he was dying, tried to set down and lost control."

"Yeah, he most likely had no choice." He turned to her. "Stay with me and keep that weapon cocked, but try not to fire unless absolutely necessary." His eyes moved across the field and the jungle beyond. There was no movement, but that didn't mean the rebels weren't around. They were gathering up the weapons and...Christ...the warheads. "How's your aim?"

"Marksman," she said grimly, her honed gaze just as alert as his.

"That'll do."

She gave him a slight smile and shook her head. "I've got your back."

He chuckled, and they stayed just on the fringe of the jungle, in the shadowed patches to hide their approach. "Let's go." He darted out, and they rushed across the open ground. Reaching the plane, they circled it and then ducked through the jagged opening caused by the fuselage being ripped away.

There were still some seats left in the interior, but mostly it was a chewed-up wreck. Approaching the cockpit, still watching for any kind of threat, Kid deferred to Paige.

This was, after all, her investigation, and this was the man she'd been looking for.

He was slumped over the steering wheel, his eyes open. His body had collapsed, his flesh a creamy consistency. Insect movement made the body shift. The smell was overwhelming, his body in full decay. There was a rust red stain on his shirt near his lower abdomen that ran down the seat and pooled and dried on the floor.

It was a horrible sight, but Paige didn't balk or flinch. He bet she'd seen a lot worse. He sure the hell had. She donned gloves. She was all business. So far, she'd been an asset in the field, holding her own. He admired her professionalism and her courage. His gaze traveled over her dark hair, pulled back in a simple ponytail, remembering the silky feel of it. She was compact, curvy, and in charge, with beautifully expressive tiger-eyes.

"He bled out, died either during the landing or shortly thereafter." Her voice was a clinical flat tone, noting the facts and keeping everything neutral. "I'm surprised they didn't destroy the plane and him with it."

The rebels hadn't even given a damn about him, just left him here to rot, and part of his disgust was because a human being had been neglected like this. Even though he'd committed illegal acts, he'd been a former marine. Kid couldn't help but think about how that compared to his dad. Had Anderson been lying just to get to him? Or had his dad not been the man he'd thought he was all these years? The not knowing was tearing him up inside.

Was Paige right?

Was he so busy trying to prove himself that he wasn't rising to his own level of potential? That it wasn't enough to be like his dad, but he needed to be his own man, on his own two feet. Stop living in his dad's shadow.

Any way he looked at it, he still wanted to do his father proud.

Paige continued to snap the pictures she needed. Searching the body, she came up with his damp wallet.

She flipped it open, and just inside, the ruined picture of him and his mom smiled at them. Paige studied the driver's license. "David Duffield." She sighed as if the first leg of her investigative journey had culminated in his dead body. "It's him, and this is the correct plane. But, Ashe, my boss never said anything about warheads."

Kid's lips thinned. "Maybe he wasn't informed about them. The navy only gives out enough information to get the job done. It was obvious they didn't want to broadcast that Anderson and his crew got away with ballistic warheads."

"I hate it when we're supposed to be on the same team and we get stonewalled." She pulled out an evidence bag and dropped the wallet inside.

"That is a bitch, but the name of the game. You have what you need?"

"Yes," she said, stripping off the gloves and giving the body another look. "He shouldn't be left here like this. We'll make sure he at least gets a burial. He just wanted to help his mom."

Kid nodded, liking that about this woman, her compassion. She might not be in the military, but she got the gist of the leave no man behind concept.

"Let's get out of here and back to the ATVs." The smell in here was overwhelming, the heat and the humidity of the jungle only adding to the thick and still air.

They made their way to the ragged opening, but Kid saw a shadow slide across the small windows. He alerted Paige, but she'd already seen it. He moved to intercept, silently, quickly, waiting for the bastard, his knife in his hand when the guy cut across the opening.

Shooting him at close range with Paige's weapon would have been effective, easy—and way too loud. The six-inch razor-sharp blade was just as effective and far quieter, but it came at a cost when the man instantly countered Kid's attack and fought back, blocking his first strike.

Then elbowing him in the ribs, sending pain radiating out, but Kid didn't let him go, nor loosen his hold. The guy kicked and squirmed until Kid body-slammed him hard into the side of the plane and stunned him enough to wrestle him to the ground. He got in one deep cut to the guy's gut and jerked the blade upward, hard.

As added insurance, Kid took the rebel's head in his hands and twisted, hard and fast, breaking the guy's neck. The sound was unmistakable.

Another rebel came around the structure and raised his sub-automatic, but Paige plugged him right between the eyes, the report of the gun loud.

Shouts echoed around them. He reached down, snatched up the dead guy's weapon, and grabbed Paige's hand. Access across the field to the ATVs was cut off as rebels came running out of the woods.

With bullets cracking at their heels and whizzing by them, Kid kept up his pace. They crashed through the jungle, speed valued over hiding at this point. Kid burst in short spurts with the sub-automatic as he ran.

They were being herded, and he had to believe that was to give the rebels an advantage against them. Then Kid saw it. A suspension bridge and the rim of a gorge. He noted there were slats missing. He remembered reading something about it—the semi subterranean waterfalls. They had no choice. Picking up his pace, Paige right behind him, he made for the bridge. As soon as he stepped on the bridge, he saw men on the other side blocking their escape. He brought up the weapon and as the structure swayed with their weight, without stopping, kept up a continuous burst that scattered them. Condors, displaced from the craggy perches above them, flew in agitated circles.

Paige picked off as many as she could. When they reached the end, rebels behind them, Kid veered to the right and skirted the gorge, displacing rocks and scree as he raced to the desired location. To the right was a sheer drop to the river. The path was nothing but a mere shelf cut in the face of the cliff, and to their left rose the smooth walls of black, frowning rock. Just below the falls, a pool. A sixty-foot drop was their only chance of survival.

He glanced behind him and rode the trigger until it clicked dry. Throwing the weapon down, he took Paige's hand.

"Do you trust me?" He looked deep into her eyes, realizing what he was about to do was on a scale of crazy he had yet to explore, as crazy as getting involved with her. Falling for her in a way that left him speechless, breathless, and wondering how he'd ever understood what it really meant to fall in love, be in love, get lost in love before Paige. But he was batshit crazy over this woman, and he wasn't afraid to do something that would give them a fighting chance. It was better than zero, and he liked their odds. Both of them were survivors.

"Yes," she said sincerely, reverently as she locked her gaze to his.

"Wrap your legs around me and don't let go." He wrapped his arms around her and looked down into the sheer drop, half a gallon of adrenaline instantly drop-loading into his veins, switching on every survival instinct he had. "Hang on."

He leapt off the cliff just as the rebels from the bridge reached them. It was as if everything slowed down. Paige's gun discharged in rapid succession, deafening him as bullets *zinged* and *zoomed* past them, the reports of the weapons reverberating off the granite walls. She released her clip, never letting go of him in the process, shoving another one home and continuing to fire.

She was magnificent.

~

HANG ON.

It sounded like what a superhero would say just before he took to the air.

Paige watched the cliff's edge fall away, but she kept pulling the trigger, hitting the men standing there, laying down covering fire and giving them a better advantage as they plummeted. Little details registered in a blink of an eye: the soft silk of his hair against her wrists, the strength of his solid, muscular body holding her close, his even breathing, calming her without even trying. The bravery and guts all wrapped up into the sheer beauty that was Kid Chaos.

But there was more to him than that. So much more, and she wanted to explore it all. She saw beneath the human shell, the intimidating and intense gaze, the devastating looks, and the humor to the man he was inside. Just as compelling as everything else. He was meant to be like this —audacious, fearless, determined. Even in his vulnerability he was bold and daring, showing her a part of himself that he'd kept reserved, private, secret.

She wouldn't want him to be any other way. She loved

that about him. Everything about him. Even the way he killed, grace personified, brutal, masterful and without any wasted effort. He was a warrior.

And she wanted him to be hers. The knowledge of that sunk deep down to her bones as they hit the water, the impact taking her breath away, the kind of impact that mirrored her reaction to Ashe.

The cold hit her like a runaway truck, knocking the breath out of her, her gasp caught in her throat as she clamped her mouth shut to keep precious air from escaping. She felt almost sick with the sudden awful cold shocking her system, but he wouldn't let her go, wouldn't let her rise to the surface. Bullets hit the water in a bizarre slow-motion slide, hot, sizzling lead gliding through cool, stalling liquid, leaving behind streaking white conic tails.

Then he started to swim, still holding her, a flip of his upper body and lower like the tail of a dolphin. He knew where he was going. He already had a plan, and she was safe here with him.

Of course, he was a SEAL, and this was the sea part. He was as at home in the water as he was on the land, as he was when her sky had been falling. He'd jumped out of heli-copters and planes. What was a small cliff?

She looked up at the man holding her so close, watching him concentrate with a calm, resolute look on his face. He had no doubt they were getting out of this alive. She felt it in his steady heartbeat. She saw it in his eyes, the utter commitment he'd made when he'd jumped into thin air.

There was no doubt what would happen if any one of those rebels crossed into his space. He would take them out one by one.

Kid Chaos.

Her lungs were about to burst just as he brought them to

the surface under an overhang of rock. She took a gasping breath, sucking in oxygen as he continued to breathe steadily. "You have nerves of steel," she whispered. Her lips quivered, and her body began to shake now that the air was hitting her wet head.

He directed her to the edge of the river. The rebels couldn't see them; he'd made sure of that. He navigated the soft embankment and froze. Paige followed his gaze, and she wondered if the universe felt they needed an additional challenge.

Drinking not far from them was a mountain lion, its tawny coat ruffling in the breeze. Its pink tongue came out repeatedly, siphoning the liquid for a cool drink of water.

Ashe rose slowly, taking off his wet hoodie and pulling out his knife. "Stand close to me," he said, his voice subdued and hard.

She rose and did as he instructed. The cat raised its head and turned to look at them. It was big, so she suspected it might be a male. Ashe stood his ground, the look on his face as intimidating as hell. He started to back away, and the cat watched them go for a few steps, then rose from his drinking crouch and followed their movement.

"Keep moving," he said. "But don't turn your back and don't run unless I tell you to."

"I'm out of ammo," she said, and he nodded, not taking his eyes from the animal.

Just when she thought he was going to lose interest, he broke into a leaping run right at them.

13

Cris pulled up to his house and sat for a minute looking at the home he'd built for her. He'd given up everything he'd been for her. The moment he met her, he knew it was all he wanted. They had fought this morning, and it wasn't like him, but he'd been so stressed worrying about Ariane and the kids' lives, his business, the people involved with him whom he supported. Anderson had betrayed him, his own partner.

But he had to realize that Anderson had always had the plan to use Cris's business as a cover for his illegal gun smuggling. He had been naïve, and it could cost him everything.

He got out of his truck, grabbing up the flowers—sunflowers, her favorite—from the seat and went inside. The smell of the delicious food that Ariane was preparing made him relax a little. He stepped into the foyer and tripped. Looking down, he saw that it was Jhosselin's llama. That kid never went anywhere without her favorite stuffed animal. He bent down to retrieve it, ready to yell to her that she wasn't supposed to leave her toys in the hall. But his heart traveled into his throat when he saw the blood. It was fresh, still wet.

He looked up, and with his heart pounding, he ran into the kitchen. "Ariane!" he yelled. But there was no answer. The eerie quiet of the house unnerved him. His chest heaved, and he ran for the stairs and tore up them two at a time, calling for them. "Jhosselin! Riky!"

They weren't there.

He ran back downstairs and turned off the stove, panic twisting him into a pretzel. Maybe she'd gone out. He was so desperate, he was now making things up. He'd call her. That's what he would do.

He dialed her cell.

"Hello."

His blood ran cold.

Bryant Anderson.

"I warned you," was all he said. Then he hung up.

Cris cried out. He grabbed the flowers and beat them against the counter until the sunny bright blooms were nothing but stems, the petals scattered on the floor like his dreams. He fell to his knees, covering his face with his hands, and wept.

Pulling himself together, he went up to his bedroom and reached up into his closet for a locked strong box. He opened it with the key on his ring. Inside was a gun. He'd bought it for protection a long time ago when he was living in a very bad neighborhood. He took it out and loaded it.

He left the house and went down to the warehouse. When a guard tried to stop him, he shoved the gun in his face, disarmed him and continued inside. Bryant was at his desk working like it was any normal day. He pushed through the glass door and pointed the gun at him. "Where is my family, you son of a bitch?"

Someone hit him from behind, and he sprawled forward, the gun discharging and the bullet *thunking* into the ceiling.

Bryant laughed as Cris's arms were jerked behind him and he was unceremoniously forced to his feet. Bryant hit him in the gut and he doubled over, the blow sending pain through him and taking his breath away.

He grabbed him by the back of the neck and forced him toward the monitor, shoving his face against it. His heart plummeted to his toes. "Remember what I said?" he murmured. "I told you to mind your own business and here you are, getting involved."

"If you harm them, I'll kill you!"

He grabbed Cris's collar and pulled hard on it, knocking him into the wall. His head bounced off and disorientation and pain made him sink to his knees. Reggie and another man dragged him upright.

"You want to know where your family is?" He crouched down and sneered. "The Russians have them."

"Oh, God. No. You fucking psycho."

"I'm not the one who made this difficult. They want what they paid for and you are working against them. They didn't like that."

"What do you want!" he yelled.

"Who is Paige Sinclair?"

"I don't know."

"You don't."

"I don't. I swear."

"Well, this is what you're going to do. You're going to find out, and when you do, you're going to tell me." He grabbed Cris by the shirt front. "If you don't, you, your family, and all your employees won't survive."

He nodded to his lackeys and they dropped his arms. "Now get out of here."

Cris landed in the street, and he looked up at the sky, shame and helplessness running through him like poison.

There was no way out of this that would save everyone, and he had to save his family. He didn't care about himself. He cared about Ariane and his beautiful Jhosselin and mischievous Riky. He cared about Paige and about Ashe, who was a good man. But with his family on the line, he'd do anything, even betray the lovely Paige and her Navy SEAL.

ASHE BRACED to take the full force of the cat as it barreled toward them, but this was the last straw. She wasn't going to let this happen. She stepped in front of him, raised her hands and yelled at the top of her lungs, staring the cat down. The animal put on the brakes, his back paws sliding in the loose stones. She picked up one and threw it. It hit him right on the nose and bounced off. He snarled and backed up. She threw another and screamed again. "Go away! Scat!"

He started to backpedal; then, like a male who had encountered an angry female of any species, he turned tail and ran.

There was a choked sound behind her, and she turned expecting Ashe to yell at her. Tell her she was out of her mind. But instead, he was doubled over. At first, she thought he might be hurt, but then he rose, and his face contorted. He stumbled backward, and a peal of laughter rushed out of him, and even though he tried to remain on his feet, he fell down on the ground and rolled around laughing even harder, clutching those rock-hard abs.

She set her hands on her hips. "What the hell is so funny, you crazy bastard? You just jumped from a cliff like you think you have wings!"

"You just *scatted* a *mountain lion*, babe, like he was a domesticated kitty." He covered his eyes and laughed some more. She marched over there. The heated exchange with the cat had warmed her some, but now she was getting cold again, shivering, and the sun was going down. They didn't have time for hysterics.

"Ashe. Get up. We have to go." He didn't move, just kept laughing. It was contagious, his laughter deep and rich. She reached down to shake him, and before she knew what was happening, he'd reached out and grabbed her, sprawling her onto his chest in a blink of an eye with his quick reflexes.

She gasped when she felt how hard he was. Aroused? Here in the middle of nowhere with mountain lions roaming and Kirikhan rebels trying to kill them, with a job to do and the dire threat of warheads in the hands of those rebels. What was he thinking?

But then he groaned, low and soft, his hips thrusting up into hers. She was thrown forward, and as soon as she touched him, she could feel the heat of him through his shirt, along with the way his heartbeat accelerated. *She* made his heart beat faster. Not a mountain lion, not a sixty-foot fall, but her. God, he made her feel like the sexiest woman on the planet.

"Kid Chaos with a hard-on while we've just escaped death twice. You really are batshit crazy."

Those aching blue eyes popped open, his face soft and tender. "It's the adrenaline, babe. Always gives me a hard-on. I want to fuck you, Paige, right here, right now. Who gives a damn? The water? Plants? Rocks? Fuck me. I need you to ride me hard. Ride me, babe."

The possessive tone of his voice, the serious, piercing, protective look said more than words ever could—that maybe, possibly, she was beginning to matter too much. How could that be? She wasn't supposed to feel this way. And, yet she did. She felt so much for him, beyond any fling. This was completely off the rails, this thing she had with the boy wonder. He slid his hand between her legs, tugging on the button of her pants, then delving inside to find her wet and tingling core.

He grabbed her by the nape of her neck. "Undo your shirt. I want your nipples in my mouth." His grip was gentle, his voice deep and demanding. With trembling fingers, she reached for her buttons. "That's it, babe. Let me see you." She pulled the shirt open and hiked up her bra, gasping at the exquisite sensations that tumbled through her from his fingertips. "Lean down," he put pressure on her nape, "and give yourself to me." She was powerless to resist. He clamped his mouth over the hard tip, and she cried out as she arched against him, the sound reverberating against the rock.

Everything receded until there was only Ashe in her world. He stroked her between the legs, his warm wet tongue swirling around her nipple, the suction making her buck against his hand. She was going to stop him and focus on the job. Really, she was. But she was tired of always thinking about work, and he made her needy as hell, and this felt way too damn good to stop. So she let her eyes drift shut, let the sensations take over, let Ashe take over, and promised herself she'd get herself right when they were done. Promised herself that she'd come to terms with Ashe and his effect on her.

Just as soon as he made her come. Again.

She was still shuddering, still jerking against his hand and the oh-so-clever fingers he'd slid inside her, when he was already slipping them out and shifting her, stripping her of her pants and undies, taking her mouth even as he breathed, "Let me the fuck in."

She wanted him in, all the way into her body, her heart, her mind. The raw truth of it was she craved the feel of him, filling her up, as she'd never craved anything before.

He was already freeing himself, panting and moaning every time she moved, every time she looked at him. He'd barely freed what had to be bared when he was jerking her down on top of him. She pushed down as hard as she could, grinding on him, glorying in the long groan of satisfaction she wrenched from him as she clenched her still twitching muscles tightly around him and rode him with the kind of freedom, abandon she'd never experienced before. It was amazing.

His hands were on her hips, his mouth on hers, his tongue deep inside, just as he was, thrusting, and she took both as fast and as deep as she could. She felt him gather beneath her as her own climax built. She bit his bottom lip, making him growl and buck higher, which made her cry out as the glorious friction of him filled her over and over again. She tightened her fingers in his thick hair and held on as his fingers sank into the soft flesh of her butt, likely marking her there as he tugged her harder, faster, against his now bucking hips.

He reached deep, sending waves of pleasure through her, and she arched back, working to keep him on that sweet spot. And her arching took him over the edge, groaning, swearing, as he pistoned inside her while coming in a shuddering fury.

She clung to him when it was over, and he clung just as tightly to her, clutching her to him, even as she struggled with the emotions that filled her to bursting, her fingers still in his hair, her face buried in the crook of his neck.

Their breaths came in heavy pants, and she slowly became aware that she was damp and sweaty. The air had grown heavy, fog coating them, only making them even more damp. She'd never experienced such ferocity like what they'd just done. It was always like this with him. She shouldn't be so moved by it. If anything, she should be bashing herself for letting him sidetrack her to such a wanton degree when they had so much responsibility riding them. What would her father think? Scratch that, she shouldn't be thinking about her dad when Ashe was still deep inside her.

But all her life she'd thought about him, and what she'd had to do to earn his affection and admiration, his trust. She had worked so hard for that. But Ashe had come into her life and blown everything into smithereens, and she was seeing what it would be like on the other side of barren, because that's what her life had been up until now. Empty, barren, lonely. So damned lonely.

This was what she could have if she let go and let herself believe that love and affection didn't have to be earned, but were unconditional, free, and felt so fucking good. Like this.

Of course, the danger and suspense certainly heightened their sensations, so there was that element, as well, feeding into all this. Maybe she could finally find not only the balance she'd only realized now that she craved, but also what was possible with Ashe in her life.

None of which explained the burning sensation that

gathered behind her tightly squeezed eyelids. Nor her reluctance to let him go, to look him in the eye and once again force herself to put this—whatever the hell it was with him —back in some kind of controlled, heart-proof box.

But he wasn't laughing anymore. He was still holding onto her, his face buried in her hair as if he wasn't ready to let go, either. He was still recovering, that's all.

Not that it mattered.

She willed herself to move, to gather herself, put her head back in the appropriate place—on the job and not reveling in the pure physical and emotional connection with him. But at the first hint of movement on her part, his arm tightened around her, his fingertips dug more deeply into her hair. So she did what felt natural and right. She pressed her lips against the damp, heated skin of his neck, the kiss sweet and gentle. God, this man. And when he kissed her temple, she kissed him again, drawing her mouth closer to the hard ridge of his jaw before nuzzling against his scratchy cheek, marveling that his boyish face could feel so deliciously like a man's. She homed in on that tantalizing mouth like a heat seeking missile, and he turned his head and captured her lips with his own.

They kissed softly, silently, reverently. Every moment of which quenched her thirst for him in a way that the fiercest declaration of affection never could.

She did move then, but he captured her face between his palms before she could slide completely off his lap. His expression was as serious as she'd ever seen it, his gaze locked onto hers so intently it was as physical a connection as the kisses they'd just shared. There was a stunned silence between them, the power and essence of which she saw reflected in his gaze as well.

It was a relief to know she wasn't alone in reeling from

the magnitude of what she'd felt had happened just now, even if she couldn't define it. She had no idea where this would go or how he felt. The breadth and depth of her emotions alarmed and thrilled her.

He grinned and held her gaze for the longest moment. Then he took her hand and kissed the palm. "That's the most fun I've ever had beating hypothermia," he whispered.

She closed her eyes and laughed. She couldn't help it. "We didn't have hypothermia," she whispered.

"Wanna go for another dip until we get chilled again? Go for round two?"

She just kissed his teasing mouth, enjoying the lights in his eyes. "Oh, Ashe, what am I going to do with you?"

"I think you did me pretty damn good. This is hands down the best damn time I've ever had in the field. Normally, I'm with a bunch of trash-talking, sweaty, dirty, unkempt men. You beat them all hands down, babe."

She laughed. "Geez, that's a great compliment."

"Oh, I guess that's easy," he said, a full Ashe, shit-eating grin on his face.

"Yeah. I'm sure most men would rather have this than that."

"Hmm, but I do love the guys."

She punched him in the shoulder and reached for her clothes, even now reluctant to part from him, but they had to find shelter and warmth. Night was approaching fast. They also had to come up with a game plan. They had to get back to the city, and as soon as she had cell service, she was going to call her boss and get an NCIS and SEAL team out here to deal with these thugs. She was also calling Cris next and warning him about Anderson and the danger. It was the least she could do for him. He had a family to protect.

They started walking, and from what she remembered

of this area, it was pretty barren. He looked at his diver's watch, which had a compass, and said, "If I'm not mistaken, there are Quechua Indians who live out here to farm coca— coke. It's a seasonal crop."

She nodded.

She looked over the bare, shattered, and split crags that reached many hundreds of feet above the trail, and some even stood in a leaning position so that the tops actually hung over the narrow passageway as if threatening to topple down at any moment; below, the steep slope was covered with huge boulders which had fallen from the towering masses above. They moved from barren rock and scree into the forest. Bright orange-red birds flashed through the deep green of the forest like fiery comets. Green toucans and tiny, pretty little parakeets flittered around.

They crossed a dry, narrow bed of a stream which was filled with rocks bearing the imprints of leaves and also fossil shells.

Breaking out into a clearing or cultivated area, Ashe shaded his eyes. In June, there weren't any farmers left. They had gone back to Cochabamba to winter, visiting their plantations only three times a year, supervise the gathering and packing of the leaves, and sell the harvest and live on the proceeds until the next one.

The huts were vacant, and it was child's play for Ashe to get inside. The interior was a low, one-room, board structure. It had a small fire pit, and after searching they found wool blankets and sheets for the bed.

The rebels would probably be looking for them, but now that it was dark, there was very little chance they would find them way out here. They stripped down and dried their still damp clothes near the fire. The bed was made out of straw, but comfortable enough for them to lay down side by side.

They ate power bars and rabbits that Ashe snared with a piece of twine and an apple that had been left in one of the barrels.

It was warm and cozy beneath the blankets with the fire going and her stomach pleasantly full.

She thought about how fragile life was, how she only got so much of it and that working herself to death didn't have the same appeal it had before she'd come to Bolivia. The people lived here so simply and happily. Could she let go of her own shit long enough to embrace a new mindset? Could she live without the specter of her need to prove to her father that she was worthy of his affection and love just for herself?

She wasn't sure that would work and losing her father's respect would be devastating. NCIS and her promotion seemed distant, on a different continent.

"Hey," he said softly, "you're pretty far away."

She turned toward him, settling onto his chest, running her hands over his hard muscles all the way down to that delicious dent just above his hip. "I was thinking that I was so caught up in watching my father all those years take me for granted, that working hard was the only time he seemed to notice me."

"Aw, Paige, that must have been so hard." He cuddled her close. "Has something changed?"

"I don't know. It's twisted up like your situation with your dad. I feel like if I pull a thread, it'll all come unraveled, and I won't know what to do with all the remnants. It scares me."

"You? The woman who told a mountain lion to scat? Impossible."

She laughed and thumped his chest. "You are completely impossible."

"Nope," he said, his voice going husky. "I'm so easy, babe. You make me so damn easy."

She was a jumble of emotions. Her sexual state had rather suddenly and unexpectedly gone from a coma into overdrive, with a man who was practically a stranger, a situation she wasn't even close to sorting out.

He covered her and used his knee to nudge her legs apart. She could feel how hard he was as he settled there. There went the world again, shrinking down so small, so infinitesimal.

There was only him, the weight of him holding her down. "My body is crazy for yours. All you have to do is breathe to turn me on." He eased her leg up around his waist, fitting himself to her, testing her, then he slipped inside all the way, making a deep guttural sound that made her sex clench around him. "Nothing like it on earth," he said. "My hard dick inside you, tight and wet. So good," he moaned.

She started to say something, but he stole her words with his mouth, opening it wider over hers, pulling her tighter as his hard body and thick cock consumed her, and he kissed her long and wet and deep, over and over, making love to her mouth, to her tongue and her lips. "I just want you, all your wet softness, all your sighs of surrender."

He pulled out and then thrust back into her so slowly, the magic of his body washing over her again and again.

His thrusts made him a part of her, fueling her needs that had been just as overwhelming as the last time she had been like this, naked and wanton beneath him. He filled her, not just with his body, but with his pleasure and the sheer power of his desire. His hands were on her, gliding over her skin, holding her, strong and sure, leaving no part of her untouched. He'd known exactly where he'd wanted to go, and he'd taken her with him.

It was all so achingly lovely, to just feel him inside her, on her, all over her. She slid one hand down his chest, her fingers pressing against those tantalizing hard muscles, to the dark hair that covered his groin. She loved the way he felt, all hard, lean muscle moving on top of her, each flex and thrust of his hips pushing him deep inside her.

She knew him, knew this could go on endlessly until they transcended conscious thought, until they reduced themselves completely to taste and touch, sight and sound and scent. It was eroticism poured into her skin. It was stamina and otherworldly delights. It was strength and the willingness to surrender. It was amazing. It was the reason he was called Kid Chaos.

Long minutes flowed into each other, sliding across the night, until she no longer existed outside of him. His heat was hers, infusing every pore. The taste of him on her. She moved, and he moved with her, as one, until he tightened his arm low around her hips and pulled her against him. All movement stopped, then, except for the slow slide of his other hand up the middle of her torso and between her breasts, until his hand came to a stop at the base of her throat. His palm was so hot, pressing her back into the bed. He branded her; bound her. It was dominance of the most primal kind imaginable, and it demanded submission. His gaze held hers, dark and glittering, his hair falling thick across his forehead as he pulled her even tighter against him.

When he pressed into her, heat flashed across her body. Sweat broke out on her upper lip and brow. He made that boy wonder move again, and a tremor started deep, deep inside her. He felt it, she could tell by the darkening of his gaze. A feral smile curved his lips, then his eyes drifted closed and his head went back. He moved her against him, pumped into her, his teeth bared, a low growl coming from deep within his chest, getting her hotter, making her wilder. She wanted him. She wanted this, all of it desperately. Her legs tightened around him, and with his groan echoing in her ears, she felt the first pulsing jerk of his release, his cock so hot and hard inside her. Molten heat pooled in her groin, and when he thrust into her again, she was with him, drowning in ecstasy, suffused with pleasure so deep, she felt it in her bones, down to her soul, so full of him, he was a part of her.

Kid Chaos had instead turned her world upside down into some kind of crazy kaleidoscope of beauty and understanding. Instead of chaos, he'd brought order in his own beautiful way.

Afterward, she turned toward him and he gathered her close.

From the moment she'd laid eyes on him, she had thought he was going to be one of the greatest adventures of her life, but he was more than that, so much more.

14

Early morning light woke her, and she roused from sleep, fully awake. She opened her eyes to Ashe. She didn't want to wake him, and even though she wanted to touch him, she kept her hands off him. But she looked.

Looked her fill, he was so beautiful. The sun was warm, heating up the small hut. He'd kicked off the blanket, leaving himself naked to her gaze. He had smooth, tanned skin, but as she studied him, she noted imperfections. He had a long diagonal line down his back, several raised round wounds, and other nicks and scars. The body of a warrior, marred by battle, but still so gorgeous. All she could see was that he was a work of art, his body a living sculpture of muscles beneath his skin. Lean and highly defined.

He shifted, sending those muscles rippling, and he turned so his face was pressed close to hers, his breathing still even and steady.

Everything about him was steady, and she hoped, hoped like hell she hadn't drawn him into something that would get him hurt, this precious man she'd found in the wilds of Bolivia. Her chest heaved, and she covered her mouth, realizing that this was all going to be over and this...thing with him was going to come to an end. That was what they had agreed on. He'd go back to San Diego and his deployments, and she'd go back to her job, another case closed, her promotion secured, increasing her hours. She'd have what she'd worked so hard for—her own team.

She'd see Atticus graduate, the last boy out of the house. He'd grow and train into a man like Ashe. Oh, he should be so lucky to be a man like him, but she knew he had the foundation and was already an amazing person. Then it would be her and her father working and living together, neither of them really living.

Her breath hitched, and her eyes flooded with tears. She'd been there for her father and her brothers, cooked, cleaned, worked, nursed, and nurtured them. But now she realized she'd never taken a thing for herself.

She closed her eyes as the tears squeezed out. She felt his fingers on her face, the tips brushing at the moisture. His breath was warm, his body solid as he pulled her into his arms, kissing her cheeks where the tears had left tracks. "Aw, babe. Talk to me," he said softly, his voice husky from sleep.

"I was just thinking about Atticus."

"Your youngest brother?"

"Right. He wants to be a Navy SEAL."

"And that's making you unhappy?" He sounded worried, and she'd never heard that tone before.

"No. Not that," she said, opening her eyes and meeting that intense gaze.

"What then?"

"Soon he's going to be gone and it'll be just me and my dad."

"That's making you unhappy? Living with your dad? Or is it the empty nest thing? I know you're not his mom, but you've been like his mom since he was in diapers. Those feelings are normal, sweetheart."

He was trying so hard to understand her. Her heart turned over, and there in a one-room hut in Bolivia, naked and vulnerable, open and real, she fell in love with a man she'd known less than a week. It was lust at first, until she'd gotten to know him, but his attempt to try to understand her, try to support her and comfort her was the kind of man she wanted forever. But she was trapped between what she wanted and what she had planned for. Ashe hadn't been in the plans. He was just this big, beautiful, irresistible force who had hit her like a freight train and knocked her whole world out of kilter.

She was at a loss on how to make this work when she felt so burdened by all the baggage in her life.

She cupped his face because he was being so sweet. She kissed his mouth, lingering for a heartbeat. "Thank you for trying to get it. But, yes, sometimes you come to a crossroads and everything hinges on the choice to go right or left. The one thing you do know is you can't go backwards."

"No. That doesn't work," he said, his eyes serious and direct. "But doesn't mean you can't go sideways or on a tangent. Leap up or lie down until you figure it out. Making a choice is important. Taking your time is just as important."

He cuddled her closer, and they lay there for a few more minutes until Ashe tensed. She heard it the same time he did. The sound of an engine.

Scrambling out of bed and hurriedly getting dressed, they stood to one side of the window as a beat-up Jeep motored into the little cluster of huts. The sound of the Quechuan language carried easily on the air.

Both of them relaxed. It was one of the caretakers checking on the building.

"Looks like we got ourselves a ride."

An hour later, they were back at the Range Rover and heading back to the city. As soon as Paige got a signal, she called her boss, gave him the information and the coordinates. He told her they were scrambling a joint SEAL/NCIS team and would be there by the afternoon. The NCIS team would secure the warehouse in the city, and the SEALs would handle the rebels at the crash site. Her second call was to Cris.

When he answered, she said, "Cris, I need you to listen because this is important. You and your family are in danger. You should get out of La Paz at least until tomorrow."

"Why Paige?"

"I'm afraid that Bryant Anderson is the man I've been searching for since I came to Bolivia."

He sighed heavily, and his voice sounded strange. "Who do you really work for?"

"I'm sorry I had to lie to you, but I'm undercover for the Naval Criminal Investigative Service. I'm a federal agent, and Bryant is working with Kirikhan rebels. He was the mastermind behind stolen military weapons in California and responsible for the death of two military policemen. I need you to promise to get out. Take Ariane and the kids to your in-laws just until it's safe to come back."

"I think he's storing those weapons in our warehouse. I could get you inside."

"You can?"

"Yes, I have the code. I could give it to you." He made a grunting noise, then said, "Where are you?"

"Almost to La Paz. What is the code?"

As soon as she hung up, she turned to Ashe. "We'll go to the warehouse and make sure the weapons are secure. They have no idea we were at the crash site, and I'm pretty sure it was hard for them to get a description, but we could have spooked them. It's possible they could be getting ready to ship them out of the country. I don't think we should wait. Cris gave us the code. We could do a looksee and then report back to the teams."

He nodded. "You trust him?"

"Yes, I do. He's not part of this."

"Okay, but we're going to need some firepower."

She nodded. "My boss has us covered."

"Okay," he said. "Let's do this."

Ashe parked several blocks away from the warehouse, and they made their way around to the back where the side door opened up into the storage area. Her boss had supplied them with automatic weapons.

Paige keyed in the code, and they slipped inside. Ashe put his hand on her shoulder after only a few steps.

"I don't like this," he whispered. "I prefer to do recon before we do any type of assault." He was very busy watching the door and waiting, focused, and looking damned deadly with the way he was holding his weapon, which oddly enough almost made her feel safe.

His gaze slid to her again, his face grim, and suddenly—oh, quite suddenly—all she wanted to do was retreat. "I know," she whispered back. "This feels off. Let's get out of here."

The lights came on, and Anderson and his buddies strolled out into the center of the warehouse, Norris and Reggie training their weapons on them. "Leaving so soon? But you haven't been introduced to our guests." Two hard looking men stood behind the lackey brothers. Kirikhan rebels.

Paige's heart went into her throat, and then she saw Cris

and it plummeted to her shoes. His face was battered, and he had his head bowed.

She closed her eyes, letting out a shaky, frustrated sigh. She closed her hand so tightly she could feel the sharp edges of her fingernails pressing into her skin until Anderson's flunkies snatched their weapons out of their hands.

Anderson clapped Cris on the back, and he winced. "Thanks to Cris, we're done with the cat and mouse game."

"Cris," she whispered, his name broadcasting her disappointment, realizing that she'd made a terrible error, one that was going to get all three of them killed. She'd trusted him, let down her guard and made the most colossal mistake of her professional career.

She hated to doubt herself, tried to shake it off, but it was a tricky, invasive emotion. She'd never been this wrong before.

But tonight she was, she thought. Tonight felt different. Tonight she was afraid.

"I'm sorry, Paige. Ashe. They have my family."

Her gut clenched hard, and she looked at Ashe whose expression was flat, calm, and lethal.

"Bryant, you're committing treason, not to mention murder counts and theft of government property. Those warheads...you know what they'll do with them. What kind of man have you turned into?"

At the mention of the warheads, the two rebels swore and started shooting rapid Russian at Anderson. He held up his hand and turned to her, a dose of stone-cold silence.

"I'm a federal agent and Petty Officer Wilder is a Navy SEAL. You harm us and you're looking at the death penalty." Her voice rang with authority inside the cavernous warehouse.

This time he laughed.

Norris grabbed her and flex-cuffed her wrists, then pulled her close, his breath hot and unwelcome on her neck. "You're mine, sweetie."

Ashe leaped at Dean and his attack was so fast, so brutal, none of the men there had a chance to move. He pushed him against the wall, his arm across his windpipe. Paige saw that Dean couldn't breathe, and Ashe had every intention of making sure he never took another breath.

Reggie hit him in the head with the end of his rifle. Ashe let go and fell to his knees as Dean started choking and backpedaling away. Then Reggie flex-cuffed his hands behind his back.

He grabbed Ashe by his shirt collar and dragged him over to Anderson, pulling him to his feet.

"Dean, you can have the girl, but hold off just yet. Petty Officer Wilder and I are going to have a chat."

Anderson punched Ashe so hard in the gut that he doubled over and went to his knees. Then he smashed his knee into his face and knocked him onto the concrete. Blood splattered from a gash on his cheek, running down over his jaw and neck. Anderson grabbed a handful of Ashe's hair. "I've had about enough of you, navy boy. Just like your damn father, never know when to quit. Well, after I put a bullet in his brain, that stopped him cold."

Ashe's face contorted into such a mask of pain and agony, Paige's stomach clenched, his roar feral and anguished just before he head-butted Anderson and knocked him completely off his feet. Ashe rose in one powerful push of his thighs and rushed over to Anderson, ready to stomp his face when Reggie grabbed him from behind, clamping his arms tight around Ashe's arms and waist and hauling him away. The big man could barely hold him as he thrashed and fought to get free.

"You fucker. You're a dead man," Ashe said, and it was more potent, crazier because he was so damn quiet. She ached for him.

Anderson rose from the floor and turned toward her. He raised a pistol and pointed it directly at her. Ashe stilled, his harsh breathing suddenly hitching.

"Attack me again, and I'll fucking blow her head off."

Ashe clenched his jaw, fury rolling off him in waves, and he gave Anderson a narrow-eyed, lethal gaze. If looks could kill...

"That's better."

Reggie shoved him, and Anderson grabbed him by the throat. This time Paige tried to move, but Dean grabbed her and held her back.

"I'm going to ask you once and only once. Then you have five minutes to make a decision. If it's the wrong decision, she dies. No second chances."

"What do you want?"

"The ETA of NCIS and Navy SEALs. Where and when?"

Paige made a soft sound. She was forcing him to betray his country, his team just like he'd done to Cris. Ashe, who would go to his death before he'd put his brothers in arms in mortal danger. But then his eyes met hers and they softened, the anger banked.

Oh, God, Ashe...no.

∼

ANDERSON TURNED AWAY and Ashe wanted to kill him with his bare hands.

"This is some kind of revenge for what happened with my father," he bit out, keeping his voice calm despite the demoralizing dread he felt. He would do anything to protect

Paige, but give up the coordinates, betray his team? He'd taken a vow. If he broke that vow, he'd break his honor, and like vines that had entwined too tight, all of that was mixed up in his own father's honor—or was it lack of honor?

He'd trained hard, honed his body into a killing machine, but where a SEAL excelled wasn't his body, it was his mental toughness, it was making decisions on the fly, it was all about winning every goddamned time, against the toughest odds, against the toughest enemies.

Memories of being tangled up with her, of holding her, taking her, the warmth of her body, the smell of her skin... Standing here in agony with the threat of losing her, he knew without a doubt that he was in love with her, the real kind, the kind that held no illusions. His heart beat as if in slow motion. In this place, in this time, he was her partner, and all the mental toughness in the world wouldn't save him from the devastation of being the reason Anderson took her life.

If he could buy them some time, any time to get back in the game, that would be the win. The NCIS team would find an empty warehouse, but his teammates, his close friends, his brothers would find a freaking small war.

She was helpless, bound, but the look on her face, that defiant, tough-girl stance made his heart beat double time. He took a breath. If he gave up this information, they would be ambushed, and he'd have to live with it for the rest of his life. Ruckus, Scarecrow, Cowboy, Hollywood, Blue, Tank and Echo, and Wicked.

But they were Navy SEALs, and battle was what they did. Live to fight, fight to live.

"Time's up," Anderson sneered. "What will it be?"

There was no contest here, no choice. He gave up the information. Betrayed them and took the hit against his honor, against his trident, against everything he'd ever stood for.

In that act of betrayal, he found what he was looking for. Found the answers to his questions once and for all. He might have followed in his father's footsteps and gone into the SEALs because he was trying to be worthy of his father. But right here, right now, he made his own decision, was his own man, and that decision was to be fearless, take batshit crazy to a new level.

He didn't have a fucking death wish. He delivered death to the enemies of the country he served even, and especially, if they were her native sons. He met Paige's stricken eyes, watched as tears slipped down her cheeks in wet tracks. He wanted to live. He wanted her to survive. And in that moment, he understood Cris's betrayal to save his family. Thought about that precocious little girl, the smart, charming boy, and his beautiful wife.

The big doors started to open, and the tail end of a truck, its staccato beep warning it was backing up, pushed through the metal doorway.

They were loading the weapons, and he couldn't do a damn thing about it. But he heard what the rebels said and tucked the intel into his memory.

No matter what, they were going to all get out of this alive. He was going to see to it.

They started to load the boxes, and the two rebels left. "Dean, she's all yours."

Every muscle in his body clenched. He met Paige's eyes and his message was loud and clear though he never uttered a word. *Stay alive, fight, win. Babe, I'm coming for you.*

He stared Dean down, and Kid could tell he was scared of him. "You're a dead man."

Reggie cracked him from behind, right in the same

motherfricking place he'd hit him before, and pain exploded in a flash burst. He fell to his knees, but his eyes never left Dean's as he backed away, his hand wrapped around Paige's arm.

"Take them to the village. I don't want any blood in the warehouse. Kill everyone. I'll take care of the SEALs." Anderson turned to go. "Oh, and Reggie, save these two for me."

Cris exploded from the floor and went for Anderson's throat, screaming at him, but Reggie grabbed him from behind and wrestled him away. Cris continued to scream until Reggie hit him in the temple and Cris went out like a light.

Through it all, Kid watched as Dean dragged Paige away, and they disappeared out of the double doors.

The muzzle of the gun dug into his back, and Kid wanted to shove it—

"Get up."

He complied. He was eager to get back to the village where Cris's family was being held, where that goon was taking Paige, where his brothers were coming in to kick ass. It was time to take back the night, and he was just batshit crazy enough to do it.

After forcing Kid into the back of an SUV, Reggie tossed Cris on top of him, shut the back door, and got behind the wheel.

About fifteen minutes into the trip, Cris woke up. He groaned and looked at Kid. "I'm sorry. I didn't know what to do," he said, his voice ragged and desolate.

Kid captured his battered gaze. "I do," he said. "Pull yourself together. If you want to save your family. Do exactly as I say."

Hope lit his eyes and his head came up. He nodded.

DEAN HAD TRIED to engage her in conversation from the moment they got into the truck. He'd actually buckled her into the seat, and that almost made her laugh. She knew what he was planning the moment he got her to the village, and it wasn't going to happen. She wasn't going to allow him to take something she wasn't willing to give. Her body belonged to another man, her heart his. She couldn't help but wonder if she had focused more on the job and less on Kid Chaos if this would have ended up differently. But now they were all in mortal danger. Dean was just as big a psycho as Anderson and hellbent on taking what he'd wanted from her the moment she'd met him.

He kept squeezing her leg, sliding his hand too close to her groin, but going no further. She couldn't help wondering if it was because of Kid's threat. That look on his face...my God, she got scared and nervous from those deep blue pools broadcasting mayhem, promising pain, delivering retribution.

She couldn't believe he'd given up the coordinates for her, for Cris's family.

She took a breath, reminded herself to stay calm, to stay focused, to not give in to the wave of panic trying to wash over her. Men like Dean underestimated a woman, every time, but she wasn't just a woman. She was a seasoned NCIS agent, and this POS wasn't going to intimidate her.

After the interminable ride where she'd wanted to throttle him several times for touching her again and again, she was ready to scream. He parked the truck and came around and got her out. Dragging her toward one of the small huts, she started counting down in her head. When they reached the door and he pulled her inside, she turned and hooked his ankle. With a deft swing of her leg, he went down in a very satisfying tangle of arms, legs, and automatic gun. She turned toward the door and started to run.

She got all of ten feet before she was hit from behind.

"Not that easy, wild cat," he said with a laugh. "I like them feisty."

He dragged her back, and when he got there, he threw her on the bed.

Advancing on her, he climbed on top of her and got into her face. "Fun times." He pulled out a knife. "Did I also say that I liked it when they screamed? Pain and fucking go so well together...don't you think?"

Dean's dark gaze held hers, and there was no mercy there.

15

The second the back of the SUV released and before it had fully retracted, Kid grabbed the big man's wrist, pushing the semi-auto down and away from their bodies even as he slammed the palm of his right hand straight up under Reggie's chin. He felt the bone give way, and he was betting he'd broken the bastard's jaw. The gun fired—too late to do the man any good. From the angle, Kid knew the bullet went into the bumper of the car.

He'd had plenty of time to use a maneuver to break apart the flex cuffs and free himself. Then he'd released Cris. He was ready when they stopped. It was a fight for their lives.

He kicked backward at Reggie, connecting with the man's torso, the subgun flying out of his grip and landing somewhere in the shadows. Cris went for him before Kid could stop him, and Reggie backhanded him to the ground. Dazed, Cris worked at trying to get up. But Reggie dismissed him. He knew where his mortal opponent stood, and his attention went back to Kid, his look as heavy as a charging bull elephant. With a flash of white teeth against the dark skin of his face, he pulled out a knife, the kind of knife Kid loved.

"Let's see what you got, commando."

Long, sharp, the edge was honed to a killing edge, glinting in the moonlight. Yeah, he had knife envy. As soon as he took that knife, he was gutting the bastard.

Kid blocked his first strike, and at the apex of Reggie's next swing, he instinctively went for control, grabbing the man's wrist and using his leverage to swing the merc around and slam him into the side of the SUV.

With that maniacal grin on his face, Reggie rushed Kid, his bigger bulk knocking him into the side of the car. Backed up against the vehicle, Reggie bore down with the knife, his muscles bulging, sweat breaking out on his brow. He pressed his arm closer, bringing his hand nearer and nearer Kid's neck, pushing hard, forcing the knife toward Kid's jugular. The guy was bulldozer strong, like a freaking machine.

Fuck.

Kid kneed him, threw an elbow strike, blocked an incoming punch...and kept holding the knife at bay, twisting Reggie's wrist and forcing the lethal tip in another direction.

He took a blow to the body, and then another. Mustering his strength, he slammed Reggie even harder into the SUV, but the merc wasn't one of those CIA spooks. He was a warrior, and his blows came fast and hard, one after the other, each one a pile driver. The bastard caught him up the side of the head, and pain shot through Kid like a whip crack. Then another strike came at him sharp and fast and deep.

Fuck.

He knocked Reggie's next blow away and twisted under the man's other arm, bringing it over his shoulder and jerking it down hard, leveraging it against Reggie's elbow and having the satisfaction of feeling the joint give way.

Reggie let out a surprised grunt.

The knife fell to the ground from his suddenly nerveless fingers.

But even as Kid went for the knife, Reggie's good arm snaked around his throat, holding on tight, squeezing him hard and dragging him down to the ground where Cris was struggling back to a sitting position, pulling himself up against the SUV, his eyes glazed with pain.

He curled his legs around Kid's thighs, his hold punishing. Kid worked at his forearm, but it was huge and sweaty, hard to get his fingers around it.

He struggled and bucked but was unable to break his hold as the edges of his consciousness went gray.

He was gasping for breath, the pressure against his throat pinching off oxygen, his struggles using up whatever stores he had. He reached down, frantically searching for the knife. When his fingers curled around it, he was almost out of time. He jammed the business end into Reggie's thigh. The big man howled and let him go but grabbed the back of Kid's head and slammed it against the side of the vehicle.

Kid bounced off, disoriented and reeling, his vision graying again. If he passed out, it was all going to be over. But Reggie, despite the broken joint and the upper thigh laceration, was on the move. He grabbed up the knife and climbed onto Kid, who was flat on his back. He pinned Kid's arms down with his knees, his weight trapping him.

He raised the knife. "I guess Bryant is going to be disappointed."

He had seconds to live.

Sonuvabitch.

He tried to twist clear, heaving his body up and out from under, but he was bucking a solid two-forty hulk off his chest, and that goddamn knife was going to pierce his heart before he could do a damn thing.

Except a shot rang out.

From where he was, buried under Reggie's bulk, he heard the gun go off, loud and cracking, an explosion of sound. He felt Reggie's body jerk hard and then slump on top of him, felt the violent dynamic energy of the merc's whole being still reaching for him, still in the fight despite his broken elbow joint, and then he felt Reggie collapse, all the fight and energy draining out of him in an instant.

He dragged himself out from under the limp body and immediately snatched up the knife. He saw Cris, the rifle's muzzle smoking, his battered and bruised face full of rage.

Impressed with his steadiness and his recovery enough to actually pick up the weapon and hit the guy in the dark made him one lucky Navy SEAL. "Good shot," he said, and with a tight-lipped mouth, Cris nodded.

Reggie's breathing was ragged, and he clutched at his lower abdomen. He knelt down in front of the guy, bringing them face to face, and pressed the tip of his blade into the side of Reggie's neck. The guy knew what came next.

"You can bleed out here in this jungle, Reggie," Kid said. "Or you can tell me where Cris's family is." His tone was flat and empty, and Reggie could read him loud and clear. It was in his fierce black gaze and in the strength he was using to keep from showing any weakness.

Yeah, Kid figured Reggie was considering his ultimatum very seriously.

Not as dumb as he looked.

Reggie was thinking, staring at him, and struggling with

the pain that had to be exploding through him, blood seeping through his fingers.

Now it was time for him to think about betrayal and what he needed to do. Anderson wasn't just a boss to Reggie, that had been clear to Kid. He was his friend and they were close. Anderson trusted him explicitly.

Good.

"It's a one-time, limited offer," Kid said, pressing the blade in a little deeper. Then Cris walked up and set the muzzle against Reggie's forehead. A few days ago, Kid would have thought this man wouldn't hurt a fly, but all bets were off when Cris's family was in danger.

"Where. Is. My. Family!" Cris put his finger on the trigger, and Reggie said, "Last hut down the end of the street."

Kid opened his mouth to ask about Paige, but Reggie collapsed, his eyes rolling up into his head until only the whites were showing, all the tension going out of his body.

Kid stood. He had only moments to save everyone. Cris's family, Paige, and his brothers in arms. He was torn, then he closed his eyes. The SEALs could take care of themselves. They had signed up for this, even as guilt and anguish washed through him. *Paige.* More anguish, worse, deep, penetrating. She was a federal agent, and she also knew how to handle herself, but Cris's wife and his two children were total innocents, caught up in horrible, terrifying circumstances. If he didn't get them out before the shooting started...they were going to die.

Torn in three different directions, Kid growled out his pain.

"Let's go get them," he said, and dipped down to search Reggie. He pulled out the SUV's keys. "Get in and drive it down to the end of this lane as close to the hut there. See where I'm pointing?"

"Yes. Thank you for doing this. Even after I got you into this terrible mess. Betrayed you."

"Look, we don't have time for confessions and redemption right now, Cris. Paige is still out there, and my friends are on their way here."

"Right. Okay." Kid took the semi-automatic out of Cris's hands and after another search found three more magazines.

Cris started up the engine and Kid was on the move. He crouched low and ran along the crude fence line of piled stone. The sheep *baaed* as he passed them, nervously moving around in their pens. There were plenty of rebels in this area. He was just lucky they were preoccupied with the arrival of the SEALs and too far away to worry about a couple of gunshots. He came around the back of the hut and carefully peered into the window. There were three rebels—one was harassing Ariane—and the two children were huddled in the corner, Riky holding his sister, both of them terrified. They had ripped Jhosselin's little pink coat; there was dirt on her face, tracks from her tears. His jaw clenched, all his protective instincts mixed in with the rage. Bastards.

He couldn't help it. He wondered if his father had gone through the same kind of dilemma, caught between saving the SEALs that had died with him or the family.

Kid had an added layer of stress. Paige. He was compelled to go after her, almost to the point of pain, but he knew what his duty was here. She knew what his duty was as well. She would agree. He knew it down to his soul.

But, if he lost her... He cleared his mind. He couldn't think about this, not about her, not about his father. Kid would do what his own heart and mind told him to do.

He slipped up over the sill and vaulted into the room, *bam*, the first one went down, *bam, bam* the second tango was blown away, and Kid turned just as the third brought up his rifle. But Kid was faster and a much better shot. The guy never even got his finger on the trigger.

Cris burst through the door. Ariane cried out his name and ran to him. Kid rushed to the kids and picked up the little girl, who bit her lip but didn't dissolve into tears. Brave little thing. Grabbing Riky's hand, he said. "Let's go."

They ran to the SUV. Pulling open the door, he ushered Riky in, and while he was setting little Jhosselin in the seat, she leaned over and kissed his cheek. Ariane was already pulling her own door closed. "Get out of here and don't stop for anything."

"Good luck!" Cris said as Kid closed the door on the sweet family, and then Cris gunned the engine, the tires tearing up loose stones and grass. He barreled out of the small village.

Kid turned toward the rest of the huts. Paige was in one of them, but he had to take out the rest of the rebels. They were going to eliminate any witnesses.

He refused to have that blood on his hands.

He shouldered the strap, pushing the gun to his back, and pulled out Reggie's beautiful knife. Stepping forward, he melted into the shadows and disappeared. It was time to go on the hunt.

Hang on, babe, I'm coming for you.

~

PAIGE'S HANDS WERE FREE. The flex cuff had snapped from the force of her fall and her weight and Dean's coming down on top of it.

Three successive gunshots went off, all in a row. That

was five altogether, but it was clear Dean was antsy. He raised his head and turned it toward the window.

"Ashe is coming for you," she whispered.

Fear swam in his eyes before he pushed off her, slapping her hard across the face. The stinging pain thundered into her cheek, watering her eyes.

He went to the window. Paige rose off the bed and shook out her arms and hands, rolling her tingling shoulders.

Then she took two breaths and let them out. Dean turned and looked at her, then did a double take. His eyes narrowed when he saw her unbound, but not running, just standing there.

He brought up the gun, and Paige said calmly, "You need a gun to handle a woman, Dean?" Then she made soft clucking noises. His gaze narrowed even further, the bravado of his ego taking over his common sense. She was banking on that, and this asshole didn't disappoint her. Men like him liked to think they were superior to women. Hurting them? That was just one of his perks. Once again, he underestimated her. It was going to be his fatal mistake.

She was an NCIS agent, and she'd had the best training money could buy.

He set the gun against the wall and chuckled. "You wanna spar, missy? Let's see what you've got."

She raised her hands into a fighting stance and smiled coldly. "No, let's see what you've got."

He bellowed and rushed her. Ready for his brute force move, Paige easily sidestepped his dash, using her foot to kick him in the ass and knock him off balance. He crashed into the wall with a grunt. With a howl of rage, he rushed her again, swinging at her with a powerful punch. She knew if it hit her face, he'd probably break her jaw. She ducked, kicked, and struck out with the side of her hand, a stunning blow knocking him down. He stayed down for a few seconds, then raised his head, shaking it like a wet dog. The man couldn't shake it hard enough to get some sense in it.

He reached out and grabbed her leg, jerking her with such force, she landed hard onto her back. He scrambled to get on top of her, but she had the presence of mind to bring up her knees, and using her feet, she propelled him violently off her using her legs as a powerful fulcrum.

She flipped up to her feet from her back, a move her instructor told her would come in handy. She turned, running for the gun, but he caught her from behind. She went with the hold, turning into it and bringing her leg up and out in a stunning roundhouse kick that went straight to Dean's solar plexus. He went down hard, doubled over.

He was trying not to kill her because he wanted her alive, which was not a comfort. Far from it. The realization only spurred her on to fight harder, faster against him. He was holding back, and that was her advantage. But she had no qualms about killing him.

She was good, but Dean was a warrior, and sooner or later he was going to gain the advantage. She'd gotten in a couple of powerful hits, even heard something crack, but she wasn't going to hold him off forever. She was drenched in sweat. Her head was ringing from one of his blows she had been just a tad too slow to block. He was hard on the attack now.

Block. Parry. Strike.

She was running out of time, barely keeping him at bay. He grabbed her around the waist and squeezed. She cried out and boxed his ears, sending him reeling away from her, but his fist connected with her chin and she collapsed to the floor. She had to get up, run.

Time slowed.

She heard a hissing sound, instantly followed by a loud snap as the door burst open, banging against the wall.

Dean struggled up, a murderous look on his face. He didn't care anymore about not hurting her, killing her. It was in the chilling, cold depths of his eyes, but two quick successive shots all but blew his head off.

Blood spattered. Dean stumbled back.

Kid Chaos.

He stood silhouetted in the doorframe like a phantom in the pale mist, his hands clasped around the subgun.

"*Paige.*" His gaze locked on her as he dropped the weapon and rushed to her, sliding to the floor and gathering her in his arms. She buried her face in his chest, breathing hard and letting his strength wrap her.

"I knew you'd come for me."

Above her Ashe closed his eyes, rubbing her spine, his usually steady heartbeat racing.

She tipped her head back and met his gaze. In a breath, he was on her, his mouth rolling heavily over hers, his hands riding up her back to lodge in her hair. She wanted it, wanted more. She wanted so much freaking more. And from one heartbeat to the next, she realized that working hard, giving up everything meant jack shit. Giving yourself, building something, making a life was what she wanted. Not the barren existence she'd been living. Ashe showed her that affection and attention didn't come from giving up everything, it came from giving everything. Everything.

"We've got to go, now," he said, and both of them froze. The faint *whop, whop, whop* of a helicopter's rotors broke the quiet of the night.

"The SEALs," she said. "Oh, my God. We won't make it in time."

Then together they said, "The ATVs." The ones they'd

stashed in the jungle when they were investigating the rebels. He went to Dean, took the gun holstered at his hip along with any ammunition he had on him.

He turned, poised to run and then he stopped, grabbed Dean's rifle. "Ah, Dean was the sniper that killed those Bolivian police. Hello, baby," he crooned. He shoved the subgun into her arms and took up the rifle, slinging it over his back. "Now we're talking," he said confidently. Then they were off and running.

Cowboy thought about his conversation with Kid. About going home, about what Kid had said about his father. Cowboy thought again about his own circumstances and going home after this op was over. As a teenager, he'd had the big kind of shoes to fill as Kid did, only Cowboy's father hadn't been in the military. He'd been a hard-core, bucking-bronc-breaking, cattle-roping, calf-branding, fence-riding cowboy. The real deal. He was also one tough son of a bitch. His regret was just as real.

His gut churned, and it had nothing to do with the op and everything to do with his disgrace and shame by association. The father he'd looked up to had destroyed not only his own reputation, but Cowboy's as well.

They were getting closer to the DZ and the Kirikhan rebels, and not a SEAL on this bird didn't know everything there was to know about them. They were a pain in NATO's ass, hooking up with terrorists. Killing civilians and blowing up shit all over the world to draw attention to their cause. They were ruthless, fought to the death, and were happy to kill anything in a uniform.

It was just the six of them deployed off the USS *Annen-*

berg—Ruckus, Hollywood, Scarecrow, Blue, and Wicked. Tank had stayed back with Echo. As Cowboy peered out the chopper's porthole, he saw jagged peaks, then deep, dark, lush jungle with dots of livestock he thought were sheep and a couple of llamas. As they reached their destination, the all go came through the comms. Cowboy scanned the terrain below, then he saw it, the downed plane wedged up against a thick tangle of trees, the chewed-up scar a great place to set down a chopper.

We're almost there, Kid.

Something streaked across the bow of the chopper.

"RPG. Evasive maneuvers!" The co-pilot yelled. Cowboy stiffened. Hollywood pulled open the door and braced his feet on the runner. He set the .50 cal to his shoulder and started shooting.

Cowboy hated it when his enemies started connecting to each other, and there was no doubt this mission was compromised. It made the hair rise on the back of his neck, because if there was one thing he and his team didn't believe in besides unicorns and the pot of gold at the end of the rainbow, it was coincidences of any kind.

Kid had saved his ass in the Darién Gap, and now it was his turn to have his back, and the Kirikhan rebels were just about to get a taste of a fully operational Wes McGraw. A hard-core, bucking-bronc-breaking, cattle-roping, calf-branding, fence-riding cowboy. One tough son of a bitch.

But Dad, you and I had a very different view of honor.

As they dodged another RPG and Hollywood continued to sling hot lead, Cowboy was just waiting for touchdown, then it was game on. *Hoo-yah.*

~

WHEN THEY REACHED THE ATVS, Kid said, "You drive." She mounted the oversized four-wheeler and Kid slid on behind her. She took off and headed straight to the crash site at full throttle. The woman was just as fearless as he was.

Just as she broke out of the trees, there was a pocket of rebels, and several of them had tubes to their shoulders. Kid rose as she raced over the rough terrain, planting his feet on either side of her, bracing himself against the runners. He tapped her shoulder twice, and she slowed the vehicle down a few notches.

He sighted on one of the rebels and took a breath, then held it, aiming for body mass. He squeezed the trigger, automatically compensating for movement and the jerking motion. The man dropped, and there was a shout. Several of them turned toward the ATV and opened fire. One of the men with another RPG shot off a rocket right at them. It missed its mark but was enough to flip the vehicle and knock them both to the ground.

Dirt and rocks rained down, momentarily stunning them. "Paige?"

"I'm fine."

Automatic gunfire chewed up the ground next to them. He grabbed her arm, and they scrambled over to the ATV that was now on its side. The Black Hawk was still airborne, and Kid smiled when he heard the .50 cal. Hollywood was throwing lead.

He turned to her. "I need you to lay some cover for me." She nodded and prepared to pop up and keep the rebels at bay. They had taken cover behind the plane. As soon as Paige opened fire, he rose and picked off as many as he could through the scope.

Well, that took about five minutes to go straight to hell.

So much for all his well-laid plans for the night, all his

running around like a goddamn chicken trying to keep all the other chickens out of trouble.

The area between the plane and the rebels, including Anderson, didn't offer much cover. But Kid was going to run that bastard to ground. It was part of Paige's mission to bring in the man responsible for those MPs' deaths. Dean was dead, and Reggie was most likely gone, too. So that left only Anderson to take the fall.

It was clear the woman beside him had combat training. NCIS agents were assault ready, but she was damned impressive. He was breathless at the speed with which she acquired a new target and kept them pinned down and desperate to get off their own bursts of rapid fire.

The Black Hawk landed now that the RPG threat was neutralized. He saw the SEALs deploying. It would be a matter of time before this was mopped up.

"Anderson," she said low and determined, jamming another clip into the magazine, then rubbing at the right side of her chest. Kid saw a figure break from the plane and race off into the night. Paige didn't hesitate. With bullets still flying, she broke cover and sprinted after him. Cowboy shifted their way, his gun coming up, training on her racing form. Kid shouted as he chased after her, and Cowboy lowered his weapon.

It was time to bag Anderson, and he was going to make sure that he covered Paige's back.

16

Anderson ran. This whole fucking thing was coming down on his head. Tonight, that NCIS bitch and Pete Wilder's kid had bested him, killing off those ruthless rebels like they were Boy Scouts. It was time to cut his losses. He had a chopper waiting along with the warheads and the other half of the salvaged weapons. He'd still get his payday, talk the Golovkin buyer into a better deal.

After this score, he decided it was time to retire. Maybe a beautiful tropical location where he could grow coffee. Yeah, maybe it was time to get out while the getting was good.

He knew things, people. He was connected. His twenty-five years with the CIA had given him a network of informants, government officials, criminal bosses, warlords, drug lords, and some of the lowest bottom feeders on the planet. When he got clear, he was putting a bounty on both of their heads. Paige Sinclair and Ashe Wilder wouldn't live past the month.

He also knew assassins.

If Cris and his family had survived, he was going to do that one personally, kill the beautiful wife and children in front of him and let him live. That would be something that would give him great satisfaction while he enjoyed the tropical sun on the veranda of his plantation. Cris had screwed him over in this mess of a deal.

He also had an ace in the hole. His Washington, DC contact.

He had enough dirt on the guy to make sure things happened.

~

Paige's blood was running hot and fast, pumping through her veins as she pursued Anderson. The monster was in her sights. If he thought he was getting away with all this, with murder, he had another think coming.

The night and the jungle slid by her on either side. Ashe called out her name, but she kept on running. She had to finish this.

Behind her there was a burst of gunfire, and when she glanced over her shoulder, she saw Ashe on one knee, taking out pursuing figures. Dark silhouettes were moving toward her, too. The SEALs. In the distance, she could see the chopper. As soon as Anderson broke from the trees in front of her, the rotors started turning.

Anderson turned, and she saw the glint off the pistol he carried. He discharged the weapon, and the bullet missed her. Off to her left, several men came running, opening fire on her. By this time, those dark silhouettes had caught up to them. Kid was almost to her position. The SEALs opened fire as well, and the rebels ignored her and faced the larger threat.

She stumbled but righted herself. Anderson was almost to the chopper. But she had gained on him. Her breath was labored, the thin air slowing her down. Shortness of breath would be expected. But she had acclimated. Maybe it was because she had been running full out.

With a whine and a roar, the chopper took off, and Anderson screamed at the top of his lungs. They had to have seen the SEALs bearing down on them. With most of their troops killed or being systematically taken out, the rest of the rebels had cut him loose.

He stopped and set his hands on his knees, knowing he had nowhere to go. She caught up to him, keeping the automatic weapon trained on him, the adrenaline rushing through her in waves, her heart beating hard and her breathing strenuous.

Anderson turned and scowled at her. "You fucking bitch!" he yelled, then dropped the weapon, raising his hands in the air. With Ashe and the SEALs covering him, she walked up to him.

"Bryant Anderson, you are under arrest for the theft of government property, for treason in selling those weapons to the enemy of the United States, and for the murder of Corporal Ronald Miller, Corporal David Hong, and Petty Officer Peter Wilder."

Her stomach lurched and sweat poured down her face. She felt dizzy, and the right side of her body pulsed with pain, getting worse and worse. She turned and tried to walk. Oh God. She dragged a breath into her lungs—and it hurt, just like everything else.

She took a halting step and gasped, the pain building up in her. The next step felt like when they had taken that leap off the cliff to the river below. Falling...she was falling.

"Paige!"

She hit the ground and tried to push up. If she could just get to her feet, she would be okay. She used Ashe for leverage, dragged her feet beneath her. The whole world was going black and white with every passing second, her attempts to breathe torturous.

"Ashe, I'm all right."

"Shh, babe. Shh. I'm here." His arms came around her, strong but gentle, helping her, sliding behind her back and holding her upright.

"Geezus," Cowboy said. "She been hit?" He turned and called out. "Blue!"

"Ashe, I—" She wanted to hold on, to hold on to him, to hold on to herself, but she couldn't.

She was sliding inside, slipping away. She started to tremble—tremble and shake, right down to her veins, right down to her pulse, her heart, and her bones.

"I've got you," he said, tightening his hold before she was gently laid down on the ground, her shirt ripped open and a gorgeous man with gray eyes leaned over her.

"No blood, but this bruise. Was there an explosion?"

"Yes, an RPG, but we were okay. Now she can't breathe."

"I think her lung is collapsing. Get the chopper here. She needs to get to a hospital."

"Paige," Ashe said, his voice so soft, so anguished. "Stay with me, babe. Don't go."

"I-I can't. I—"

"Fuck can't, babe," he growled, "That's not in our vocabulary. You hang on."

She couldn't breathe anymore, her breath trapped, pain twisting inside her.

With the last of her strength, she grabbed Kid's arm as she saw the Black Hawk hovering above her like a big, black insect. "Tell them I love them."

"You're going to tell them yourself."

She closed her eyes, and that beautiful man with the

golden blond buzz cut and the clear, pure blue eyes said, "One patient, adult female, semi-conscious. Tension pneumothorax. Code Red."

WITH HIS HEAD in his hands, Kid sat by her bedside. It had been hours, he'd lost track. Unable to sleep or eat...hell, it felt like he was the one who couldn't breathe. The blast from the RPG's shock waves had hit her and caused internal trauma, collapsing her right lung, but thanks to Blue's amazing medical skills and his needle decompression of Paige's chest cavity, he'd kept her alive until they got to the closest hospital. She was breathing easily with no permanent damage. They had to insert a chest tube until her lung healed. Now all she had to do was recover.

A hand curled around his wrist and his head popped up. Paige, her eyes glazed, stared at him. "You look like hell, a gorgeous dark angel," she whispered.

His throat got thick, and he covered her delicate hand. "Paige," he said softly. He had no idea where she wanted to go from here. He was hoping that she was going to tell him that when they got back to San Diego, they could at least date. He knew this was supposed to be temporary, and without being able to help it, he felt the pressure of his job sliding between them. He would have to warn her about his deployments. His absence had caused the two women in his life to leave him; one had given him back his ring, and the other had thrown him over for a safe banker.

Kid Chaos wasn't safe.

He wasn't easy.

He was in love with her. He'd never known what it really meant to be in love, not until now, not until her. Fear of losing her to death was now replaced with just simple fear of losing her in his life.

He was a crazy bastard.

But she had made him see that his boldness was just a part of him. He had weathered the information about his father, but before he could fully put that behind him, he had another trip to make. But that could wait.

She drifted, her eyes closing.

"Paige? Where do you want to go from here?"

She sighed, and her eyes blinked a couple of times, then closed. He thought she'd gone to sleep when she whispered, "Only temporary."

His heart plummeted, shredded, turned over and tightened in his chest as it shriveled into something hard and aching. She was reminding him they had decided to keep it simple. He'd agreed.

He closed his burning eyes as they stung, his throat feeling full. "All right," he said. Just then there was a commotion at the door, and a man walked through with three men flanking him.

He rushed over to the bed and grasped her hand as she opened her eyes. Tears welling, he said softly, "Baby. How are you?"

She smiled and said, "Daddy."

Kid stood and backed away as her family crowded in. Her father, lean and tough, the boys, Leo, Knox, and Atticus each with concern and love shining in their eyes. She'd raised these guys, and he couldn't be prouder of her. But now she was in good hands, and he could leave. Prolonging the inevitable would only hurt more. Better a clean break.

A hand landed on his shoulder, and he turned to find Cowboy. He and the other guys milling around outside had been taking turns checking up on her, but they were more worried about him. Even her boss had been here, a big man with a shock of dark hair.

The NCIS team had been able to waylay the truck carrying the crates of weapons after another firefight with the rebels who had been killed down to the last man. He grimly told Kid that the warheads hadn't been among the crates.

He was sick that they got away with them, but this wasn't over. The SEALs would recover what belonged to the United States Navy.

His eyes felt gritty and heavy, but every time he closed them, he saw her on the ground, her plea for him to tell her family that she loved them. He was still adamant that she would tell them herself.

Now she could.

"Hey, man. What are you still doing here? Don't you have that wedding to get to? Michelle is your favorite cousin. I'm sure you don't want to miss it."

"If you need me—"

"I don't need you and that ragtag bunch out there to wait any longer. I have things to do. So get out of here. Kiss the bride for me."

Cowboy looked to the bed where Paige had gone back to sleep. The doctor came in and started to talk to her family. They were nodding and taking in the information. He retreated and ended up bumping into Blue. He turned, and Blue said, "The prognosis looks good for her. She'll have to be in the hospital for a few days. I think they're moving her to the States tomorrow. She'll have a chest tube for a bit, and that'll work to re-inflate the lung in about a month."

"Thanks, man, for saving her life."

He nodded in his modest Blue way. "You and her?"

"It's over. She just wanted something temporary."

"Aw, man. I'm sorry. Some things last as long as they last."

"True that. I'll see you back in Coronado. I'm heading out."

"We are, too. I'll see you back there."

Kid walked to the nurses' station and asked for a piece of paper. He wrote Paige a note, keeping it light. He handed it to the nurse and asked her to make sure she got it, then he was in the elevator, then out of the hospital.

He got a ride back to Paige's place and packed up his belongings, avoiding looking at the bed; then he left her key in the tray on her foyer table, locking the door on his way out.

He took a cab to Cris's house and after knocking, the door opened.

Ariane didn't say a word, just wrapped her arms around him and hugged him hard. Jhosselin yelled, "Ashe with an 'e'!" and flew like a pink missile to him, latching onto his leg. Riky was more conservative and held up his hand for a knuckle bump. Then Cris materialized out of the kitchen, his face mottled with bruises, stitched gashes, and scrapes. But his eyes were shining with happiness and welcome.

"Will you let the man in the house, you three. I think we owe him some breakfast."

After Ashe ate and was kissed and hugged some more, Ariane shooed the kids away from him and off to school.

"I can never repay you for what you have done for us. My company, my livelihood, and my heart, you have given them all back to me. Know that any time you want to mountain bike here, it will be on the house, and there is a guest room reserved for you and the lovely Paige. I hope that you and she will be very happy."

His heart heavy, Ashe just nodded. He couldn't talk

about Paige, not even to Cris. He was still raw from leaving her. At the door, he went to shake Cris's hand, but the older man pulled him into an embrace.

"God bless you, Ashe, your country, and your warriors. I am forever grateful."

He took a cab to the airport and booked a flight to DC. He slept all the way, his dreams filled with Paige. When he woke, he made his way to the Pentagon, then to Lieutenant Colonel Tom Davis's office. When he reached the aide's desk, the man said, "Do you have an appointment?"

Kid shook his head. "Tell him it's Pete Wilder's son."

The man relayed the information and the door immediately opened. "Ashe, what a surprise! Come in."

Ashe followed Tom into his office and closed the door. They made small talk about his mom and his sister and nieces. Finally, Tom said, "I get the feeling this isn't about catching up."

"No, it's about my dad." Kid outlined briefly what had happened and who he had met.

Tom's lips thinned. "I don't know if what Anderson says is true, Ashe. But I commanded your father's unit, and I can vouch for his character just as I did when I talked to the Medal of Honor Committee. He embodied values that can't be taught. He was selfless, fearless, and a damn fine SEAL. Brave to a fault. I personally can't believe he was ever involved with anything illegal or dishonorable."

Ashe swallowed hard. He realized that he was going to have to go on faith here. Decide that his father was a good man who gave his life for those family members, just as Ashe would have done for Cris's family.

"In my opinion, the apple didn't fall far from the tree." Tom smiled. "You're a lot like him, Ashe, a large, loud personality who makes everyone laugh. But when it comes

time to get down to business, you are a consummate professional. Hold that tight in your heart for your dad, and I
know that he's looking down and is so damn proud of the
man and the SEAL you've become."

He rose and held out his hand, and Tom shook it. Then
Ashe saluted him, turned, and left. He walked to the subway
and traveled to Virginia where he caught a cab and was
soon on his mom's doorstep.

He knocked, and when she opened the door, she
wrapped her arms around him. "Oh, Ashe, it's so good to
have you home."

She brought him inside, and Emma, his sister, rushed to
him, throwing her arms around him. His nieces, Sofia and
Grace, each wrapped their arms around his legs. "Wow," he
said, looking into Jay Marlowe's eyes. "There's a lot of
estrogen going on here? Save me, man."

His brother-in-law laughed and shook his head. "Come
between you and your admirers? No way, man. You're on
your own."

Hours later, after his gifts had been handed out, his
mom had examined the cuts to his face, and his sister's
worried eyes had made him feel guilty about upsetting them
both, he retired to the back porch and the sultry summer
night. His mom came out with a piece of apple pie with ice
cream on top and handed it to him.

"How are you, Ashe?"

"I'm doing good, Mom."

"And your vacation riding a mountain bike down a
death road. Was that fun and exciting?"

"It was." His tone was subdued. He freaking missed
Paige so much he thought his heart was going to collapse.

"Doesn't sound like it." His mom gave him a skeptical
look.

After a moment, he gave her just the briefest information about meeting Bryant Anderson and what he'd said
about his dad.

Her eyes flashed. "I don't care what he said," she
snapped. "He obviously never knew Pete. He was a
wonderful man, faultless to a T. You can be assured that he
would never betray his country. That would be like
betraying us, and that is something that would never
happen. He was dedicated to the navy, the SEALs, and us. I
swear, Ashe. I wouldn't lie to you."

"I know that, Mom." He set down the plate and wrapped
his arms around her quivering body. She was so angry, he
could feel the waves washing over him.

After he let her go, she cupped his face. "What else
happened in the highest capital city in the world? There's a
sadness to your eyes I recognize that often has to do with the
opposite sex."

He heaved a sigh and picked up the plate, taking a bite
of the cinnamony apples and ice cream. "I met a woman, a
strong, amazing woman, and she turned my life around, but
relationships between a SEAL and an NCIS agent can be
complicated. So, I'm here and she's there."

"I'm sorry. I do want you to be happy."

He nodded. "I know. It's all fine. Things work out the
way they're supposed to." He took another bite, the crickets
loud in the silence, the moon bright in the sky. "Mom? How
did you really feel when I told you I wanted to be a Navy
SEAL like dad?"

"I was proud and freaking terrified. But I knew you. I
knew you had to do what was important to you, regardless
of anyone else's feelings. Your dad would be proud of you
whatever you chose to do. You didn't have to prove anything
to anyone, Medal of Honor or not. It was nothing but a hunk

of metal, and the honor didn't come from bestowing the medal, but from your dad's sacrifice." She pulled a box out of her shorts pocket and pressed it into his hand. Ashe opened it and stared at the medal nestled in blue velvet. She curled her hands around his and squeezed. "Never forget that. The apple didn't fall far from the tree."

She smiled, kissed his cheek, and left him with his pie and his dad's medal.

TWO WEEKS LATER, he was deep in Mexico rescuing a high-level banker and his wife from a bunch of kidnappers. They were in the back country, and the LZ was miles away.

"Kid! For the *love* of God! *Donkeys*?" Ruckus shouted.

The first in the string *hee-hawed* like he was offended. Kid rubbed the animal's forehead and said, "Hey, he didn't mean it. He doesn't know you like I do." He heard Ruckus growl. He faced his LT. "They're fast and they're sturdy. You said to find some transportation." He looked as innocent as a child.

Scarecrow laughed, doubling over. Hollywood dissolved against one of the donkey's flanks. It was just the four of them this time out. But it had been enough to free the married couple and take care of the pathetic kidnappers. Well, that was until they stumbled on some drug runners. Then all hell had broken loose. But with his rifle and scope, Kid had done his job.

Long story short, they had subdued the bad guys, and Kid had found their donkeys. No Jeep in sight.

Scarecrow wiped his eyes. "You did tell him to find transportation, LT. Beggars can't be choosers. This *is* transportation, just the four-legged kind."

Ruckus ran his hand over his face, working hard not to crack a smile and lose some of his hard-ass reputation. "Dana is going to love this newest Kid story."

Kid grinned. "I'm working up a whole repertoire. I'm a legend, LT."

"You're something, all right," he said under his breath. "Jackass comes to mind."

Hollywood wheezed, "He should fit right in."

Ruckus looked at the donkeys, the exhausted and bewildered civilians begging him for a reprieve. He sighed. "All right, mount up. We're getting out of here."

Kid rubbed the donkey's soft nose. "See, I told you he'd come around."

Hollywood couldn't stop laughing all the way down the trail.

Scarecrow leaned over and said, "Man, you always have us covered. You're the bomb." He tapped fists with Kid.

"High ho, Silver," Kid called out and tapped his steed with his heels and held on when the placid animal took off like a shot.

The apple didn't fall far from the tree. Those words flowed through his mind, mimicking his mom's and his dad's commanding officer's. Tom and Mom were right. He would hold the memory of his dad as he always had. He was finally getting it that he was not only worthy of his father, but strong enough to step out of his shadow and walk his own path, knowing that being a Navy SEAL was all he'd ever want. His commitment to his team was solid, his commitment to the navy was strong, and his commitment to himself was unbreakable.

Now if only he could get Paige back. His life would be complete.

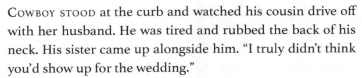

COWBOY STOOD at the curb and watched his cousin drive off with her husband. He was tired and rubbed the back of his neck. His sister came up alongside him. "I truly didn't think you'd show up for the wedding."

"I almost didn't, Erin," he said.

"It was a long time ago, Wes. Can't you forgive him and let it go? Mom and I miss you so much." She clasped his arm, and he turned to look into her blue eyes. "No, I can't. He betrayed us." He clenched his jaw. *He ruined everything! He ruined my reputation and took away everything I wanted!*

"Are you going to at least stay for a few days?"

"No," he said flatly. "My plane leaves in three hours."

She sighed, her voice teary, and he clenched his jaw even harder.

"Darlin', don't." He pulled her against him, his arms wrapping around her as she pressed her face into his chest.

"Your high school reunion is in a few months. Why don't you come home then? Stay for a while and attend."

He thought immediately of Kia, and the temptation to find out what was up with her was overwhelming. But where could that possibly lead? He lived in San Diego, and she lived here in this community where he would always be known as 'that coward's kid.' He wondered what she thought about him.

There was nothing he could do about what people gossiped about. It had been ten years, and he missed his family.

"Please, Wes. You barely know your niece and nephew. They ask about you all the time. Mom is not getting any younger. The reunion is over a weekend, a few days."

He gritted his teeth, hating that he had disappointed his

family and hurt them. Her tears were tearing him up inside. She looked up at him, more tears welling. He swore softly.

"All right, a few days," he said gruffly. It would give him a chance to put this Kia business behind him. He'd find out she was married and off limits, or the fantasy of the past years didn't hold up in the light of day. "I'll come back for the reunion. I can't say how long I'll stay," he said without committing.

On his way out of town after leaving his teary family, Cowboy couldn't help himself as he drove where his heart resided. He parked at the ranch gate, a pole arch used to have SWEETWATER carved into the crossbar, but now there was a fancy sign with flowing, wavy lines underneath iron black letters. Those wavy lines had been their brand, the ranch that should have been his birthright, that he had planned to take over and run when he'd finished college. His throat tightened when he saw the sunflowers swaying against the wooden fence posts, they were particular favorites of his mom—"a dollop of sunshine," she'd always said.

He remembered planting them so long ago with his dad, who made sure she had some every day to place in a watering can she set on the hand-hewn kitchen table where both the hired hands and the family took their meals. The memory hurt so much he turned away from them.

He vaulted the fence with ease; not much stood in his six-five way. He walked, knowing he was trespassing, but unable to help himself. This walk down memory lane would only open up old wounds that had never really healed up like they were supposed to. He saw a group of buildings off to the right and gazed at the spread that used to be his playground. Everything was so familiar. His throat closed and his breath hitched. Nothing...not a thing had changed.

The lane curved down into an open area, branching off to the big white arena where he'd trained horses. He felt a rush of warmth as the house and other buildings filled his view. The huge old-fashioned house, which faced the gravel driveway, looked recently painted, its green trim—their colors—standing out sharply from sparkling white. A veranda stretched across the front, and old rockers that had been crafted by his grandfather still sat as if beckoning him for a rock and beer that had been his granddad's routine at the end of the day.

He'd been born there, and he'd spent all his young life there, rooted in this ranching country. In fact, the McGraws had been one of the original settlers in these parts, one of the American families who had been given huge land rights when the nation had been new. His ancestors had been running huge herds of cattle when this part of Galveston was still a territory. But that had ended in the study on the east side of the house.

Ended their roots, ended their legacy, robbed him of his birthright, destroyed their honor. His chest filled with a volatile mix of regret, anger, and sorrow.

It had been his dad's responsibility to all those gone before him to keep it running. But he'd failed his ancestors, his family, and his son.

He looked down and kicked a clod of dirt, then raised his head again. Off to the right were the barns and corrals filled with horses. The cattle—Brangus and UltraBlack, their glossy coats glinting against the rays of the sun—were grazing off in the distant pastureland, and beyond he could see the ocean sparkling beneath the stark blue sky.

He saw a man trotting on a palomino, its glowing coat like liquid gold, white mane long and thick on its neck, and its tail swishing. He wondered fleetingly if it was Sunshine, his horse, but he would be too old to work the ranch now and must have either been sold, passed, or had been put out to pasture.

The man spied him, and Cowboy withdrew, heading back to his vehicle, putting it in gear. He'd better skedaddle, or he was going to miss his flight. His cell rang, Kid on the other end of the line. He started to talk, and Cowboy's heart sank. He'd had high hopes for him and Paige. It seemed like Kid had finally realized that he was picking the wrong women. He said nothing and listened.

After he hung up, he regretted promising his sister that he would come back. He would most likely be as disappointed as Kid was. In a few months, he'd have to endure the gossip and the condemning looks. Conversations held behind hands and in whispers.

That's Jack McGraw's son. He took the coward's way out when he committed suicide ten years ago and his family lost everything...including their dignity, pride, and honor. How can you ever recover from that?

PAIGE SAT on the patio and wanted to scream. For the last thirty minutes, she had four grown men at her beck and call. They had just removed the tube from her chest, and it was good to get the damn thing out, to breathe normally. But she felt she hadn't done that since Ashe had left the hospital, nothing but a lame-ass note to explain his absence. *It's been fun, babe. Later.*

Fun? It was more than that, and she knew it. He knew it, too. So his sudden disappearance had to do more with him than with her. Because she had wanted more, wanted to talk to him about taking their new relationship further. She'd wasted so much time already.

"Can I get you anything?" Atticus asked.

"No! God, you all are driving me crazy."

Atticus frowned, looking a bit confused. Her baby brother had grown into a handsome man, dirty blond hair, a strong, maturing face with sultry brown eyes many young girls noticed first about him. He was lean and muscular in that transitioning way from teenager to adult. "I just wanted to help. We were worried about you, Paige. Geez."

She took a breath, trying to tamp down her irritation. It wasn't Atticus's fault, or any of them, really. She was just mad at the world right now.

"Why don't you get to one of them video games, boy?" her father said.

He nodded and left after Paige gave him an apologetic smile.

"What's up, baby?"

"Nothing."

"Uh-huh. Spill, chickadee."

She told her dad, the whole thing pouring out of her. "I love him," she blurted.

His father's brows rose. "I remember a pretty devastated young guy, dark hair, sitting by your bedside. He didn't look that happy-go-lucky."

"He didn't?"

"No, sweetie. If you want something, what do you have to do?"

"Ask for it."

"Exactly."

He was right. She was not one to mope around, but said what she thought, and damn the consequences.

"Daddy, you love me for who I am, don't you?"

His brows rose again, and he laughed softly. "My girl, that's a given. You've been my right-hand gal for so long, it makes me almost nervous to think about you not here. But I wouldn't want you to put us first anymore. The boys are grown, and we handle ourselves now, thanks to you. I'm seeing myself a pretty little thing I met when I was bowling the other night. Don't worry about us anymore."

"It just seemed that you only noticed me when I was working hard, and I got it in my head that the only way to get your attention and affection was working hard. I kind of carried that with me into my job at NCIS."

He sat forward and took her hands, enfolding them in his big ones. "Did I? Dammit, Paige. I'm sorry. That's not true. I love you more than anything, honey. Whatever you do. Throw away that notion and get on with your life. Don't do what I've done all this time, bury yourself in work and loneliness. It's no way to live."

"You're right." She stood up and headed for the house.

"Where are you going?"

She turned and smiled at him over her shoulder. "To get on with it. I have a man to see about some fun."

She grabbed her keys and purse and headed for her car. She drove to Camp Pendleton and walked into the NCIS office. Her co-workers greeted her warmly. She stopped at Mike's desk, and he said, "Sinclair, I told you I didn't want to see your sorry backside until six weeks was up."

"Yes, sir." She couldn't help smiling at his clipped tone. This was Mike at his caring best.

"Are the six weeks up?"

"No, sir."

He looked up, his face stern, but with a twinkle in his eyes. "Then why are you here?"

"I need to access my computer. It'll only take a couple of minutes."

"Is this personal?"

"Yes. I—"

He held up his hand. "I don't want to know about it." He folded his fingers and indicated with his thumb as he jabbed it toward her desk. "Carry on. Then get the hell out of here."

She smiled softly, then went to her desk and pulled up Ashe's record and carefully transferred his address to her phone. She shut the file. "Mike?"

"Yeah," he said, looking over at her.

"About that promotion?"

He straightened and nodded.

"I think I'll pass."

His brows went up and he smiled. "I can't say I'm not sorry about that, but are you sure? You deserve your own team."

Her co-workers whooped and fist bumped each other, and she laughed.

"Thank you for the opportunity, but I want to stay put. I need a better balance."

"You got it, Sinclair. Now get out of here."

It took no time at all to get to Ashe's townhouse. But when she knocked, there was no answer. Disappointment and a healthy dose of anger twisted in her gut. It had been two weeks since she'd woken up at the hospital in San Diego where her father had her transferred for better treatment on home ground, and she didn't want to wait another day to talk to him. Then she heard the loud male banter coming from behind the complex. She followed the voices and noticed a bunch of men down the hill on a basketball court. Then, one of them going for a layup against some pretty big odds caught her attention. He was lean, muscular, a shock of black hair with heavy bangs, and batshit crazy. Her heart soared.

"Ashe," she shouted. All of them froze, and she took off at a run. When she got close enough to see his shell-shocked face, she yelled again, "What the hell do you think you're doing?"

"Paige?" His voice squeaked.

She marched across the ground, eating up the space between them, then onto the court and past all these huge guys. In front of his team members, she grabbed his sweaty T-shirt, breathing the scent of him in and propelled him against the chain link. "You left me unconscious in a hospital bed, and when I woke up, you were gone with the sorriest excuse for a note. Who are you kidding, Ashe? Fun, my ass. We have more than that! Way more." Several of the men laughed, riveted to her chewing him out. "So, I repeat, what the hell do you think you're doing?"

He took a breath, his expression going defensive. "Trying to save my heart from being torn out again. You said this was fun, too!"

"I was trying to be cautious around you, you idiot. But let's be clear. I want you in my life. Do you want me in yours?"

She shook him, and the tall dude next to him said, "Ashe, you better come up with a good answer, or I think she's going to kick your ass. I'll help her."

"Shut up, Cowboy."

"He's right. I will kick your ass."

He closed his eyes and pinched the bridge of his nose. Then they popped open. "Fuck, yeah I want you in my life, but you said—"

She cut him off and planted one on him. That mouth,

that gorgeous, smart mouth that she couldn't get enough of, would never get enough of. When she came up for air, she said, "I'm in this forever, Ashe "Kid Chaos" Wilder. F-o-r-e-v-e-r. Tattoo that on your ass. Because it's permanent."

Several of the guys clapped, and several intoned deep *hoo-yahs*!

Ashe gave them intimidating looks, but none of them budged. One leaned against the fence, another folded his arms, and another one leaned on Kid's shoulder. Ashe shrugged him off. "So help me, Cowboy..." He turned his attention back to her, cupping her face. "I need to know you can go the distance with me, Paige. I can't...go through...I thought I loved Mia, but I had no fucking clue. I'm batshit crazy about you, and if you take my heart—hell, who am I kidding? You already have it. If you keep it, I have to know."

"Through thick and thin, come hell or high water, I'm all in."

"Are you sure? Because it's hard to be with a SEAL. We demand so much, and that's a lot to ask of anyone. Look what it's done to countless relationships, mine included. Right now, all this is a new challenge for you, but what happens when the novelty wears off and the never-ending work and responsibility turn into a never-ending grind? What then?"

Her gaze was unwavering, and her voice was steady as she answered softly, "I would never pack up and leave, Ashe. I'm not made that way. You'll never come home to emptiness or a returned ring. My arms, my heart, and my soul will belong to you." She gently took his face between her palms. "I'll love you for the long haul."

The muscle in his jaw twitched, and he abruptly looked away, his expression open. She got it. The collapse of his two relationships, especially the one with Caitlin, had left some scars. Maybe the wounds had healed as he said, but he had been badly hurt, not once, but twice. That had to weigh heavily on his mind. She watched him, compassion stirring. He slipped his hand into her hair, cradling her head against his shoulder. Enfolding her in a close embrace, he nestled his cheek against her hair.

"We haven't much time left," he whispered, his voice low and uneven. "And I don't want to waste time talking about something that's old news." He kissed her, passionately, showing her how much he'd missed her. When they parted, he said, "I love you, too, babe. More than I can say."

"I think you said it pretty darn good."

"Well, my house is just right over there. Let's make up for lost time before I have to leave on an op."

She turned around and was immediately faced with some happy guys. They high-fived Ashe as he moved through them. She stopped at the last guy, recognizing him instantly. "Blue."

"Yes, ma'am."

She went up on her tiptoes and kissed him full on the mouth. "Thank you for saving my life."

"Yes, ma'am," he said, his cheeks coloring while Ashe looked daggers at him.

She grabbed his arm, laughing. "Let's go."

Once inside Ashe's house, her phone rang. It was her brother Leo. "Let me soothe one of my brothers that I'm not dead in a ditch. If I don't answer, he'll just keep calling."

Ashe nodded and went upstairs.

She took a few minutes to assure Leo that she was fine.

"Hey, woman," Ashe shouted from upstairs. "Get up here so I can get my dick so deep inside you, you'll scream out my name."

"Don't tell me what to do unless you're naked!" she yelled back.

"Oh, babe. I'm naked all right."

She took a much-needed breath and headed for the stairs, muttering under her breath, "This living together thing will sure beat loneliness hands down."

She'd take Kid Chaos naked, dressed, mad, passionate—any way she could get him. All the time, all the way. For forever.

EPILOGUE

TWO MONTHS LATER

Kid stood at the Sinclair pool with a stopwatch. "Come on, Atty, you can do it," he said.

Paige came out on the patio and looked around. She frowned. "Where is Atticus? He still has homework to finish. You know it's his senior year and he can't slack."

"He's...ah...training."

"Again?" She marched over to him and said, "If he doesn't finish high school, he can't go into the SEALs."

"He's not going into the SEALs after high school. He's going to the US Naval Academy in Annapolis, Maryland. He's already applied. Then he's going in as an officer. I'm telling you, babe, he's the real deal. I've never seen anyone handle himself like your kid brother."

"What? You're making him go to college? My brother loves academics, but he loves English the best. His favorite writer is Hemingway. He's won prizes for his writing. What the heck is he going to major in?"

"Whatever he wants." Kid shrugged. "What's wrong with

English? SEALs come from all over with different backgrounds, even Rhodes Scholars."

She glanced into the pool, and her face blanched. She looked at him and sputtered. "Oh my God! Ashe, you didn't." She went to jump in and help her brother who was resting at the bottom of the pool, holding his breath like a boss.

He grabbed her around the waist and held her. She struggled, but he wouldn't let her go. "He needs to be drown-proofed."

"You tied his hands and feet!" She tried to push away from him, but it was useless.

"Yeah," he said like she was dense. "That's required. I'm simulating the test exactly how he has to do it in BUD/S." He clicked the stopwatch. "Okay, it's time. He's got to get the oxygen mask at the bottom and come to the top. Then he can get out."

Sure enough, as they watched, her baby brother used his whole body to swim down to the mask, get it between his teeth, then head for the surface. Ashe said, "C'mon, man, you can do it."

Caught up in Atticus's struggle, Paige said under her breath, "C'mon," then louder, "Oh, God, he's doing it!"

When Atty broke the surface, Kid dropped his stopwatch and jumped in. Grabbing him and dragging him over to the lip of the pool, he released his bonds. Paige, who was now on her knees, ruffled his hair. "That's my baby brother."

"Paige," he said caught between laughter and pride. "Stop."

After they were out and Atticus had the towel draped over his shoulders, Kid said, "Way to go, Hemingway."

"Hemingway?"

"Yeah, it's a good call name, don't you think?"

A big grin split his face. "I guess it is." He sobered and

looked at Ashe. "You're a great teacher." Then he got this level, grown-up look on his face. Atticus glanced over at Paige. "When you going to ask my sister to marry you?"

Just at that moment, she looked over at them and smiled, and his heart felt as if he'd gotten nailed by a ten-ton truck. He had given a girl a ring once and she'd returned it to him, his future with her over. He was determined that when he asked Paige to be his wife, she would be the last woman he ever asked. "None of your damn business, kid."

"Well, when you do and you need to consider a best man, I'm available."

Kid chuckled and ruffled his hair, laughing. "Good to know."

He got up. "I'd better get to my homework. See you later, Ashe. Thanks for helping me."

"That was part of the deal. You go to the academy, I help you get into SEAL shape and ready for BUD/S."

SHE ROLLED her sore shoulders against the soft cushions. They'd eaten dinner sitting on the floor in his living room area with the city lights glowing soft and indistinct in the darkness. The food had been good, but the company she kept was better. They had laughed themselves silly when Kid told her about the Mexico op and the donkeys. She'd had an opportunity to meet the whole team and, *wowza*, what a bunch of intimidating, gorgeous hunks. So, she could imagine the look on Ruckus's face when Kid had shown up with those animals.

After that, they had held each other in companionable silence, and they must have drifted off.

Her Navy SEAL, combat ready, combat trained, special

operator in more ways than one. His place had turned into hers when he'd asked her to move in with him. It was the next step in their relationship, and it felt good. Her brother and dad had helped pack her up and move her. It had been a family affair.

Now she wished she'd taken some painkiller with her meal, her soreness from moving telling her she'd been pushing herself too hard. She was galvanizing herself for him leaving tomorrow to deploy to someplace she didn't know. But now that she'd met his team, she felt a little better to know he was in good hands.

He'd known while they were eating that she was dreading tomorrow, and he tried to be upbeat with the donkey story, but she couldn't help it. She'd miss him like crazy.

Feeling the need to be close to him, she kissed him on the cheek, very carefully so as to not disturb him. But Ashe was a light sleeper, and she had to admit that she knew that, too. He stirred and snagged her waist, dragging her closer, wrapping her in his arms. She smiled as he nuzzled her neck. "Hey, babe," he whispered, then dropped off again for a bit.

Cohabitating with him was going to be so good, but again not easy. Surrounded by Ashe's life here in his home, she had plans to make it more livable. Like curtains and art and some comfortable furniture. Things he hadn't handled, well, because he was always on the move and rarely home.

That sent a pang to her midriff, but she took a deep breath. She would make it into a home with home-cooked meals, clean sheets, and a managed life while he was off fighting for his country. She wanted to support him through it all, and she would.

She kissed his mouth, deepening it to get a rise out of

him. She felt his grin beneath her lips. "You trying to get me naked so you can tell me what to do?"

She chuckled, and when he rolled on top of her, she looked up into his wonderful face. "What if I am?"

"Hmmm." He nuzzled her neck again. "I think we'll have to have a race to see who can get naked faster. Go."

She started to unbutton her shirt, and he didn't move a muscle. She looked up at him. "Are you cheating?"

"What?"

"You're not even trying to beat me."

"I'm no dummy," he said softly. "I can't get enough of seeing you naked, and I like it when you tell me what to do when you're naked."

"You are—"

"Amazing."

She closed her mouth. "Yeah, that, too."

"Ha, ha," he said and captured her mouth, kissing her for real now, dragging her deeper under his spell. Before she knew it, they were both naked, and neither one of them cared who was doing the ordering. Pressing her down on the rug, his hands were as hard and demanding as his mouth and his shaft as he came up between her legs, nudging her legs apart. "Getting to the good stuff," he said on a gasp as he seated himself deep inside her.

She'd never get enough of Ashe, and she could only thank fate that had sent him on a bike trip to Bolivia, sent him to Going Down Wilderness Excursions and right into this orbit where she was now, them revolving around each other, their special gravity called love gluing them together.

Her family loved him, and she loved him beyond measure.

Before she knew it, it was morning, and Ashe was carrying her to their bed. He was fully dressed in camouflage with his duffel packed. "I've got to go, babe. We have debriefing, then we're shipping out this afternoon."

She caressed his beautiful face. "I love you, Ashe. Stay safe."

"I love you, too, Paige. I'll be back. I promise."

She nodded. He shouldered his pack, and then he was gone.

An hour later, she got up and did her run, showered, and dressed for the office. Once at work, she got down to business.

About an hour later, Mike's phone rang, and after answering, he sat up straight, frowning, his eyes glittering. *Uh-oh.*

"When?" The grim lines on his face deepened. "Are you sure?" He leaned back and let out a breath. "Dammit!"

Her co-workers' heads came up, and rightly so. They exchanged looks. That tone wasn't good.

He slammed the phone down.

"What is it?" Paige asked.

"Anderson is dead."

She sucked in a shocked breath. "What? How?"

"Hit when he was being transferred. Some bold shooter took him out. Sniper round to the head. We've got nothing on those warheads and weapons! He died before revealing his contact in DC. Son of a bitch! I'm heading up to TacOps." He was going to talk to the director at headquarters in DC from their specialized, secure area with a big screen on the far wall and equipment and computers to the left.

She watched his retreating tight shoulders and sighed. *If only...* Finding those weapons was not only an NCIS priority, but a navy priority as well. She was sure they hadn't heard the last of this. Her gut clenched. *Six* ballistic warheads. *God.*

As mid-morning rolled around, she heard the strumming of a guitar, and then Ashe's rich, deep voice singing behind her. "The Power of Love." She stood up and turned around, saw Cowboy, Kid's best friend walking behind him, both of them in their uniforms. People in the cubicles were standing up, watching him slowly walk toward her.

The lyrics brought tears to her eyes, and he stopped in front of her. Cowboy's knowing smile reached all the way to his attractive whiskey eyes. She laughed out loud when he still sang the 'lady and man' lyrics wrong.

He finished out the song, his voice rising with the notes. People were clapping and smiling as she wrapped her arms around his neck. "You are unbelievable," she whispered. "I'm so in love with you."

"You're beautiful, so beautiful." He kissed her.

"I thought you had to leave."

"We finished the debrief early, and I wanted to say I love you one more time before I go." He took a breath and met her eyes, his so warm and filled with the love he'd just declared. "Paige, I was going to wait until I got back home, take you out for dinner and ask you this by the water at that place we love on the docks."

"Ask me?" Her heart was feeling so tight in her chest, just like when her lung had collapsed, only with a lot more anticipation and no pain. "Ask me what?"

He got down on one knee and looked up at her. "Will you marry me?"

He offered her the velvet black box, and when she opened it, the ring nestled inside. And she thought about Caitlin and how much she had hurt him, how she wasn't able to handle this man and his absences, but Paige had no doubts in her heart or mind.

"Oh, God, so many yeses."

Cowboy laughed and pumped his fist. "Hoo-yah!" he said, and Ashe stood up and took the ring out of the box and slipped it on her finger.

"We'll celebrate when I get back. Start planning the wedding. I don't want to wait too long." He turned away, and Cowboy smacked him on the back of the head. "Oh," he handed her a piece of paper. Here's my mom's number and address, and my sister, Emma's. Call them and go meet them."

"Without you?"

"Yeah, it won't matter. They'll love you, too."

Cowboy tapped his watch.

"I've got to go." He kissed her several times before they left. She couldn't bring herself to tell him about Anderson and ruin the mood. There would be time enough for that later.

Over the time he was away, she did just what he asked. She missed him like crazy, but each time she looked down at the ring, she glowed with such happiness.

"So, you're just telling me this now?" Kid said as Cowboy reclined against a boulder, his weapon braced against his inside thigh. They were back in Mexico. But there wasn't a donkey in sight.

"Yeah, it's no big deal."

Kid took another bite of his MRE. "You hate going home, but now you're *going* to your high school reunion? Sounds like a big deal to me."

"Me, too," Blue said, sitting down.

"Oh, dang it, now we have the whole peanut gallery."

"One guy isn't the peanut gallery," Scarecrow said.

"Right." Hollywood sat down. "But the more the merrier. Spill, big man."

"Oh, geez," Cowboy said. He explained what had happened when he'd gone home for the wedding."

"Your sister crying would do me in, too. I have a sister, and I couldn't resist her. I get it," Kid said.

"That's not everything," Cowboy said, looking sheepish.

"What's the other reason?"

"Kia Silverbrook, a girl I knew in high school. I didn't talk to her then."

"The one that got away?" Hollywood said thoughtfully. "I don't know what that's like, but I bet it bites. I say get her out of your system."

Scarecrow shrugged. "Be decisive, man. Right or wrong, make a decision. The road of life is paved with flat squirrels who couldn't make a decision."

"Great. That's your advice. I'm roadkill?"

"Um..." Scarecrow looked confused. "No." Then he said it again.

"There's no need to repeat yourself. I ignored you fine the first time."

The guys laughed.

Blue took a breath and said, "Cowboy, regret comes from the things we don't do but wished we had. If you're attracted to this girl, make a move."

"Naw, it's a fantasy. She lives in Texas, and I'm, well, I'm with you punks."

That got more laughter. "You're doomed," Kid said and clapped him on the back.

"I say, there's your chance. Get her done," Hollywood said. The guys meandered away.

Cowboy leaned over and whispered, "I don't know. She's different. She makes me feel different."

"Scared?" Kid asked under his breath, making sure the guys couldn't hear him. "That's not a bad thing." He nudged him. "Suck it up. You're a SEAL. We can do anything."

As the guys started giving Cowboy a hard time about his love life, Kid's had fallen into place. He couldn't wait to get home so that he could love Paige in every way.

When the day finally came and he walked off the plane, he was confused. He didn't see her waiting for him. But as he came up the walk, there were balloons and welcome banners everywhere, a wonderful aroma coming from the backyard. When he went inside, everyone was there. Not exactly what he had hoped for because he wanted to get into her before he actually had to socialize.

But when he spied his mom, sister, and nieces, he was overjoyed to see them. They hugged each other tight.

Then he kissed and hugged his future bride.

"What is all this about?"

"Oh, we're getting married next weekend. I have a ton of things for you to do."

"We're getting married?" Could one man be this happy?

"It's batshit crazy, but you told me to be ready." She smiled. "What is there to wait for? I have a million things to talk to you about."

He took her hand and said, "If you all could excuse us." He dragged her out of the backyard and up the stairs. Before she could protest, he was kissing her and hiking her dress up to have his way with her hard and fast up against the wall. Once they could breathe again, with her wrapped in his arms, he whispered against her fragrant skin, "Okay, give me the million details. I think I can concentrate now."

She started to talk, and he nodded, his heart full. There was a time when he thought he was going to be a failure at this shit his whole life, but then this woman had drop-loaded into his life like one-hundred percent adrenaline. Now all he had to do was hold on.

He watched her face as she talked and thought: *It's going to be one hell of a ride.*

Thank you for reading *Kid Chaos*!
Reviews are appreciated!

Book 3 in the SEAL Team Alpha series, Cowboy, is next. A trip home, an old, guarded secret, and the woman he couldn't get off his mind add up to one heck of a homecoming for Wes "Cowboy" McGraw. For him, things changed ten years ago, now he going to find out the truth. Will it make him or break him?

GLOSSARY

- Comm - The equipment that SEALs use to communicate with each other in the field.
- DZ - Drop zone, the targeted area for parachutists.
- HALO - High altitude, low opening jump from an aircraft.
- HVT - High value target
- Klicks - Shortened word for kilometers.
- LRRP - Long-range reconnaissance patrol.
- LT - Nickname for lieutenant.
- LZ - Landing Zone where aircraft can land.
- MRE - Meals, Ready-to-Eat, portable in pouches and packed with calories, these packaged meals are used in the field.
- Tango -Hostile combatants.
- SERE -Stands for survival, evasion, resistance, escape. The principles of avoiding the enemy in the field.
- Six - Military speak for watching a man's back.

ABOUT THE AUTHOR

Zoe Dawson lives in North Carolina, one of the friendliest states in the US. She discovered romance in her teens and has been spinning stories in her head ever since. Her heroes are sexy males with a disregard for danger and whether reluctant, gung-ho, or caught up in the action, show their hearts of gold.

Her imagination runs wild with romances from sensual to scorching including romantic comedy, new adult, romantic suspense, small town, and urban fantasy. Look below to explore the many avenues to her writing. She believes it's all about the happily ever afters and always will.

Sign up so that you don't miss any new releases from Zoe: Newsletter.

You can find out more about Zoe here:
www.zoedawson.com
zoe@zoedawson.com

OTHER TITLES BY ZOE DAWSON

Romantic Comedy

Going to the Dogs series
Leashed #1, Groomed #2
Hounded #3, Collared #4
Piggy Bank Blues #5, Holding Still #6
Louder Than Words #7 What Matters Most #8

Going to the Dogs Wedding Novellas
Fetched #1, Tangled #2
Handled #3, Captured #4
Novellas (the complete series)

Romantic Suspense

SEAL Team Alpha
Ruckus #1, Kid Chaos #2
Cowboy #3, Tank #4

New Adult

Hope Parish Novels
A Perfect Mess #1, A Perfect Mistake #2
A Perfect Dilemma #3, Resisting Samantha #4

Handling Skylar #5, Sheltering Lawson #6

Hope Parish Novellas
Finally Again #1, Beauty Shot #2
Mark Me #3, Novellas 1-3 (the complete series)
A Perfect Wedding #4, A Perfect Holiday #5
A Perfect Question #6, Novellas 4-6 (the complete series)

Maverick Allstars series
Ramping Up #1

Small Town Romance

Laurel Falls series
Leaving Yesterday #1

Urban Fantasy

The Starbuck Chronicles
AfterLife #1

Erotica

Forbidden Plays series
Playing Rough #1, Hard Pass #2, Illegal Motions #3